The Group

The Jack Series, Volume 2

Todd LeRoux

Published by Todd LeRoux, 2024.

THE GROUP

First edition. February 27, 2024.

ISBN: 978-1738317585

Written by Todd LeRoux.

Also by Todd LeRoux

The Jack Series
The Group
The Cradle Operation

The Quest
The Beginning

Standalone
The Jinn
The Wanderer
The Quest
The Island

Watch for more at https://www.toddleroux.com/.

For all the men and women working to make the world safer for children. Thank you so very much.

The Group
a Novel
By
Todd LeRoux

Chapter 1

JACK WATCHED AS THE sun rose over the Eastern mountain range in the starving country of North Korea. Standing in the morning light, Jack thought about the man he had killed the night before. No one was going to mourn the dead man. The bastard used his position in the military to kidnap young boys and girls to sell into slavery. His biggest clients were the so-called elites of the world. These sick people thought they had the right to own others, to buy children for their sick twisted desires. Jack knew he had made a difference the night before. He also knew it would take more than one assassination to fix the problem.

Jack looked to the southwest. He knew his friends were waiting for him back at their camp. A camp set up and run by a secret unit of the U.N. This unique Unit of the U.N. was so secret it was thought to be a myth from the cold war era. The men and women who sat in the general assembly in New York thought the Chinese made up the story of the Unit in an attempt to take world attention off their genocide in Tibet. The Unit's reason for existing was to end mindless military violence against innocent civilian populations worldwide.

Jack didn't like what he was forced to undertake in the name of gaining peace. Jack knew he was saving some innocent child from a life of torture and degradation. Jack wondered if he was genuinely making a difference in the world. Standing still, he watched the sun rise over the mountains. Jack was about to start his hike back to the camp when his com sat device beeped. Holding the Unit up so he could look at the screen, Jack silently cursed the object and then tapped in his code. As he waited for whatever information was about to download. Standing still, Jack watched a small Asian deer make its way through the forest.

Richard sat and read the report of another rape and murder of a young girl. The woman sitting across his desk was the head of security for the secret United Nations unit. To look at him, no one would have guessed the rotund Richard was the head of the Unit. Richard was the one person who was responsible for all the good it accomplished over the last decade.

"I can't sit around and hear about some child molester raping and killing young girls," Joan said as Richard read the report.

"I think Jack is in the area. If he hasn't turned off his GPS and radio, we'll get a message to him." Richard said. He laid the report on his desk. Richard never looked at the pictures in reports of this kind; he knew what the images would hold. It was the same no matter where they were, whether it was here just outside of North Korea or in Africa, Bosnia, or South America.

The bodies of the young looked the same, battered and broken. Their faces were bruised and torn as if the beasts of myth had been set loose on a world of unsuspecting lambs. Taking the file, Richard placed it in his safe and locked the door as he left his office. Inside this secure compound, hidden a mountain range separating North Korea from the Sea of Japan. Richard stood surveying the monitors of the main information gathering room called 'dark watch.' From dark watch, Richard, along with the men and women who worked within this special Unit created by the U.N. founding countries. Those being Canada, Britain, the United States, along with Australia. France was a founding member, though it did not participate due to hurt feelings over the U.S. invasion of Iraq. Russia had become a cold war enemy by the time the Unit had been created.

Jack, Richard, and the Unit had been responsible for the destruction of the largest, most violent organized crime syndicates to come out of Asia in the last two hundred years. The head of this syndicate was the CIA station chief in Hong Kong. Now, the man sat in an unknown prison. Upon his capture, Richard seized all the money of the syndicate. This money was now used to fund the expansion of the prison. Standing in the dark watch monitoring room, Richard thought the world seemed to slip further into insanity. Jack started looking forward to the afternoon when the rain would fall in this part of Asia. The pounding rain helped if Jack stood still and let the rain fall on him. It seemed to wash the world's filth off for a short time. Jack heard his GPS beep at him; it was the signal Richard was trying to make contact with him. Like other times he was torn on whether to answer it or just let the thing go on beeping until its batteries died.

"Go." Was Jack's standard way of answering the beep.

"U dash one one, stand by for Alpha zero." The voice of a com operator came over his earpiece.

"U, this is Alpha, have a job if you want. Information is forthcoming, need reply ASAP, out." Richard's voice said in his ear. Leaning against a tree, Jack cursed. He had been out trying to find the target for a week now. His target hadn't been where the fuck-ups at Intel said he should've been a week ago. Now Richard wanted him to find another; Jack took off his backpack. He needed to see a small video screen inside it. Opening the screen, he attached it to the satellite GPS he carried and watched as the data download started. It was a file sitting on a rock. Jack read the file. Like Richard, he didn't look at the pictures as they downloaded. Jack understood why Richard asked for an answer quickly. The bastard in this file needed stopping, in the permanent sense of the word. Jack unhooked the video screen and then called 'dark watch.' Once he coded in the correct phrase and numerical sequence, Jack gave his two-word answer. Richard was hoping he would hear those words.

"Happy to." Then a click, Richard knew Jack had ended the connection. Richard also knew they wouldn't hear from Jack until the monster in the file was eliminated. It wasn't that Jack was happy to kill this man. Richard knew Jack would be thinking of the innocent girls this bastard raped and then strangled. At the same time, putting a bullet in the fuckers head wasn't going to cause him any lost sleep. Luckily, it hadn't taken Jack long before he was in the right spot to find the target. Sliding under a bush, Jack had a good vantage point to watch for his target. From this point, he could watch the intersection where two roads met and merged into a single track in the jungle. If his target came down either road, he would take him.

Maung loved his life; he had boys to listen to his stories and jump when he said jump. He also had girls whenever he wanted. Of course, when he was through with them, no one would ever have them again. Maung smiled as he drove back to his headquarters.

Jack could hear the rattle of the small diesel engine powering the jeep through the jungle of this part of Asia. Jack could see his target sitting behind the wheel with a smile on his face. Jack often wondered why all serial killers held the same smile. It didn't matter if it was Ted Bundy, John Wayne Gacy, or Richard Ramirez. They all had the same vacant shark-like smile surmounted by dead doll eyes, eyes that never seemed to reflect light. Instead, they seemed to drink in light and gave nothing back but a void. A dark place, it's as if their soul cried out for more, never to be sated. The only way for them to gain peace was to inflict pain and terror on others.

Maung smiled as he remembered the girl he had taken the week before. She only screamed. Last night the girl fought. He was impressed by how hard she fought him; he carried her nail marks on his face and chest. She had bit him hard enough to break the skin. Maung could feel himself getting aroused just thinking about the girl, she scared him, and he loved it. She fought right up to the point where he felt her die. The monster Maung never felt or thought anything again.

Jack watched as the smile grew and spread over his target's face. Reaching with his thumb, Jack snapped off the safety on his M200 USMC-issued .408 cal rifle. Breathing easy, Jack waited for Maung to center in his trijicon acog scope. Jack settled, breathing in, out, in, then he let half his air out and held his breath, listening to his heart as he gently took up the trigger slack. When the shot came, it was as much a surprise to Jack as it would have been to Maung if he had heard it. Checking through the scope, Jack could see the partially decapitated corps driving the jeep into the bushes. Jack knew his target was dead; the screaming engine of the jeep called out the fact the dead man's foot held down the throttle.

Now Jack could never be accused of being environmentally conscious. He hated unnecessary noise, so after breaking down the M200, he walked to where the jeep sat. Its tires had dug and flung away the dirt from under them when it came to rest against the tree now firmly holding it. Reaching in, Jack turned the key, killing the engine, then threw them into the jungle. As for the lifeless form of Maung, well, let the bugs eat their fill, Jack thought. Looking back to the mountains, Jack started making his way back to camp, to his friends. Jack came back to camp the same way he often left, silently. Someone would find Jack sitting in the mess hall when the crew went in to start their preparations for breakfast. The morning crew would find Jack had somehow unlocked the mess hall and made a pot of coffee and sandwiches. The former head of the mess hall complained about Jack doing this to Richard. The former head of the mess was told as long as Jack didn't burn the place down, he was to be left alone. The new man in charge of the mess didn't mind Jack coming in before he did. Hell, the man even gave Jack a key, so he didn't have to break in.

"Your back." The cook told Jack.

"Yep, eating too good out in the bush, came back so you could toughen me up," Jack said as he smiled over his coffee.

"I'll toughen you up all right." The cook threatened with a large cleaver and a smile.

"I left the pot," Jack said as he got up.

"Could you let Richard know I'm back and in my quarters," Jack asked as he stood to leave? The old cook nodded and held up a cup of coffee as thanks, then watched as Jack walked out the door. The older man watched Jack with a look of concern. He knew what Jack did. He also knew from personal experience the toll it took. The one thing he didn't know was the training Jack received starting at a very young age. No one in the Unit knew how young Jack had been when his training had begun. Even less knew about his past, how his parents were murdered, and Jack was tortured into forgetting them.

The cook also knew Jack had other things on his mind. The first was his partner, the man who was usually at his side was back in London waiting to have an operation for a brain tumor. Though the cook never met the man, the Tibetan sounded like a man who would be good to know. The ex-marine, now cooking for the Unit, watched the door to the mess slowly close behind Jack. Like so many other people involved with the Unit in this part of Asia. Eugene heard the rumors of how Jack came to be with the Unit. Eugene had been in the Marines long enough to know you don't take the scuttlebutt to heart.

Jack had taken all his gear to his quarters before going to the mess hall; now, after the coffee, all he wanted was a hot shower and his bed. As he walked across the compound, he nearly walked into a redheaded Chief Warrant from the British military, though she was not British. Jack excused himself, and in one of the most beautiful

Irish voices Jack had ever heard, she told him it was no problem. Jack watched as the Irish chief warrant walked towards the mess hall. Standing in the middle of the compound, Jack wondered if he should have a second cup of coffee. Though he wanted to, Jack just couldn't bring himself to turn around and follow the Chief.

Jack was showered and dressed when a polite knock announced Richard; he waited for Jack to call 'come in' before he opened the door.

"How are you this morning?" The portly English man asked as he took a seat in the only chair the small private quarters had.

"Fine, Richard, the secondary target was where *'you'* said he would be." Richard noticed Jack put emphasis on the word 'you.'

"Yes, about that, we have a problem; I need you to come over to the shack right away," Richard said. He smiled as Jack nodded and then held the door for him.

"Jack, anytime you want to talk about Tran, you know I'm here. I also miss Tran; he is a friend, a dear friend." Richard said. He knew Jack wouldn't talk about his Tran, the man who helped him get out of Tibet. As Richard left Jack's room, he gently pulled shut the door. Richard knew Jack wouldn't talk about Tran for fear that somehow talking about him would cause the tumor to get worse. Though how things could get worse for the man was hard to guess.

"I know Richard, I would rather keep my own counsel on this subject," Jack said as they walked out into the sunlight of the Asian morning. The shack, in reality, was called the intelligence and communications building; everyone called it the shack. This building was where intelligence was gathered from satellites under the control of founding nations, as well as their own assets in the field. Jack hated this building, he told Richard on more than one occasion. 'The people who worked in this place needed to be taken out into the field and given a real-world education.' Richard was still thinking about Tran when he was caught off guard by Jack's voice breaking into his thoughts.

"You know I looked for the son of a bitch for a week before he showed up. I'm getting sick and tired of these fuck'n fools telling us it's a sure thing. Then I get out in the bush, and it turns out it was less than a sure thing." Jack said as he and Richard entered the shack. A young guard stood beside a biometrics scanner. He watched as Richard and Jack swiped their identification through a reader, then placed his hand on a palm reader. Once the light at the scanner went from red to green, the guard nodded, and the men were allowed to pass.

"I know, Jack; I have had a word with the head of the intelligence gathering on more than one occasion. He tells me what he and his people do is not an exact science." Richard finished. Richard and Jack stood in front of another door. Jack smiled as he held up a hand to stop Richard from entering his passcode.

"Let me," Jack said as he entered his code. Jack knew the head of this department had, ever since his arrival, tried to have Jack's security clearance revoked or at least downgraded.

"If you must," Richard said as he stepped aside, smiling. Richard knew doing this gave Jack a firm advantage over the new Chief of intelligence. Jack could see David Johns standing in front of a large plasma screen. This was one of five serving as a viewport for a real-time down-looking satellite. David knew Jack still had security clearance above his. This was Jack's way of rubbing his nose at the fact. Jack smiled at the man, then turned with Richard in tow and entered David's office.

David could see Richard had taken a seat behind his desk. David knew Richard did this as a sign he was the boss; it pissed the younger man off. Richard was the head of the worldwide Unit. David couldn't say anything. However, Jack was sitting on the only other chair, which left David standing. Cursing under his breath, David slowly walked towards his office.

"It seems we've had more problems with your Intel, David." Richard began.

"The Intelligence was fine; I can't help it if your golden boy gets lost." David snapped as he looked at Jack. Richard knew David had taken a dislike to Jack the very moment he had stepped off the chopper.

"Well, I tell you what, David, I think Jack here is right. I think he needs to have a spotter with him, you know, so he doesn't get lost out there." Richard said, smiling. Jack waited; he'd seen Richard smile before. Jack knew when Richard smiled, it signaled he had made his mind up about something.

"Jack is going to take some time off, about three days, then he's going to go back out there to find and bring back Nauge Ping. You will be going with Jack as his spotter, so he doesn't get lost, as it were." When Richard finished speaking, Jack started laughing.

"The hell I am!" David said.

"I'm an asset to this Unit, not some weapon you decide to send out in the jungle. Besides being out, there is the job of... well, let's just put the plain truth out in the open... it's for less intelligent individuals." David asserted. Jack looked at Richard and then started laughing. David knew he had made a mistake, a terrible blunder. David knew he was more intelligent than the people he was forced to work with. However, to blurt out the fact was something he shouldn't do, he couldn't do. David's mother and his uncle told him on different occasions. He would have to hold his tongue and intellect in check, or others would try to make a fool out of him for their own gains.

"See ya later, boy genius," Jack said, then patted David on the back. Richard never moved out of the chair he occupied, at five foot eight and one hundred and seventy-two pounds. David wasn't what would be called a big man, but with his jet black hair and green eyes, he had a face peopled remembered.

"I have no idea where it is you came to the notion you are more important than anyone else. Let me tell you one thing, mister, after the little speech you just gave! I would just as soon send you to the Antarctic to gather intel on the local terrorist cell. Instead, I'm going to tie you to Jack for a while. If you're lucky, he'll teach you something." When Richard was done berating David, he stood up and left the office before David could say anything. David knew letting Jack and Richard get under his skin had been a mistake. Now he would have to go out into the jungle with the man. The man was responsible for ending his family's power in the U.S. government. No one knew he was the adopted son of G.W. Hollyford's sister. Mary adopted David when he was two years old after her husband died of cancer. Mary loved and doted on David. She gave him all he ever wanted until she became ill. Then the evitable happened; David stood by and watched as cancer killed Mary before his twelfth birthday.

G.W. took David in and showed him the way the government worked. If you have money, then you can be in the government. If not, well, then too bad. G.W. sent his own son to the best schools in the country. The old man sent David to all the same schools. As far as David knew, his adopted uncle and mentor was dead. The family was disgraced because of these people. They found a secret in G.W.'s past, a secret the old man tried to hide, and Richard and Jack used it against him. Then rub salt into the wounds of the disgraced family. They froze his uncle's assets and seized all properties, bankrupting the family. David watched as Richard walked to the door. David knew once he sold the information about this secret Unit to the Chinese. Or to any of the other governments these bastards have interfered with. He would have enough money to restart his family's power and wealth.

Chapter 2

JACK OFTEN THOUGHT about the friend he met in the mountains of Tibet. Tran lost everything to a Chinese Colonel when the man tried to rape his little sister. She fought the Colonel and took his eye, then slashed at the man with his own knife, ruining him as a man. For this, the Colonel had his men kill Tran's family. Tran found Jack descending a mountain; on this mountain, Tibetan Buddhist monks lived in a grand cave system. In these caves, the monks help people who've been hurt and escaped the Chinese military. Together he and Tran found the men who had taken from them and hurt them. For Tran, it was the Colonel. For Jack, it had been General Trang; each man killed his tormentor. In the process, they found and freed four BBC journalists, men they now called friends.

Along with Richard, he knew friendship. The men he called friends couldn't understand what it was to be bonded by the fight for each other. Now Tran was in a fight Jack couldn't help him with. No bullet wound threatened his friend. There was no one man Jack could hunt down and have justice from. No, the thing Tran fought was a tumor growing in his friends' brains. Jack still remembers the look on Tran's face when he found out. Tran smiled and thanked the doctor for his help, then left the office.

That night he set up a Buddhist shrine and sat in the lotus position on the floor chanting. Jack remembered Tran chanted for three days, then came to the table where Richard, Tomas, William, Jerry, and Scott with Jiao sat sipping tea, waiting to see him. The rest of the day they spent laughing and reminiscing. The men took turns getting up to fetch things for the very pregnant Jiao. When they would sit down, each would tease Scott for taking advantage of her. Scott would blush and tell them it was the other way around.

Tran used meditation to hold on long enough to see Jiao and Scott's baby brought into the world. September fifteenth at three am, the little boy came into the world; Tran was there to see him. They were all at the hospital when Jiao went into the birthing suite. Scott and Jiao told Tran they wanted him to be there as the baby's uncle and godfather. Tran saw a life born into this world; he later told Jack it was a miracle. Tran touched every finger and every toe to make sure they were there. When he touched his little head, the baby stopped crying and looked at him. Tran told Jack it was then he knew this one child would be great.

"It is in his eyes; the eyes are the windows to the soul. When you hold him, you watch for the soul. If you see it, you will see the old and wise Buddha." The next night Tran left the house he had grown to love on the island of St Martin of the Scilly Islands in the English Channel. It was hard for Tran to go to a hospital, knowing Jack and the others would be out in the world.

Nevertheless, it was Jack who told him to get well, then he would come and help again. Jack hadn't told anyone; he was scared Tran wouldn't make it through the treatment and surgery. Jack knew he should call Jiao and Scott to ask how Tran was or if he needed anything. Jack thought if he did, he would jinx Trans chances of getting better.

Richard found Jack sitting in the mess hall, sipping at a cup of coffee. Jack looked up from his cup; he knew Richard had news about Tran. Inside, Jack dreaded to hear what the word was. If he could've changed positions with his friend, he would have. Anything so he didn't have to listen to what Richard was going to tell him.

"You heard from the doctors?" Jack asked.

"Yes, I have; for a change, it's good news the tumor is responding to treatment and has shrunk; it is small enough now, and the doctors say they can operate." When Richard finished, he was smiling. Jack nodded; he was going to say how it was nice to have a bit of good news. Eugene came over to the table and placed a bottle of bourbon down. Jack looked to the former Marine and then to the bottle of Jim Beam bourbon on the table.

"Sounds like good news, good enough to have a drink," Eugene said. Even though the new head of the mess hall never met Tran. Eugene knew from the stories the men and women told about Tran he would like the man when or if he ever met him.

"How long before they operate"? Jack asked.

"It should be over the day after tomorrow, and we should know how it went the next day. So why don't you take your time off and stay in camp until we hear the outcome." Richard offered. Jack stood and offered a toast to Tran and his health; the three men nodded and tossed down the bourbon. The three men stood silently for a moment; they each remembered others they wished to have a drink with. Others lost to the battle with time and illness. Jack thanked Eugene, the beefy cook for the Unit, then turned and left the mess hall heading back to his quarters.

"Thank you, Eugene, that was a good thing. I needed a drink, and so did Jack." Richard said as the older man nodded.

Richard spent so much of his in contemplation, filling out forms and filing reports. It amazed some people he could do this without much thought put into the task. Richard was one of the few people on the planet who could genuinely multitask. He could fill out the forms needed for the founding countries of the Unit. While Richard was filling out reports and paperwork, Richard could ponder other problems and then arrive at the required answers while finishing reports. People were amazed at how he worked, and Richard was amazed others thought it was something special.

"Excuse me, sir." Chief warrant officer Joan O'Driscoll said as she knocked on Richard's office door.

"Come in, Chief, lovely day," Richard said.

"Yes, sir, it is truly a fine day. I wanted to talk to you about something personal." Joan said as she walked to Richard's desk.

"Personal, I'm here for my people. What is it you need, time off or a friendly shoulder?" Richard asked.

"I would rather we talk outside in the open air if that would be all right?" Joan offered. She watched as Richard stood and nodded his head towards the door leading out of his office. Neither of them said anything until they were out in the fresh air.

"What was it you wanted to talk to me about, Joan?" Richard asked the strikingly beautiful redheaded Irish Chief. To anybody who heard Richard ask her, it seemed she was going to ask for time off. To take care of a personal matter of some sort.

"Well, I have a new relationship in my life. I have you to thank for it, though I don't know if you will approve." Joan said as she and Richard walked behind the mess hall. When they walked around the far corner of the mess hall, Joan had finished what she wanted to tell Richard. Now she watched as Richard stopped and looked up at the puffy white clouds floating across the pale blue sky above the jungle canopy. Joan knew when Richard found out David was the adopted son of Mary Hollyford-Johns. The sister to G.W. Hollyford, the man Richard and Jack imprisoned on a Scottish island in the north sea. Richard told Joan David could have joined the Unit and hidden his past for one reason only, and it looked like Richard was right.

"Is this relationship going to harm your working for me?" Richard asked, already dreading the answer.

"No, however, it will harm your working relationship with David Johns." Stopping, Richard looked at the Chief. He could almost read the story in the Chiefs' face and knew what she was going to say before she said it.

"And you know this for certain, there can be no doubt." Though Richard knew there was no doubt he suspected something like this, or he wouldn't have had a sweep done in the first place. Joan looked at Richard and then pulled out a small plastic case. Inside the case was a tiny surveillance device.

"Where did you find this little poison pill?" Richard asked as Joan held a very sophisticated surveillance audio video bug in her left hand.

"I hate to tell you, it was in your office, hidden in the acoustic tile above your desk. We planted one of our own in David's office. I have to tell you, Jack was right to request you have him watched." Joan said. Richard watched as Joan returned the bug to the small plastic case and put it in her pocket.

"But why, why would he do this?" Richard asked.

"Money, he could blackmail the Unit. Threaten to release the information to the press if you don't pay." Joan surmised. Though Richard didn't want an answer, he knew she was right.

"Go get Jack; tell him to meet me in the gym," Richard ordered as he started across the compound.

Jack lay on his bed; he had taken his second shower of the day and tried to fall asleep to no avail. He was going to turn off the television when a knock came on his door.

"Hold on a sec." He said as he walked to answer it. To his amazement, the redheaded Chief was standing on the other side when he pulled it open.

"Richard needs to see you right now; he's in the gym," Joan said as Jack as he fumbled with a T-shirt. This was the first time Joan saw

Jack without a shirt. His scared body told her of years of pain. It also told her of a man with a will to survive just about anything.

"What's it about?" Jack asked as he closed his door.

"Can't say," Joan said as she turned to lead the way down the hall.

The cook watched as the little prick turned his nose up at the coffee. Eugene folded his big arms over his chest as he watched David. Eugene joined the Marines when he was eighteen and grew up drinking their coffee. It was the same coffee Jack made when he returned from the jungle. Their coffee could strip the grime off a tank track. Instead, this little prick wanted some kind of cafe coffee. Eugene knew the type he wanted. It was a low-fat cappuccino with chocolate sprinkles or some shit along those lines.

"You know it wouldn't kill you to make good coffee," David said.

"Sure it would; if I made the coffee you like, then we'd all look like you, ya fuck'n halfwit. If you don't like it, bring your own." The old Marine said as he threw down the cloth he was using to wipe the counter.

"You can't speak to me that way. Do you know who I am?" David sputtered as he stood, shocked.

"Yeah, I know who the fuck you are. You're the sniveling whining sack of shit who hasn't shut up about the food or coffee since you stepped off the chopper." Eugene said as he crossed his beefy arms.

"Richard is going to hear about this. I want you off this base, and if you're lucky, you won't end up in the brig!" David hissed as he stormed out of the galley, with a chorus of laughter following from the people eating lunch. He couldn't believe a lowly piece of shit cook would disrespect him in front of lesser people. Now he knew what his uncle had meant about the rabble who trip up great men.

Jack could see Richard sitting on one of the benches in the gym; he had never seen the man so agitated before.

"What's up, mustachio?" Jack asked. He hung this nickname on Richard when his friend tried and failed to grow a mustache. Richard smiled at the name he came to like.

"Well, you were right," Richard said, knowing Jack would hate being right about the man, even though he disliked David Johns.

"Well, I'm right about a lot of things; you're going to have to give me more of a hint," Jack said as he sat beside his friend.

"About David Johns, you were right about him when you told me not to trust him. Joan here found a bug in my office. So we can go under the assumption he's recorded everything for at least a month." Richard told Jack. He looked at his friend and then at Joan. Jack hadn't liked David from the moment he laid eyes on him. To be right about a bad feeling he had about David was something else.

"As we speak, Joan's team is going through your quarters just in case. They'll check mine next, then, as David goes off duty, they'll check the main center. I want you to lay low for the time being, ok." Richard said. Even though it sounded like a request, Jack didn't think it was one.

David stormed across the compound to the Intel shack; the guards could see him coming. Word traveled faster than David; the men at the front of the shack knew the cook had chewed him out. They even knew the cook called him a whining sack of shit and a halfwit. Now David stormed in through the door and angrily tried to swipe his card. After the third attempt, he realized he had the card backward. David knew he needed to calm down, he was too close for the cook or Richard to get under his skin now. David was forced to look like it was business as usual. It would give him time, and all he needed was time. Sitting in his office, David decided he had enough of this place, and he had enough evidence to bring Richard and Jack out from the shadows. With the aid of the press, he could sell them to the highest bidder. Looking out the window of his office, David wondered what he could do to make their lives as hard as possible.

David knew what he was going to do. He smiled as he thought about his plan; he would upload a virus into the intelligence network. He could do it from his own computer station right there in his office. It would take a day or two to download the virus without anyone noticing. He could upload it in the morning before anyone came on duty.

"Well, how long do you think we have before old Dave goes off the reservation?" Jack asked Richard.

"No more than a day or two, I would think; if he was smart, he would be trying to think of an out right now," Richard said.

"We can't just let him walk around knowing what we do," Joan said.

"Your right. I'm going to give David some administrative time off, you know to cool down." Richard told them.

"Can I watch?" Jack asked, hoping he could try to push David's buttons again. Jack thought of the man as a simpleton; he loved to get the spoiled man riled up.

"I want you to inspect weapons in the armory across the hall from my office in case he tries to run," Richard ordered.

"Can I bring a loaded clip into the building with me?" Jack asked though he knew what the answer was. Instead of getting a response, Richard just sighed and walked out the gym door. Jack grinned as he hopped off the bench rubbing his hands together.

David muttered to himself as he walked to Richard's office. He wondered what the fat bastard wanted now. God, he was getting sick and tired of all the bullshit he had to put up with.

"Yes, David, I want to talk with you; I have heard about your verbal scuffle with the cook, along with what took place in your office earlier today. I feel you need some administrative time off. Nothing too long, of course. Four or five days should do it." Richard watched David John's face go from white to ashen, then red, now it hovered around the purplish color. Richard thought the man was going to have a stroke, then the color lightened, and he smiled.

"I think your right, Richard; a week off will do me a world of good; get my head on straight, that sort of thing," David said and smiled, then he left Richard's office. Jack watched from the armory as the man they suspected of planting surveillance equipment in Richard's office and, as it turned out, in his own private quarters. David turned and walked down the hall with a smile on his face.

"I don't know, Richard; that seemed to be a little too easy if you ask me," Jack said as he walked into his friends' office.

"Yes, at first I thought he was going to explode, then he calmed down and said it was a grand idea, time to get his head on straight as it were. Now I know he is planning something, but what?" Richard wondered aloud when Joan walked in.

"Your quarters are now clean, Jack," Joan reported. She didn't notice how Jack sat up whenever she was around; Joan also failed to see Jack would try and hide the left side of his scared face.

What she did notice was he was a big and ruggedly handsome man. At over six foot, he was taller than most, and with a narrow waist, he looked good even in the digital camouflage he wore most days. Joan had been asked to come to work by Richard, and the British agreed to assign her to this Unit indefinitely. She arrived a month ago, and Jack had been like a schoolboy around her from the first day.

"Um, thank you, Chief," Jack said as he looked at one of the legs on Richard's standard gray metal desk. Richard decided if it were left up to Jack, the man would die alone and a confirmed bachelor.

"I have a plan," Richard announced. "You two are going to keep an eye on our little would-be spy. When you catch him in the act of whatever it is he's doing, you grab him, and we scare the hell out of him." Richard said.

"I'll take the night shift if you want," Jack said, looking at Joan.

"No, the two of you will work together, as in at the same time." Richard finished.

Jack knew what Richard was trying to do, and he was embarrassed his friend thought he needed to go to such lengths to set him up on a date. The word date echoed around Jack's head; how long had it been since he had a date. Jack thought about it and couldn't come up with a month, or year for that matter. Hell, he didn't have anything to wear to a date. The only woman who had been in his life was a high-priced call girl. She was an American who, at the time, was living in Hong Kong when he met her. She would come over for a roll in the hay once in a while. Then things went sideways with Mike Styles, and he escaped from the prison in China. Mike tried to get information out of her, even though she had none to give. Jack saw the pitchers of what the bastard did to her; she didn't even look human when Mike was finished. Maybe he was getting ahead of himself; Richard never mentioned anything about a date, so he could be jumping to conclusions.

"Make it look like you two have a budding romance starting." Richard finished saying. Jack failed to hear any of what the man said except for the words budding romance. When Jack heard the words 'budding romance,' he turned to Joan, who was smiling at him. All Jack could think to do was shrug his big shoulders and watch her walk away. As Jack watched Joan walk to the door, he thought she threw a little more hip action into her walk; he wasn't sure, though. Jack left the office and walked across the compound to his quarters. Sitting in his quarters, Jack wondered what to wear to his made-up date with Chief Warrant Officer Joan O'Driscoll. Everything he owned was some kind of camouflage. He knew Richard was standing outside his door by the way the man knocked.

"I have some clothes you might want to sort through and see if any will fit, and I brought shoes for you. Now I can tell you the ones I like. Also, I can tell you black goes well with everything." As Richard gave advice, Jack stood and looked at his friend.

"Did you do this in the hopes of getting me a girlfriend, or was this really for security reasons?" Jack asked. He looked over some nice button-down shirts and a sports jacket.

"For the security of the unit, of course," Richard said. He was feigning being shocked. Jack thought about telling Richard shouldn't bullshit a bullshitter. Instead, he just smiled at Richard and turned back to the pile of clothing. When Jack picked out what he wanted to wear, Richard looked at what Jack picked and nodded his approval. He chose brown slip-on oxfords with a pair of light tan cotton slacks and a light blue cotton shirt topped with a tan sports jacket.

"I think you'll look the part of the romantic," Richard said as he left the room.

After watching the last of the three stooges marathon being shown by one of the public broadcasting stations from the States. Jack showered again, then dressed. Jack looked in the mirror; he thought he looked all right. Except for the heavy rope of scar tissue running down the left side of his face. Every time Jack thought about what he had gone through at the hands of General Trang and his twisted assistant, he could feel the rage start to burn in him again. Shaking his head, Jack smiled and turned from the mirror; this wasn't an actual date. Jack was determined to make a great impression on the beautiful Chief Warrant. Jack knew about his reputation of being a hard man with an even harder temper. It was this reputation Jack wanted. He used it to keep from getting caught in a conversation about his childhood. It helped Jack guard against the rage he felt at the theft of his childhood and the murder of his mother and father. For that reason, most people gave him a wide birth when they saw him coming.

When Jack left his quarters, he wondered if he looked all right or if his own ego convinced him he was up to par. Walking across the compound, Jack passed a young French Canadian analyst. She was so shocked by the transformation in Jack she turned to watch him walk past and walked into a pole knocking herself on her butt.

"Hey, are you all right?" Jack asked. as he hurried to help the girl to her feet.

"Tabernac, yes, thank you, just clumsy of me." The twenty-something said as she wiped dirt from her bottom.

"Please be careful; we can't have our pretty ladies getting all bruised up," Jack said.

Joan was waiting for him, then walking to meet Jack when she saw what had happened. Joan stood and watched as Jack helped the younger girl to her feet and sent her on her way. Looking at this man she was to work with, Joan couldn't help but wonder if the stories were true. Was his past lost to him? She knew he went to see Phillip three times a week if he was in camp. There was a rumor going around in some of the sessions they needed to restrain Jack. One of the rumors going around was during one of the sessions, he jumped from a window. They said he was trying to get away from whatever monsters lurked in the darkness of his mind. Joan thought, like some of the other stories surrounding this man, this latest was just another story someone made up.

"You ready for our date," Joan asked as she walked up to Jack.

"Ready, willing, and able," Jack answered. For the first part of the night, it seemed harmless enough. They followed David to the mess hall, where the man grabbed a box lunch and left, not wanting to stay in a place where he had been made a fool of. Jack and Joan watched David as he walked back to his quarters. The two of them watched as David ate his supper and worked on his computer.

"Let's get to the intel shack," Joan said as she grabbed Jack's hand. Jack was about to ask her why they were going to the shack, then thought he would wait and see. The guard on duty at the shack's entrance smiled at Jack as he and Joan passed through. Joan held Jack's hand, pulling him along like a disobedient child. Jack wanted to turn and ask the young guard what the hell he was smiling at. Before he could, Joan pulled him through the door and down the hall.

"I want David John's personal computer usage monitored twenty-four hours a day, all the information placed in a confidential file for Richard's Along with Jacks and my eyes only." Joan was telling one of the computer geeks who work in the Unit. These young people were rescued by Richard. All of them were saved from governments who were going to prosecute them for hacking into their supposed hacker-proof systems. Now they worked for the Unit and were free to hack into governments all over the world. Joan was talking to one of the female hackers; the girl was eighteen and had more facial piercings than Jack could comfortably count. Her hair was dyed flat jet black she wore black eye shadow and eyeliner. Her fellow hacker was another girl who shared the same taste in makeup and piercings. The second girl told Jack that he had a *wicked* scar when he first met her.

"No problem; anything to get that fucker wound up? You know David came in here and told Tish and me we were going to have to remove our jewelry, and we couldn't wear our makeup. The first day he came here, we went to Richard, and he told us not to worry. We love Richard and hate that asshole." Tosh told Joan as she hacked into David's computer. Jack was amazed at how fast she was able to break through the firewall of the laptop.

"You guys can get into his computer that fast?" Jack asked. He was amazed when he watched what David typed start scrolling across Tosh's screen.

"Oh, it's not so hard; all I did was hack in and place a little program. It copies David's keystrokes and relays them to this file. I can put the file into a sleep mode where it will collect whatever he types in his e-mails and to what address he sends them." Tosh told Jack; he started to think this hard-looking girl wasn't so bad. Tosh explained what she was doing; also, she didn't speak to him as if he was stupid. He asked a question, and she gave him the answer, simple plain no, bullshit jargon to make the uninitiated feel stupid.

The rest of the night, Jack and Joan watched as David worked on his computer, then about eleven o'clock, he called it quits and turned off his lights. Joan walked beside Jack holding his hand. She liked how he would stand still and listen to her. To him, it didn't seem to matter; she was a woman. Jack thought she was the most beautiful thing he had ever laid eyes on; Jack couldn't believe she was holding his hand. Jack knew it was only pretended; Jack knew with the heavy scar running down his face, he looked horrible. For now, he just wanted to walk with this woman beside him. When they reached the female quarters, Joan thanked Jack for taking her out around the compound and then, to Jack's surprise, stood on her tiptoes and gave him a peck on the cheek goodnight. The following day Jack could swear he could still feel Joan's lips on his cheek. Jack couldn't wait to tell Phillip that for the first time, in he didn't know how long, he slept through the night without waking from a nightmare. Walking across the compound, Jack was smiling and even said good morning to a couple of shocked passers-by. One of them was so amazed he turned to see if anyone else was behind him.

Of course, Richard was the first in the Intel shack; it was the same every morning. Going through security, the guards returned Jack's good mornings with smiles and curious looks. Jack walked down the hall and watched Tish walk into Richards's office with a file in her hand.

"Thank you, Tish; just have a seat for a moment." Richard was saying as Jack entered his office. Richard looked at Jack and wanted to ask him how it went last night; however, other matters had to be taken care of first.

"We're just going to wait for Joan to arrive before we start. She was kind enough to go to the mess and get a pot of coffee for us." As Richard spoke, Joan walked into the office with a large pot of coffee, and the cook followed with a tray of pastries. The old Marine looked at Tish and then around the office. All the young hackers loved the gruff ex-marine; he had taken Tish and Tosh, as they called themselves, under his wing.

"What's going on? You're not in trouble, are ya?" Eugene Baker retired Marine, now cook for the Unit, asked Lisa Monroe, aka Tish.

"No, Tosh and I did some work last night, that's all." She answered her unit father. Jack and Richard watched as the gruff cook patted Tish on the shoulder.

"Good girl, proud of ya and Tosh." Then walked out the door. Joan smiled as she watched Tish blush under her heavy makeup. Maybe if the girl's real father said the same once in a while instead of trying to rape her, she wouldn't be here. Once everyone had taken a seat and helped themselves to coffee and a breakfast pastry, Tish started to read from the report compiled from David John's computer use the night before.

Richard couldn't believe what he was hearing; he knew David Johns was the adopted nephew of G.W. Hollyford. The man who was responsible for the *cradle* project. The man who ordered Jack's parents killed and placed Jack into the project erased whatever memory he had as a boy. That same man now sat in a prison that didn't exist. G.W. Hollyford's son was also in the CIA. When his father had been director, he was thrown out with his father. The younger Hollyford was now serving five years for tax fraud in a Montana minimum security prison.

Chapter 3

WHEN HE FOUND OUT ABOUT David, he should have had the man removed. Richard thought maybe, just maybe, something could turn out for the best. He wanted to believe David was here in the Unit because he wanted to do some good. However, it seemed David was trying to exact revenge for his adopted family. Richard read the rest of last night's e-mails he became increasingly worried about the security and safety of this compound. Richard looked at the phone on his desk; he picked it up and pressed four buttons.

"This is Windsor one; I am calling in an Omega one priority, code Omega one deep six, six!" Richard looked at Jack and Joan.

"Get that man and bring him to me!" Richard ordered.

"Get Tosh and get her back to work along with the other techs. I want to know if there is any military movement." Richard ordered Tish. Without saying a word Tish jumped up and ran out of the office. Jack followed Joan out of the office and across the compound; he thought they should check the mess hall before going to David's quarters.

"With time off, the little shit is probably still in bed," Joan said as she pulled the door open to the male quarters. Jack knew the best way to grab someone was to do it when they were asleep. The confusion with being drug out of bed violently aided in getting them to cooperate. Therefore, when Jack kicked the door off the hinges, he ran right to the bed, grabbed David by the hair, and drug him out of his quarters. To the other men who had heard Jack kick in the door of their neighbor, then watched him drag the struggling David out by his hair. Most of them thought he'd pissed Jack off one too many times. All of them thought good riddance; none of them liked the man, and to most, David was nothing more than a pain in the ass.

"Hey, let me go. I'm going to have you charged with assault; you can't do this!" David screamed as Jack drugged him out of the building and threw him on the ground.

"Listen to me, you little shit, you're going to walk, or I swear to god I'll beat you half to death. Then drag you busted and bleeding; if you think I can't try me!" Jack said as Joan stood with her hand on her sidearm. She watched as the sulking David Johns stood and tried to brush the dirt from his pj's. Every time David would try to slow down, Jack would shove him hard enough the man would stumble forward. When they reached the security checkpoint inside the Intel shack, the guards stood aside and let Jack and Joan take David through into the main building.

"I don't know what you are doing; I will be talking to the Secretary-General and counsel about how I was treated here when I get to New York, David threatened.

"Well, I don't think I have to worry about you making it to the big apple anytime soon. Look, David, we know your uncle is G.W. Hollyford; his sister adopted you when you were young. We also know you were in contact with a Chinese operative about selling information about this Unit." Richard told the pale and shaking David.

"Now, a man in your position knows what the last charge would do to your name. You know how long you would live after being convicted of that type of treason; I want you to think about it for a moment." Richard said.

"I've been set up; I would never do anything of the sort, and as for being Hollyford's nephew, so what I never liked the man, he was a blowhard," David said, trying to find a way out.

"Joan had the hackers tie into your computer and copy everything you sent and received last night. You mentioned a price, and the spy agreed to pay it. You even went as far as to set up a meet where the exchange would occur." Richard told him. David knew he had been caught; he also knew trying to talk his way out of this would not work. Looking around the office, David then turned his panicked gaze to Joan. If he could get her gun, he could take her hostage and then get the hell out of the compound. Once in the jungle, he would kill her, then run for the ocean and try to find a boat. All at once, David jumped up and tried to grab Joan. Jack and Richard watched as David tried to get her pistol free from its holster. Jack almost laughed when Joan sidestepped and threw a punch that landed squarely on Davids's chin knocking the man out cold.

David knew he had a hold of Joan's shirt then something happened. He felt something hit him in the face. The next thing David knew, he was looking at Jack from the floor. Jack had knocked him out, he was handcuffed, and his one chance was gone; he was their prisoner now.

"Nice try; I bet you didn't think we had 'Rocky' in this Unit, did ya?" Jack asked him. David was lifted off the floor by two guards. Richard stood shaking his head, looking at the man who betrayed the Unit and his country.

"I want him sedated at all times; he is to be placed on the last chopper with Joan, Jack, and myself, is that understood?" Richard asked. The two highly trained guards nodded their understanding.

"Choppers, what choppers?" Joan asked.

"This base is no longer a viable entity. It has been compromised, so we bug out and destroy everything left behind." Richard told her and watched as Tosh ran down the hall towards his office.

"The choppers are inbound, and the barges have been set up in international waters off Vladivostok. The North Korean military is also on the move, and the Chinese are flying in a large elite unit. From what we caught on the radio traffic, they were to erase an embarrassment." The frazzled girl told them.

"That would be you, Jack," Richard said as Joan smiled. She heard the stories about him and his friend Tran. Joan really wanted to listen to those stories from Jack himself. Tosh looked at Jack; he was large, and some of the other hackers told her he would kill at the drop of a hat. They said he had to see the shrink three times a week to keep from flipping out and killing people in the camp. She didn't believe it, when Jack smiled at her she flinched.

"You shamed the Chinese government and their military; that's so cool," Tosh said.

"Ha, you hear that, Richard? I'm cool," Jack said, smiling, and watched as Joan shook her head smiling.

The choppers started to land before lunch; the first people to load out were the tech staff, with all the hard drives from the computers. Anything that couldn't be taken out and placed into a case for transport was erased. The cases themselves were wired with plastic explosives. If the chopper went down, the case could be remotely detonated, destroying the information on the drives inside. The following people to load out were the support staff; this was the medical staff, and the people of the mess hall. When Richard told Eugene he would have to leave first, the ex-marine crossed his big arms and smiled.

"Not before my girls." Eugenes smiling answer came as no surprise to Jack. What did surprise him was Richard smiled back and nodded.

"Then go and help them, please." Was all the leader of the Unit said?

Richard, Joan, Tish, and Tosh sat in the back of the large cormorant helicopter. Jack and Eugene sat on either side of David Johns was sedated and strapped into his seat, still handcuffed. Being the last chopper out of the camp, Richard carried a black briefcase with him; when he opened it, Jack could see several switches. He watched as Richard flipped each switch into the on position with one last look; the Unit leader pushed a black button. Even though they flew away from the compound and inside a large, heavy cormorant helicopter, Jack could still hear the explosions. They all could feel the blast wave as it hit the chopper, pushing it forward and up at the same time.

"What the hell do we do now?" Jack asked Richard.

"We carry on; we know David was going to meet a Chinese spy and sell him information on the Unit. I say we should talk with this man and see if he wants to tell us anything." Richard said with a smile.

"Do we still have a job?" Tish asked, hoping she and Tosh wouldn't have to return to their families.

"Oh yes, I wouldn't let a little thing like this get the best of my team," Richard said.

"We have taken care of the worst in North Korea though I would have liked to get Kim Jong-Un and put him with Hollyford and Chow. The plan was to pull out in six months anyway. The only thing we lost was the buildings and the monitors. All the information made it out and is on the barges now." Richard finished as the Indian pilot informed them they were now out of North Korean air space and over the sea of Japan.

Though they called the ships barges, these two vessels were far from the flat bottom powerless goods-carrying tubs people think of when the word barge is used. Instead, these vessels were retired by the British government and then handed over to the Unit. These ships were naval resupply ships; now, they sported freshly painted hulls of dark blue with white superstructures and cranes. The first of the ships wore her name on the stern of her hull and on both cranes. 'ARAWN' white on the stern and dark blue on her cranes. She is named after the ancient Welsh god of the hunt and underworld.

The second is identical to her sister in every way, but for her name, this second ship was called 'CAILLECH .'Her name comes from the Welsh; however, the Irish and Scottish also held this god in their hearts long eons past. Caillech was the god of weather, earth, and sky, along with the moon, the seasons, and the sun. Richard was proud of these two ships; from the outside. They were nothing more than old ships well cared for with the billions the Unit had extracted from criminal bank accounts around the world and with what Jack turned over. They were able to refit these two sturdy ladies of the seas with new, more fuel-efficient, and powerful engines. Jack loved the ships; on them, he felt free. He would stand out on the deck, enjoying the sound of the water as it passed around them. Both Jack and Richard thanked god; the Canadians were in the area, along with the British. One call, and they were out and safe.

Chapter 4

THE CAPTAIN OF ARAWN stood on the bridge wing; he smiled as Richard and Jack walked onto the bridge. He was a smaller, slim man with a lined face and sad blue eyes. Jack thought the Captain's eyes seemed to have taken on the blue of the sky. The man knew his ship and the men who worked under him. Jack listened to some of the men talk one night in the galley as the ships brought them here. One sailor said if Richard was to try and replace the Captain, he would leave with the old man. To their relief, Jack told him he wasn't the replacement. The men laughed when Jack informed them he didn't even know how to drive one of these things.

Richard informed the Captain the ship's destination would be Smith Island, part of the Andaman and Nicobar Island group in the Andaman Sea. The Captain nodded and went to one of a dozen computers on the bridge; he asked the man there to bring up their destination. In less than a minute, Jack could feel the ship start to turn to the south. He watched as the compass slowly turned to its new heading. Smith Island, it didn't sound romantic to Jack. Then again, it would be better than a fake date walking around the compound in the middle of the jungle, he thought.

"We are going to have to travel through the East to the South China Seas. Then pass the Raiu islands through the Singapore and Malacca strait. Once we reach, if we reach our destination, we'll anchor offshore and monitor the situation from satellites. I want to know if the Chinese triangulated the Unit's position from David's communications. If they have, they know we've pulled out, and the jig is up, as it were. However, if they fall short of finding it, we meet their spy and see if we can grab him." Richard explained his plan to Jack.

"Ok, so until we know how far the Chinese have made it, then I'm free?" Jack asked, hoping Richard would say yes. Nodding his head, Richard answered. Now Jack thought all I have to do is work up the nerve to ask Joan out on an actual date.

The Arawn had one hundred and sixty men and women on board. Most of them were sailors and officers of the ship. The rest were from the compound. These two ships would hunt for treasures lost to the sea in some millennia past. Both also had advanced scientific labs on board to help in the understanding of the oceans covering most of our planet. This was a stipulation of the governments who funded and founded the Unit. In these labs, scientists worked, trying to shed light on the depths of misunderstood ocean myths. The scientists would eat at different times than the crew of the ship and those of the Unit, even though they all belonged to the same entity. It wasn't that the scientists thought better of themselves; it was so they could talk about their work. It also helped the scientists feel they are not excluding others from the conversation.

Jack liked to eat at the same time as the scientists, the conversations didn't involve him, and he wasn't expected to join in. He could just listen to the men and women as they rattled on about the mating habits of this animal or how single-cell organisms evolved, from all the talk about how animals mated compared to some other kind of water creature. Jack believed these people needed to get off the ship and do some mating for themselves.

"Good news!" Richard announced as he entered the galley.

"The Chinese didn't get a chance to triangulate David's signal, so they know he was in the northern part of Asia someplace; that's about it. As for the North Koreans, they caught the signature of one of the choppers as it flew out into the sea of Japan, and that's all. So I think we're good to go with the meet on Smith Island." Richard told Jack.

Jack and Richard had talked about the meeting with the Chinese spy for three hours. Richard told Jack he and Joan were to act as married tourists taking a tour of the old British prison on the island. After Jack and Richard hammered out the rest of the plan, Jack excused himself and left the galley. He knew they would be at sea when Tran went through the operation for the tumor. This was better because the ships could communicate with London via wireless and satellite links. Jack stood behind the radio operators waiting for his call to London to go through. He was just about the point he was going to give up and leave the small communication room; the operator turned and gave him a headset. Jack was shocked to hear Jiao on the other end of the line.

"How is he doing?" Jack asked, afraid to hear the answer.

"Jack, he is going to be fine; the doctors can't believe how strong he is. You have nothing to be worried about. They have scheduled the surgery for first thing in the morning. The surgeon told us it should be over by lunch." Jiao said. In the call's background, Jack listened as Jiao's baby cried for his bottle. Jack smiled as he heard the baby boy, a flash to his mother came at that moment. The vision was so strong it forced Jack to suck in a breath. For a second, Jack thought he would be driven to his knees. The radio operator looked at him, wondering if he should get help or sit still.

"Ok, that's great. Would you tell Tran, Richard, and I called? I'll call back tomorrow afternoon." Jack listened to little Scott make happy sounds as he got his bottle. He barely heard Jiao when she told him she would tell Tran they had called. For the first time in weeks, he had a good feeling about the surgery and Trans recovery. Jack stood outside the bridge of the Arawn. He smiled as he thought about having Tran back. He thought about going to the galley for a coffee, then decided he would try to find a quiet corner to sit in and look at the night sky. Jack walked to the stern of the ship; he chose to watch the wake of the ship as she made her way through the sea. Sitting by the railing, he looked up at the stars and listened to the hiss of the foaming water. Under the sound of the ship passing over the water, Jack started to hear another sound. At first, he couldn't tell what it was or what direction it came from. Then he saw movement out of the corner of his eye, in his peripheral vision. Something black moved on the water; it was closing on the ship. Jack wanted to alert somebody; he was about to run to a call box when he saw Joan walking towards him.

"Somebody's trying to board us," Jack told her. Joan turned without saying a word and ran for the nearest call box. Jack knew it would be a running fight from there if he let the first man on the deck. He knew the first man had to be stopped. Jack knew this would be pirates because of the scientific gear ships like these carried; they were often targeted by pirates. Ships like the Arawn and the Caillech had enough computers, and other scientific gear pirates deemed both ships worth the risk of a fight. To these pirates, their lives were worth the risk if it meant an easy life for their families.

Joan reached the call box as the first grappling hook sailed out of the night and clanged onto the deck. Jack hid and waited until the first Asian face peeked over the railing. Throwing off the tarp he was hiding under, Jack stepped to the man and grabbed his head with both his big hands, violently wrenching the man's head and breaking his neck. Before the second man had a chance to get his feet on the ship's deck, his friend and leader dropped past him and disappeared into the black water. Then a large fist swung out of the night and slammed into the side of his head. The last thing the second pirate saw was the water of the ocean coming up to meet him. Jack could hear running boots coming behind him. He knew armed guards would stop any further attempts at boarding from any pirates. Jack sat on his deck chair, and security chased off the pirates with a hail of automatic gunfire. The Caillech reported no attempt had been made to board her. Also, her Captain had ordered round-the-clock security on deck. Jack sat and watched the moon and stars as they glided through the black sky; he was about to get up and go to bed when Joan stepped out of a doorway.

"You did the right thing; if they had gotten on board, then more would have died," Joan told him. She tried to lessen Jack's guilt over the killing of the pirate.

"Yeah, I know." Was all Jack could think to say. Jack looked at the moon one last time before he went in. Joan stopped him and looked into his eyes, then she placed her hand over the scar running down the left side of his face.

"You carry the guilt of killing others because you're not a monster; you're a man; talking helps." She said, then gave him a peck on the cheek again. Standing on the deck with his cheek burning where Joan placed her hand, Jack could see himself wanting her in his life. What kind of life could he give her? In reality, he was a killer, maybe not born but certainly built. Though he hoped his killings brought the world greater peace. Jack remembered an old and wise man who once said, 'There can be no peace if one man is forced to pick up arms.' Jack knew, like all soldiers know, with perceived differences comes fear, then hate.

That night the nightmares came back, but the flow was different. Every time the dream was about to reach the point where he would wake screaming. Joan's face would wash over Jack's subconscious, and the dream would change. When the night finally started to give up its hold on the earth for another day, Jack rolled out of bed and showered. He was really looking forward to seeing Joan.

The following week flew by as he spent more time with Joan and Richard going over their plan on how to handle the Chinese spy they were on their way to meet on Smith Island. Richard watched as Joan looked at Jack and how Jack tried to keep the scarred left side of his face away from her. When Richard would smile, Jack would give him his best angry look. While it was enough of a look to scare most of humanity, Richard would smile and wink at Jack.

Jack stood on the deck and watched as Smith Island materialized out of the fog that blanketed the Andaman Sea during the long watch of the night. The fog was heavy enough to keep what little sound the ship made as she passed over Poseidon's layer from rising into the air. Richard joined Jack, and he told him the Captain was going to anchor the ship in Smith Island's main harbor.

"I have made sure we are listed under a scientific vessel, so you shouldn't have any problems if you let Joan do the talking." Richard finished.

"When we're done with the relocation, I think I am going to take some time off, go back to St Martin, take care of Tran, fish, anything I have to do to get the last year straight in my head," Jack said.

"Are you all right? Do you need anything?" Richard asked as he looked up at his friend.

"Yeah, I'm fine. It's just we needed to do more than we thought in North Korea. I'm having doubts; I am wondering if I can do this and, if I can, for how long." Jack said.

"You know I have enough people to set up in the new area, so you can start your vacation as soon as we are done here," Richard told Jack as he patted his shoulder. Richard knew he was going to have to tell Phillip about his fear about Jack.

Richard worried the pace he set might be too much for the man. He worried about Jack going out into the bush for days and sometimes weeks on end. Richard knew working with Phillip, Jack managed to get back some of the moral codings his parents tried to instill in him as a child. Could he be harboring guilt over his life and the path he found himself on? When they traveled, Phillip was with them as Richard sat and talked with the Unit's counselor about Jack and the need for the man to take time off.

"I think he'll be all right," Phillip said as he looked at Richard.

"Jack's confused; he knows what he's doing is making a difference in the lives of so many. However, at the same time, he doesn't know if this is what his mother and father would have wanted him to do. You see, Richard, we have found Jack has a wonderful ability to remember his mother, not so much his father. That will come; his mother being a lawyer, taught him to beware of corruption. Also, she taught him how people should treat each other. Because of this, Jack has a real sense of right and wrong when it comes to forcing people to do things or of the killing of unarmed noncombatants." Phillip told Richard. When Phillip finished his explanation, Richard sat and stared out into space for a moment, then looked at Philip.

"So what your saying is, I did the right thing by giving him the time he needs?" Richard asked.

"Absolutely, yes, you did. It will give Jack time to realize his mother would approve of his life now. Also, she would forgive his past if he would only come to terms with the fact he is of no blame. Jack needs to grasp the fact that he was not in control of his past. This will be the hardest thing for a man like our Jack to grasp. For so much of his life was removed from his control, now he has control back. It's hard for him to contemplate ever being totally without it. In his mind, he was the authority responsible for his own past." Phillip said as he picked up his cup of tea.

"I just wish he could get to that point. I hate to see the man torturing himself over something he really had no choice over." Richard stated as the two men sat watching the waves march towards Smith Island.

Jack stood and watched as the Captain dropped anchor outside the town of Port Blair. A smaller speedboat called a launch was being lowered over the side of the Arawn. Because the Caillech wasn't needed, she stayed out at sea. From her position, she would do satellite surveillance. Thanks to the Americans, they had the best satellites in the sky watching over the area. Jack turned and watched as Joan stepped out of a doorway. She smiled and nodded to Jack, who nearly fell over when he saw her. Wearing a one-piece bathing suit with a white cotton wrap around her waist, Joan had most of the men on board staring at her, with her red hair and creamy skin splashed with freckles across her chest and shoulders.

"We should get going; we don't want to be late," Joan said as she kissed Jack on the cheek.

Joan was sitting in the speed boat when Jack climbed down the ladder, she smiled and nodded to him, and he smiled. He knew he was getting ready for a fight if the Chinese spy he and Joan were going to meet had orders to grab or kill them. Jack had someone new to worry over; he worried about Tran dying, and now he worried about Joan. This beautiful red-haired woman sitting beside him.

"Did you pack anything for the day, honey?" Joan asked to Jack's shock.

"Honey?" Jack repeated, shocked. "I didn't think I needed to." He finished.

"Well, don't worry. I grabbed some things for you." Joan said as she handed Jack a small double-edged knife in a case; it was made to fit inside the waistband of his trousers under his shirt. She also showed him an aerosol inhaler many asthmatics carried. Unlike the ones used to control asthma symptoms, this one-shot is a fine mist of a highly potent sedative. Once inhaled, the individual would be rendered unconscious within fifteen seconds. Faster depending on how close the delivery system was to the nose and mouth of the target. The last thing she showed Jack was the tinny .25 cal automatic pistol. Jack smiled, then thought he would take a chance and patted his beautiful partner's knee. To his surprise, she didn't slap him. Instead, she held his hand all the way to the docks for small power boats. Once Jack found the birth, they were assigned. He and Joan found their way into the town of Port Blair.

Jack couldn't believe this once cruel face of British rule in India was now a hospital serving the town of Port Blair. It also allowed tourists to take pictures. Jack watched as a guide told the people of the rebellion how most of the leaders were thrown in this place. As Jack watched the crowd, he was looking for a sign the spy was among them. It wasn't until the tour guide started to tell of the Japanese occupation during the Second World War a distinguished-looking Asian man stepped from the crowd.

"I have heard this before. My wife wanted to come here and see it again." The man said to Jack.

"I am new here. My wife has never heard this." Jack said. During David's questioning and with the aid of the newest member of the sodium pentothal and scopolamine family of pharmaceuticals, the traitor told Richard the coded phrase.

"I trust you had a good trip here, Mister Smith?" The spy asked.

"I had a fine trip; the people I work for think I'm on vacation," Jack told the man.

"I know we discussed an exact amount during our communications, and I don't see a means to carry it," Jack said.

"Well, my people want to make sure it is good information before we pay." The Chinese spy returned smiling.

"Oh, I'm sorry, I forgot to take my stupid pill this morning, so it was nice meeting you. Have a nice life." Jack said as he stepped back from the man.

"Hold on, I was just testing you; the money is in a numbered account in the Cayman Islands. It can be accessed at any time, and I have the account information here." The spy said and held up a piece of paper. Jack knew he wouldn't let the numbered account go until the information he was ordered to retrieve was in his hand.

"I have the flash drive at the marina hidden on my boat," Jack said. He knew this wasn't the deal; he was hoping the man was under orders to get it no matter what. Jack watched as the spy looked around and nodded his head so slightly that it was almost missed. Jack did the same and smiled to himself, knowing the Chinese spotter would be busy trying to find Jack's handlers. Joan watched as Jack talked to the Chinese spy. She was surprised he didn't seem excited in any way. She smiled as Jack turned and started towards the dock where they tied the launch. Jumping down into the launch, Jack reached under the console in front of the steering wheel and pulled out a flash drive.

"The money, please," Jack said as he held the drive behind his back.

"Let me see what's on it first." The spy said as he looked around, seeming to get nervous.

"Listen, pal, I've had other interest in this information, so if you want to see anything, then you have got to pay," Jack told the spy.

"I have to confirm it is real, not bullshit as you Americans say!" The spy said as he looked around again.

"You keep looking around; if you think someone is coming to jump me, well, you're fucked. When I grabbed this, I tripped a signal blocker under the wheel. So for the last thirty seconds, your people have heard shit; now, do they want the information, or should I sell it to the Russians. Or to any of the countries from the Middle East; like I said, I have lots of other interested parties wanting this." Just as Jack finished, he saw Joan walking down the dock; she held bags as if she had been shopping and wore a wide-brimmed hat.

"My wife is coming, so make up your mind, in or out!" To push the point, he was serious. Jack untied the line at the back of the boat, holding it to the dock. The Chinese spy looked around one more time; he would have to make this decision on his own. Just as he was going to say yes, something jabbed him above his left kidney, and the pain caused him to inhale quickly.

As Joan passed behind the Chinese spy, she held a needle in her left hand and stabbed him above the left kidney. When he sucked in air from the pain of the needle piercing his back, Joan sprayed him in the face with the sedative. Reaching up, Jack grabbed the man and pulled him into the launch; looking up, Jack watched as a hole appeared in the boat's windshield. Joan turned around to see if she could find the sniper when the second bullet hit her. The round passed through her upper shoulder, skipped off the water behind the boat, and buried itself in a beautiful yacht birthed beside them. Grabbing Joan, Jack didn't bother untying the rope holding the front of the speed boat to the dock.

Twisting the key over in the ignition, Jack shoved the throttles all the way forward. When the two-three hundred and fifty horsepower mercury engines caught, they did their best to stand the launch on its tail. Then in a guttural roar and a flash of white fiberglass, the launch was screaming out of the marina, heading for the harbor. Sitting on the floor of the racing boat, Joan looked up at Jack. He was leaning forward, trying to avoid other boats in the crowded harbor and trying to avoid getting shot by the sniper. A bullet hole appeared in the back of the driver's seat; thankfully, Jack wasn't sitting. Instead, he was standing in front of it. Joan looked behind them as Jack swerved around other craft coming into Port Blair. Joan was trying to find the sniper intent on killing Jack when the wound in her shoulder caused her to black out from the pain. Jack looked back to blood running down Joan's back, staining her wrap; he could also see she was unconscious. From where he stood, Jack couldn't tell how bad it was, or if she was even alive, all Jack could do was to try and wring more speed out of the launch.

Chapter 5

THE ARAWN WAS ALREADY pulling its anchor off the bottom of the Andaman Sea when Jack arrived with the captured spy and the wounded Joan. Before Jack could tell the medics Joan had been shot, they jumped off the ladder and started to work on her. He wanted to help; Jack, also at this time, would likely make things worse for her and the two medics. Richard waited with Jack outside the operating room as the doctor worked on Joan. Tish stopped by and asked if they had any news; thirty minutes later, Tosh poked her head in the door with the same question. Just when Jack thought he couldn't stand the wait any longer, the young doctor walked out of the surgical room. Pulling the mask from his face, the young Australian doctor smiled.

"The bullet passed through her muscle; it's the muscle that moves the shoulder. So for the next, while she won't be doing much, if she takes it easy, she'll make a full recovery." Richard and Jack shook the doctor's hand before they left; Jack wanted to stay and see Joan when she woke. The doctor told him she was asleep and would be for the night.

The spy sat on the cot in his cell at the bottom of the Arawn; he knew he had been caught. In China, if you were caught, then you were tortured. The government in China believed all the other countries in the world did the same. It was just the other countries had never been caught the way China had. Years ago, when he was being trained for his life in the intelligence service of his country, they had taught him and others how to deal with torture. The spy believed he could stand whatever they used against him; his mind wasn't a slave to his body. Jie Zheng heard the outer door open and then the guards speaking to someone. When the inner door opened, the man who met him on the island entered with a fat man. Jie sat straight and looked at the fat man. He knew from experience it was the soft-looking men who held all the power. It was the hard men who kept them in power.

"We've sent a message to your government and nearest embassy telling them of the attempt on the life of our officer by a hostile agent of their foreign service," Richard said.

"I could care less how you worded it; my government will know the truth. I was to meet a man, and this man told me he had information on a matter of importance to my country. Then I was kidnapped for no other reason than the hunt for information in matters that don't concern you." Jie Zheng said.

"With the sniper and this ingenious little co2-powered dart gun, we found on you. I do not think you were going to pay for the information in good faith. Were you?" Jack asked. Jie could see a small plastic device with a co2 canister sticking out of the bottom.

"Don't suppose you would be so kind as to tell us what the toxin is derived from?" Richard asked, not really expecting an answer. Richard smiled when Jie Zheng turned his back to Jack and him.

"Well, that's what I thought, so be it; you will be handed over to the Americans for the duration of your stay in the west. Before you ask, I don't know how long that will be because you are part of a government. Also, you have no ties to terrorist organizations. I think you will be treated well." Richard informed Jie. As Jack stood to leave, Jie Zheng stood; he stepped to the bars of his cell. He looked at Jack; it seemed, for the first time, the smaller older man really looked at Jack. Richard stopped, turned, and watched as Jie studied Jack's scarred face and the man's heavy shoulders. Standing still, Jack was about to ask 'what the hell' the man was staring at when the captured spy nodded almost to himself and then started to speak.

"I had a daughter once. She was twelve when I sent her to train for the intelligence service. Just after her twentieth-second birthday, she was sent to kill six men in India, an American, and a Tibetan. I think you are that American. You killed my daughter, her, and her friend. As her father, I deserve to know, did she die with honor." Jie Zheng asked. Jack and Richard stood looking at the man, stunned; neither of the men could believe this was Jiao's father.

"What was your daughters' name?" Jack asked. Both he and Richard studied the older spy's face trying to see if there was any resemblance to Jiao.

"My daughter was Jiao; I gave her to the trainers in the military after I shot her mother, my wife." Jie Zheng told them. When the man admitted to killing his wife, Jiao's mother. Both Richard and Jack stood looking at the man who had just confessed to everything Jiao feared.

"Why, why in hell would you kill the mother of your child?" Richard asked, shocked. Wondering if he had misheard heard the statement, or at least he hoped he had. When the man smiled at the question, Richard knew he had heard it correctly.

"When my wife was little, her father was a great man in the Foreign Service stationed in Paris. For years, he was responsible for the assets that gathered information in Europe. When they moved back to Beijing, I met and married his daughter. Some years later, my wife gave birth to Jiao. My wife was always telling her about Paris and how it was the city of love. My wife would get Jiao to draw and paint monuments of that decadent city for our apartment. When Jiao was twelve, she told me when she was old enough, she was going to be an artist and move to Paris to live." Jie Zheng said.

"My wife turned my own daughter against her country, so I took my wife to the head of my Unit. This man had been friends with her father for years; he ordered me to shoot her." Jack and Richard watched as a smile played on the spy's lips.

"Which I did happily, knowing she was the cause of my daughter's corruption. Now I need to know if I can honor her or if I should curse her name along with her mothers." Jie Zheng told Richard and Jack. The two men looked at him and shook their heads, then stepped through the inner door of the holding area. Each watched as the door was closed and locked; Jack stood looking in at Jaio's father as Richard shook his head.

"It still shocks me of the depths of evil a human can sink to in the name of a country or a religious belief," Richard said.

Jack and Richard left the cells at the bottom of the ship and made their way to the infirmary. Neither man said a word before they entered the recovery room where Joan now sat up in bed being hand-fed strawberry ice cream by Tish. Tosh occupied a chair at the foot of the bed. She was reading Joan her horoscopes for the day. Before Joan could stop the girl, she blurted out the horoscope.

"Hey, it says here, you're going to have a man come into your life, and he will bring you peace and contentment. I think it might be Jack they're talking about." Tosh said before she realized Jack was standing behind her.

"You do, do you?" Jack asked as the girls headed for the door holding hands and giggling. The two men sat with Joan and talked about how she felt and if she thought she needed any time off. Of course, Richard offered to fly Joan anywhere she wished to go. She opted to stay on the ship with them.

"That's fine. Now I was going to have you moved into my cabin, and I'll take yours. That way, you have more privacy, you know, until you're healed and ready to move back into your cabin." Richard told

Joan. Jack just smiled, knowing she would be on the same deck as he was, just two doors from him.

"I have ordered the ship to sail around the Island of Sri Lanka, then around the point of India to the city of Kochi. There we will send our prisoners off with the Americans then the rest of us will get on a plane and go to our homes for some well-deserved time off." Richard told them. Jack was already thinking about a little boat and some fishing. He wanted to get in with Tran as soon as his friend felt up to it.

It had been some time since Jack had been ripped from his sleep by the murder of his mother. Phillip said this was because he worked hard to remember her. Jack knew he had come to grips with his mother's murder and grieved in his own way. Jack still dreamed of different people and places. On this night, his mother's screams ripped him from his sleep. Turning on his reading lamp Jack could hear the dying echoes of his screams. Standing at the sink in his bathroom Jack splashed water on his face; he knew this nightmare had been brought on by Joan getting shot. To Jack, it seemed he had just gotten back to sleep when the sound of a horn intruded into the peaceful realm of St Martin and the home he had there. Standing in the open doorway of his cabin, he couldn't see any of the crew running, so Jack placed the sound of the horn in his dream. He was about to turn and try to regain the peaceful land of the Scilly Islands when the horn sounded again. Jack decided maybe he should find out what was going on. He hurried to the bridge of the ship to find Richard standing on the bridge of the Arawn when Jack entered and walked over to him.

"The Chinese have a ship closing in on our position. The Captain has sounded the horn hoping when the Chinese Captain hears it, he will back off." Richard said, knowing Jack was going to ask what was happening.

"Is it working, sir?" Jack asked as the Captain stepped out of the radar room.

"No, the bastard is still on a collision course with us, and I think he means to put a hole in our side." The gray-haired American Captain answered.

"How the hell could he do that?" Jack asked no one. Richard decided he would answer Jack's question.

"The Chinese ship is sailing under the guise of a fishing vessel. Like the Russians did back in the day, in reality, it belongs to the intelligence and information gathering portion of the military." Richard told Jack.

"With the hull able to break pack ice, it would be no problem for them to ram us and punch a hole in our hull below the water line. Then all they would have to do is back off and watch as we tried to escape in the life rafts." The Captain said. He ordered his ship to full speed and changed direction, so our ship and the Chinese were now running in the same direction. Richard and the Captain were bent over a large map reading desk when a shout came from the radar room. Jack turned and watched as the Captain hurried over to the door.

"Holy hell, I don't know who you call friends, Richard, but they dug our ass out of the fire." The Gray-haired Captain from Nantucket said as he returned to the desk.

"An American battleship on patrol in the Arabian Sea, bound for the Persian Gulf, somehow got wind of our predicament and is heading to the Laccadive Sea to see if they can help. We can hear the Chinese telling the American Captain it is none of his concern and to mind his own business. Now I know this Captain, and I can tell you the man is a real busybody, practically invented scuttlebutt. I can imagine this little intervention will cost me a good bottle of scotch, a really good bottle." The Captain said as he smiled.

"How long before we are in the Laccadive Sea?" Richard asked as he felt the Arawn rise over another in the endless marching waves which seemed to find their way around the world.

"We'll be there and anchored before the U.S.S. Winston-S Churchill enters the Laccadive Sea. However, they are going to hang around when we set you guys off in Kochi, then the Churchill will see we safely make it back out to sea again." The Captain answered with his smile returning to its usual place at the corner of his thin lips

"Well, I must say, with the namesake of the bulldog coming to save the day, as it were, I feel better," Richard announced. He thanked the Captain and left the bridge. Jack knew Richard was trying to get things sorted out, so when they did leave the ship, everything would return to normal for the crew and the Captain.

"Have Joan, the girls, and Eugene ready to go as soon as we hit the port of Kochi. First, check with the doctor to see if Joan can travel with us. I want the girls to bring their computers and any other equipment they might need on the road." Richard said as he opened a large case.

"Richard, I'm starting to think we might not get to fly home as soon as we thought. If you think we're going to run into trouble, you need to tell me right now." Jack said as he looked his friend in the eye.

"I'm not sure; that being said, I would like to be prepared just in case it turns out the Chinese are a little more insistent this time." As he spoke, Richard dialed the odd-looking phone and held it to his ear. Knowing he didn't need to hear what would be said, Jack turned and walked to where he hoped Tish and Tosh would be. By the time Jack spread the word about the slight change in plans and answered some of the questions Tish and Tosh asked, he was more than happy to go and tell Joan. She didn't have questions; she just nodded and said she would be ready. At the armory on board, Eugene was waiting and helped as Jack picked out the weapons he thought would best suit their needs. Those that would fit the girls, just in case it came to that. Eugene had no doubt about Joan's abilities. He was worried about her injury.

The damned Americans always sticking their nose in where it is not needed. Zihao thought as he paced in front of his office window. He was hoping the ship Arawn, would turn and make a run back out to sea, then he could have them torpedoed. The politicians would put a sad face on for the world and call it an unfortunate accident. If Jack and Richard and the others from the Unit Zihao, and the others in the Group wanted dead, somehow got off that ship. Zihao knew he could get at them wherever they chose to hide, and like rats, he knew they would hide. Thinking of Jack, Richard, and the journalists dead brought a smile to Zihao's lips. He watched Jack, and the Tibetan trader fight out of China and escape capture.

It was those pictures the English bastards took then helped to get to the rest of the world. Those pictures hurt China. Now every time he turned on some foreign news program, there was one of the journalists telling of how they found the graves. How they were kidnapped and held until Jack and Tran freed them. No one cared about the men they killed, or the men held responsible for the escape and put to death for their actions. However, they will care, Zihao thought. When he and the group capture Richard, the head of the Unit, and the rest of its leaders as well as the traitors and the journalists, things will be different. He would kill Jiao and her baby personally when she was brought back to China. First, he would kill the man she married, which he would do in front of her. It was time the west learned their actions had severe consequences. Zihao and the Group were going to teach the soft men in the west the price of interfering in areas that do not concern them.

Jack couldn't believe the Port of Kochi. They sailed out of the ocean into a large river. To the south was Fort Kochi, and to the north beautiful undisturbed white sand beaches of west India. Jack stood on the foredeck of the Arawn as it rounded a small island in the river. He could see ships birthed at the docks getting loaded and unloaded. A small powerboat came to the Arawn. A small polite man came on board; he was going to be their pilot for the docking procedure. An hour later, the Captain thanked the man and watched as the gangway was lowered into place. Richard told Jack and the others they would be flying out of the local airport on Wellington Island. When Richard pointed, Jack turned and could see the airport directly across the river from the port.

"We are going to have to wait until the morning; the plane is now leaving Paris and won't arrive until dawn. We are going to stay on the ship until we can fly out; it's for security." Richard told them. Jack turned to Tish and Tosh.

"I want you two to try and get back into NASA and see if you can get me real-time intel on the Chinese; I would like to know what the hell they're doing," Jack said as Richard walked over.

"I've gone against these assholes before; I don't think they'll give up without a fight," Jack told the girls.

"As a matter of fact, I know these assholes won't give up at all. It goes against their nature." Jack said to Richard.

"We're going to have to tighten security, have the men armed. Can you get the okay from the Indian government? Jack asked. Richard turned and scratched his cheek.

"I can't see why not; however, if I start making formal requests, there is a greater chance the Chinese will find out where exactly we are. If we issue small arms, give instructions no one is to use one unless fired upon first, we should be all right." Richard said.

"I don't care what port town the bastards have slipped into; I just want to know if you can get at him and kill him." Zihao Peng said into the phone, then listened to the reply, smiling Zihao gave a comeback of his own.

"Then wait until night falls, and send a team to see if the ship is in a position to be mind. If it is, then plant the explosives and detonate."

Zihao explained. He hated dealing with the older men in the service. He found talking to them was like dealing with a child. The meeting of the Group to discuss developments with the U.N. was in one hour.

Their delegation tried to reveal the existence of a secret unit within the organization. Still, they were laughed at and heckled into silence. When Zihao and the rest of the Group were shown the tapes of the general assembly, they stared in disbelief. One by one, their delegation stood to reveal the Unit's existence. Then one by one, each man was heckled and not allowed to speak. Calls for China to get out of Tibet became louder and louder until each man gave up and sat down.

"Look at what has happened; the whole world is against us. They won't even let us speak now. I think it is time for us to move with the course of action our Group has discussed for the last fifty years. We can no longer sit and watch as the world moves further and further astray. America calls itself a world leader. We need to stop this; China needs to take the helm and steer it back on the right path, the path we choose." When Zihao stopped speaking, the rest of the Group sat in silence for a moment, then each man stood and smiled. Within each man, a fire of abhorrence and the will to dominate others had been rekindled. It was going to be their time to rule, and if they failed, then Zihao knew at least the U.S. would not survive the missiles he could launch.

Chapter 6

JACK WATCHED AS THE small rubber zodiac idled down the center of the river. Sitting on a deck chair in the shadows, the men on the rubber craft were unaware they were being watched. A young Scottish sergeant stood behind Jack in the doorway. Not wanting to be seen, the Sargent waited until the craft moved off before he stepped out onto the deck.

"Interesting time for a putt down the river." The Sergeant said. Jack and the Sargent watched as the boat turned and started back up the river.

"Must like the paint job," Jack said.

"Holy shit!" The Sergeant whispered. "They're one man short!" Jack knew what that meant; one of the men had slipped over the side of the zodiac when it turned and started back up the river. That man was right now swimming towards them and would try to plant a charge on the hull of the Arawn.

"Go and get the divers over the side, then meet me on the docks. I want to take this asshole alive. If that means ripping his arms off, that's what we'll do." Jack said. The Sargent was moving before Jack finished speaking.

When Jack said to go and get the divers in the water, he wanted one special team of divers to go over the side. These five men were former U.S. Navy Seals; they had been trained by the best in dirty deeds. When they weren't hunting and disarming bombs, they were diving on some of the best shipwrecks in the world. Each of these five men thought of each other as brothers. When Jack told them of the zodiac, how it returned up the river short one man. The teammates nodded and slipped silently into the dark water. Twenty-five minutes later, the five men stood on the deck of the Arawn. On his knees in front of them was an Asian man dressed in a wet suit holding his broken nose. Frank, the team leader, was holding a disarmed magnetic mine.

"Yes, sir, he was sure as shit trying to plant this on our hull. He wasn't very smart about it, though; he was trying to stick forward of amidships. The bulkheads would have closed, and it wouldn't have sunk us." When Frank finished, Richards's face was white.

"I don't think they wanted to sink us; instead, I think they wanted to hurt us, to call attention to us." Richard finished.

"Why do that when they can sink us and be done with it?" Jack asked. Richard ordered the man to be locked in with David instead of the other man so they couldn't communicate. Richard and Jack watched as the sun turned the morning sky blood red and then orange. Jack thought it was a beautiful sunrise until Richard told him about a saying the fishermen had in the town he came from.

"The saying goes. Red sky at night, sailors delight. Red sky in the morn, sailors be warned." When Richard finished, Jack looked at his friend.

"I wouldn't have thought you to take the sayings of fishermen to heart Richard." As they stood watching, the sky warmed from orange to blue.

"Oh, I can tell you those old fishermen knew how to watch the weather when your life depends on the tide and whims of the sea. You trust in the sky to tell you whether it's safe or not." Richard told Jack as they walked back to the gangplank. Richard looked around, then walked down and stood on the dock, Jack standing beside him.

The short ride from the docks to the airport on Wellington Island was easy. Jack and the rest of the Group left the docks, turned south on NH47A, then crossed the bridge connecting the island with the mainland. Once on the island, they followed NH47A to Ps Parameswaran road, then through the checkpoint gate to the roundabout. The third exit off the roundabout to the Wellington Island air terminal was easy. Jack thought it was too easy. When things were this easy this early in the battle, they became harder later on.

Once Jack, Richard, and the others cleared Indian customs and immigration. They were allowed to walk out of the terminal to the gleaming Cessna citation x, with a top speed of Mach .97 or 977 kilometers per hour; it was one of the fastest planes within the Unit, with its two AE3007C1 Rolls-Royce engines and a few upgrades that break a few of the aviation laws in most countries around the world. Richard was confident they would reach England with little trouble. Both pilots who flew this plane were retired royal air force pilots. Each with tens of thousands of hours of flight time under his belt. Another reason to feel safe, Richard told the girls.

"These men can handle anything man or nature throws at them, so you can sit and rest easy," Richard said.

"Sir, when we take off, we are going to turn and head out into the Laccadive Sea, then we will turn east and head for Dodoma in Tanzania." The co-pilot said as he helped stow the last of the baggage.

"Why so out of the way?" Richard asked.

"It's those damn satellites, sir; the Chinese have about blanketed the European continent." The pilot replied. Richard just nodded and wished he were already in London. Ten minutes later, Jack and Richard listened as the two Rolls-Royce engines powered up. Fifteen minutes later, both men watched the ground sink below them as their plane carried them off to the safety of England. Richard watched as the earth turned below and gave away to the vast blue sea.

He couldn't help but wonder who was after them and how hard they were willing to work to get them.

"They have taken off, sir; no, sir, they are headed out to sea on a western heading." The Captain of the Chinese ship said.

"Yes, sir, I can confirm the men you told me about are on that plane." The older man said he was about to thank whoever was on the other end of the call, then just looked at the receiver and placed it back in the cradle. Turning to his first mate, a man his own age with whom he had been friends for years. He watched as relief washed over the man's face as he told him the news.

"We are done with this; Beijing informed me they have another vessel set up around the islands off the western coast of Africa. Around Cape Verde to see if they can gather any intel. We are to station here and do the same. I was told the Group was going to shoot down that plane in the wilds of Africa. The Captain said as he turned to look out the side of the bridge.

Zihao knew this plan would work, and the two men who left his office confirmed it was possible. When he had explained, he had wanted to use a Chinese missile to shoot down a small plane. However, the trick was what was left had to have an American missile signature on it.

"We can do better!" One of the technicians said as he smiled.

"We have an American missile we bought from an arms dealer who disappeared some time ago. It's even a new one and is compatible with being fired by one of our jets." The man said.

When Zihao told him a Chinese jet would not be in the area, an American plane would be doing the shooting. The men thought their leader had gone mad. When Zihao explained over some time, the Group had bought American warplanes in pieces and had gotten one in working order. Now the Group had an American F18, and it was in Africa and waiting for orders. One of the bespectacled men started to ask why the jet was sitting in Africa, then thought it was none of his business.

"We have had assets in South Africa. Everything we need is there. With minimal time everything can be ready to do whatever is needed." Zihao said, smiling, then turned to the others in the room.

"Once the leaders of the U.N. unit are dead and gone. We will start the second part of the plan to discredit the United States of America and the weak puppet group who dares call itself the United Nations." Zihao Peng said. The seated men in the Group smiled and turned to Zihao, congratulating him on his future success.

Richard was asleep when they landed in the African country of Tanzania. The airport serving the capital city of Dodoma offered local goods and an open-air food market boasting local fresh fruit. Jack and Eugene watched the girls pick out colorful silk and cotton wrappings. Tish found a woman who sold scarves and other cloth items while Jack and Eugene loaded themselves with food and water. Richard made a call to MI-6 just to check if the Chinese were up to anything when Jack and the others returned to the plane.

"I don't like it; everything seems quiet, too damn quiet. It's as if the Chinese are sitting on their hands. As far as we can tell, nothing has taken off from China, nothing unusual." Richard Jack. Once again, Jack watched as the ground dropped out from under the plane's wings. As the small jet rose into the sky, so did his hopes for Tran and the chance they could get out of this mess without anyone getting hurt. Jack knew better than to hope for the best; he had always planned for the worst, and he was breaking his own rules.

The Chinese pilot knew what he was going to do would end the lives of the people on the other jet. He'd been ordered to shoot down the plane, and like any other good soldier, he did what he was told. Mark, the older of the two British pilots, snapped his head up when the threat warning screamed its alarm.

The Chinese pilot didn't engage his radar guidance system until he had the Cessna dead to rights. When he was sure, Quan flipped the switch and fired the missile.

The first indication they were in trouble came when Mark put the Cessna into a nosedive at full throttle. He and Wayne fought to control the plane and keep the missile from hitting them. Mark fought gravity and tried to pull out of the dive. He could hear the girls screaming in the cabin. Wayne watched as the missile gained on them and waited until the last second to release the chaff and other missile deterrents. For a second, the missile became confused and faltered, then before hope blossomed, it began to track again. Mark fought the plane back out of the dive, and he listened as Wayne counted down the counteractions he deployed against the missile, as well as the distance to impact. When all countermeasures had been exhausted, Wayne turned to his older friend and, in a matter-a-fact tone, told Mark.

"It's been an honor flying with you and to have called you friend." Mark looked at his friend and told him the honor was his. Then made a cutting dive to the left as the missile exploded.

Quan watched as the pilot dodged and dove all over the sky, trying to shake the missile, but in the end, the missile won. He watched as the explosion ripped parts off the tail section and damaged the right wing surface. Quan knew with these two surfaces damaged, the plane would crash. He had been ordered to do this, not to watch as the Cessna fell to earth. Quan banked his fighter and flew away from the area, wishing he could fly off and never be found. Quan didn't know who was on the plane. He hadn't liked that he had been ordered to shoot down an unarmed unit like this.

Jack knew the Cessna hadn't been hit. He also knew you didn't have to hit a plane to kill it. Just by the sound of theirs and how fast the ground was coming up to meet them, theirs was dying quickly.

All Jack could think about was somehow he did this to his friends. He would never be able to explain why it happened.

Mark looked at his friend and knew even if they managed to bring the plane in so their passengers lived, they would most likely die. The old saying 'the pilots were always the first to the scene of the crash' echoed in his mind as he looked out the windshield. Wayne called in the mayday, but for some reason, he couldn't get a response. He had given the longitude and latitude of the attack to the static of the dead airwaves, hoping the radio hadn't been damaged in the explosion. Mark knew they had crossed into the Democratic Republic of the Congo. He also knew they passed to the north of the city of Kindu. Reaching, Mark flipped on the intercom system and shouted for Jack and the others to get ready for a crash landing. He also informed Jack where they were, what towns were the closest, and in what direction they were.

At a thousand feet, Mark and Wayne knew it was over, the beautiful Cessna X they loved to fly was going to die, and they would be going with it. Both men tried to save the plane and themselves. Now they were trying to slow the jet so the people in the cabin could have the greatest chance of walking away. With the fuel dumped, the ride to the ground was quiet except for the sound of aluminum being torn free by the speed of the descent.

At the last second, both Wayne and Mark flared the Cessna. Dropping more of their speed before they impacted the earth. Before the plane could stall, they brought the nose down and felt the plane hit. Wayne thought for a brief second both he and Mark were going to live through the crash. A bowling ball-sized stone ended his thoughts when it crashed through the windshield and crushed his skull. Mark knew his friend was dead. He watched as a shallow ditch came into view. What was left of the Cessna embedded itself into the earthen bank. The impact killed Mark instantly, as the dash of the plane was forced into the cockpit with the rest of the nose of the Cessna from the impact.

In the cabin of the plane, the only person who remained conscious through the whole crash was Jack. Getting out of his seat, he ran to the door behind the plane's left wing. When Jack tried to turn the door handle, he found it was jammed, so he turned and ran to the emergency exit above the wing. He almost yelled his joy when this exit worked, and the window popped out of the plane. Jack looked around and found Joan awake, trying to get out of her seat. Joan smiled at him when Jack rushed over to see if she needed help.

"I think I'm okay, nothing too serious." She said, wincing as she tried to stand. Jack took the time to check her wound, finding none of her stitches torn loose; he smiled and nodded to her. For the next twenty minutes, that's the way things went. One by one, the members of the downed Group stood and left the plane. When they were all outside, Jack returned to the plane and started handing out what they needed. When Jack had thrown out what was important, he also had to think about their survival in the jungles of central Africa. He watched as the two younger girls checked out each other and ran to Eugene. The older marine was in good shape and told the girls to help Joan; with her injured shoulder, she wouldn't be able to carry anything. Richard stood beside Jack and looked at the destroyed Cessna.

"If you can get the floor up in the center of the aisle, there is a weapons cache in the belly of the plane. There should be two Walther pp 22 calibers as well as four Sig Sauer P6 9mm; there should be two hundred rounds loose and four clips for the Walther and the sigs." Richard told Jack. Jack was in the aisle of the crashed Cessna. He had cut the carpet away before Eugene had climbed up on the wing.

"I need something flat, like a bar, to get the floor up," Jack said, then went back to work as Eugene looked around, trying to find what was needed. Jack succeeded in getting a corner of the panel he found under the carpet up enough to wedge a door from a cupboard into it. Eugene climbed back through the window with a heavy branch. Both men strained and grunted as the sweat dripped off their noses and chins. Just before Jack was going to say it wasn't going to work, the panel popped up, causing both men to fall back into their seats.

"Son of a bitch, this thing had more than it needed," Eugene uttered as he looked into the weapons bay.

"Go tell Richard, and I'll start throwing out what we need," Jack said as he tried to squirm his way into the damaged bay.

Richard frowned when Eugene told him of the extra weapons the plane held in the belly. Richard watched as Jack handed out the Walther and the sigs. He couldn't understand why they would have two British L85A2 automatic rifles with a total of five hundred rounds of ammunition, along with an L115A3 .338 lapua magnum sniper rifle and a hundred rounds for it.

"They shouldn't have these kinds of weapons; however, for once, I'm glad they came over-prepared," Jack said as he checked out each of the guns to make sure they hadn't been damaged in the crash. Tish watched as Eugene helped Jack with the guns. Though she and Tosh were fine, she started to shake and cry. Tish knew she should be happy they were alive. When Joan asked her why she was crying, Tish couldn't come up with a better answer than she was scared.

"We are going to have to burn the plane before we walk out of here," Jack said. He knew Richard would agree he would want to avoid some of the shared technologies from member countries getting into the wrong hands.

"Damn, I forgot we would have to walk out of here," Richard said as he stared at his feet. Jack always wore a pair of custom-made boots for his feet. After being tortured at the hands of General Trang, he needed specially made boots so the bones in his feet wouldn't ache.

He then turned and looked at the rest of the survivor's feet; stopping at the girl's feet, Jack asked.

"What the hell kind of boots are those, and are they comfortable?" Jack asked the girls.

"They are Volatile job site boots if you must know," Tosh answered as she held one of her feet up, showing off the black boot with its platform sole. Jack looked at the boot, then at the girls.

"Can you walk in them without breaking an ankle?" Jack asked as he knelt down to get a closer look at the boot.

"No problem," Tish sniffed as she held Eugene's hand.

"We wear these boots all the time, hell Tosh even chased down a purse snatcher in Paris last year with a pair on." Jack had to admit that was pretty good. Joan wore a pair of standard-issue boots, and Eugene wore the boots of a United States Marine. Then Jack looked at Richards's feet; he shook his head.

"What the hell were you thinking, Richard?" Jack asked as he stood up.

"Well, I thought I wouldn't be in a plane crash today. Thank you," Richard answered defensively.

"Don't I always say, hope for the best, plan for the worst?" Jack asked. Joan nodded her head, as did Tish and Tosh. Jack returned to the plane; he knew his feet, and Richards was close to being the same size. Dropping his spare pair of boots in front of Richard. Jack smiled and nodded, mouthing the word *planning.* Richard just shook his head as he switched footwear. Richard knew it was going to take some time before he outlived this. Nobody knew how much money Jack had hidden in different banks around the world. All Richard knew was Jack had turned over hundreds of millions of Euros when he joined him in the Unit. Jack told Richard once he had kept two of the smaller accounts for his retirement so he could buy boots.

Chapter 7

RICHARD NOW WORE ONE pair of those boots, and he knew they were worth the four thousand dollars American Jack paid for them. Jack and Eugene gathered wood and threw what they could into the battered Cessna. Once Jack was satisfied with the amount in the plane. He climbed back in and lit one fire in the front of the cabin and one at the exit point. Standing on the wing of the destroyed plane, Jack said a silent thank you to the two brave men who gave their lives to help save them. Nobody looked back as the fire started to burn; most of their clothes had to be thrown into the fire along with Richard's custom-made luggage. The only thing they could take with them was whatever fit in the three backpacks they had, along with the girl's computer hard drives. The actual computers were now burning in the plane; Tish carried one hard drive in a computer bag she had draped over her back, while Tosh carried all the software in her bag.

Jack took point and carried one of the A2 rifles; in his pack was the A3 sniper rifle, which was broken down and wrapped in a towel. While he had been in the weapons locker, he had found combat webbing and now carried extra clips for the A2 in it, and all the loose ammo was in a bag in his pack. Eugene was in the rear with the other A2; he also had a combat vest with webbing and carried his extra ammo in his backpack with what food was on the plane. Each member carried as much water as they could, and Joan was in charge of rationing it. When a bottle was emptied, it was kept so it could be filled if they found water. Jack told the girls to try to walk in the footsteps of the person in front of her. He explained it would make it harder to count their numbers if their trail was found and followed. On their first night, Jack thought they had only made fifteen kilometers before the light waned and the moon started to climb into the sky.

"What do you think? Should we push until midnight?" Eugene asked as he sat beside Jack.

"I think we're going to have to. Then we'll bed down for four hours and pick it up again." Jack said as he ate.

"Just remember these people ain't like you or me; they haven't been in the fire before. Hell, it's been twenty years for me. I hope I'm not too far gone." Eugene said, Jack, looked at him and smiled. Jack knew it had been a long time since Eugene had been in any type of combat situation. He also knew once it was learned, it wasn't lost. When Jack stood and told the others of his plan to hike until midnight, then sleep for four hours and start again. He was answered by a chorus of groans. Joan looked at him and smiled; she knew what Jack wanted was for the best. She also knew Richard and the girls were not used to this much walking. Though it wasn't the girls she was most worried about. Joan had been watching Richard throughout the day and could see his life of bureaucratic work and lack of physical exercise was now taking its toll.

Joan stood and checked her Sig and the rest of her equipment, as did Richard. Tish and Tosh both carried the 22-caliber Walther in their computer bags. Tish wanted to stay in the small opening in the forest they found. When Eugene pointed out that this is where night critters come to hunt, she was more than willing to get up and start walking.

Midnight came when Jack stopped the march. Richard and the two girls dropped their packs and flopped to the jungle floor.

Richards's feet felt like he could have walked all night. It was his legs, especially his calf muscles, were exhausted; they ached. Before Jack knew it, Richard and the girls were asleep; their light snoring did its job and lulled Joan and Eugene asleep. Jack decided to walk out of camp, so he could catch naps away from the others, as he kept an eye on their camp. Four o'clock came fast; though Jack had slept, he woke when an insect crawled over his face. From that point on, Jack dosed off and on until the appointed hour. When Jack came fully awake, he laid still to make sure he was alone; this was a force of habit. He was about to sit up and call to the others when a shadow moved. Jack watched as three men stepped out of the jungle's darkness into the moonlight.

Jack watched as the three men skulked into their camp. These three men were too interested in the three women, Tish, Tosh and Joan, to stop and look around. As the three rebels skulked into the camp, they were unaware Jack was following them. When the first man reached for Joan, the intruder was surprised to find her awake and smiling at him. Then the intruder felt Joan ram the knife Frank, the leader of the five-man seal team, gave her into his chest. The intruder's two friends saw their leader killed by the red-headed woman. When they tried to go to his aid, they heard a click behind them. When they turned to fire, Jack killed each one with one round to the head from his Sig. Jack didn't have to tell anyone it was time to go; they were smart enough to know. Jack told the rest of them to move one click east and wait.

"What the hell are you going to do?" Richard asked.

"I'm going to double back and see if these idiots have a vehicle," Jack replied as he disappeared into the jungle. Three kilometers into the bush, Jack found what he was looking for. A single man stood beside a battered 1979 stage one Land Rover, the first one built with a 'V-8' engine. He watched as this man walked over to a bush and slung his Russian-made AK-47 over his shoulder to relieve himself.

When Jack tapped the man on the back of the head with his pistol, the man came to attention.

"Keys?" Jack asked in one word, and in a comment, the man answered.

"In." Before the lone man could say another word, Jack slammed the Sig into the base of the rebel's skull. The man fell into the bush, where he had just answered the call of nature. Bending over, Jack cut the strap holding the rifle over the unconscious man's shoulder. Walking over to the Land Rover, Jack dropped the old rifle into the cargo bay. Jack was surprised to hear the truck start with ease. Turning the suv around, Jack returned to where he had left Richard, Joan, and the others.

"Safety wasn't a real concern with the men who fixed this thing up; they took off the doors and threw away the seat belts," Richard stated as he looked over their transportation. Tish and Tosh smiled as they sat in the small cargo area in the rear of the Land Rover. Eugene stood at the back, watching the nearby bush for any movement. When Jack nodded to him, Eugene jumped in with the girls and faced out the back of the truck.

"I wish we had a computer, so we could use Google Earth to find roads and get the hell out of the area," Jack said as he topped a rise in the trail, remembering how he and Tran used the search engine to find their way around Bhutan and India during their escape from the Chinese.

"Well, before we left the plane, I thought to grab a satellite phone and throw it in her bag," Joan said as she nodded to Tosh.

"I was wondering who put that there." The girl said as she opened her computer bag and took out the phone. Smiling, Richard took the phone and turned it on.

"Half a charge; it's better than nothing," Richard said. He dialed a number he knew wouldn't have shown up on any of the Intel the Chinese had on the Unit.

"We should go to Uganda, my sister has property there, and she keeps staff in the house. They are good people and have a lovely family; also, they know me, so we will be welcome. Once there, we can fly out of the international airport back to England, where we can turn things around and go after the *Group* in China."

Zihao listened to the report as it came into the Group live from Africa.

"Sir, the plane is burnt; it wasn't caused by the crash." Captain Zen Wong was explaining.

"If the crash had caused this fire, we would find a trail of debris. Also, inside the plane, I can see ashes from a wood fire. I think the people who were on this plane lived. They did this to cover their tracks." The Captain finished. Zihao ordered the Captain to follow the escapees if he could. He was also to report in every hour on the hour. When Zihao ended the call, he turned to the others in the Group.

"Gentlemen, we do not have to wait for the Captain to confirm the deaths in Africa. Instead, we move forward with the plan as it is laid out. We have found a weakness in the U.S. and its national security administration. Like so much in America, the leaders of this agency believe they are the best and will not listen to the younger generation. The young people of America are lazier than their parents; they want everything, but they are unwilling to work for it. So we offer them what they want, and they work for us. When they broke the code, we happened to be there, and the young man who had the brains and the knowledge was given what he deserved, a lethal injection of our new toxin." Zihao smiled as he told the rest of the Group how the child of a leading American Senator died in his father's house of a supposed heroin overdose. Now he and the Group could peek into the N.S.A. and see what little secrets they were keeping on people around the world.

"When the world finds out how the U.S. has been listening and reading their e-mails, the outrage will force the U.S. to stand alone. Her allies will be forced to acknowledge they didn't know the extent of the information gathering being conducted by the N.S.A." When Zihao finished. He knew how Chairman Mao felt on that glorious day when he declared the People's Republic of China had come to exist.

"We can start this activity with the exposure of small bits of information. Our people in America will start to send leaked information to the news media of America. The glory-hungry reporters will do the rest." One of the other generals in the room said and smiled.

Chapter 8

MONDAY MORNING IN WASHINGTON DC, a day most leaders in the information gathering and analysis' branches of the American government wished they had to do over again. A young, reasonably unknown reporter was sent an e-mail from an anonymous source. The e-mail told her of personal information as well as private documents. These had been gathered about her and the rest of her colleagues. The secretary of homeland security was giving a press conference that Monday morning. Wendy Cameron stood; she asked why the N.S.A. and homeland security felt it was necessary to gather information on her and others in the journalism field. When the answer was she was mistaken, Wendy pulled out her notepad. She read some very personal e-mails from her fiancées i. p. address to her computer. Then she read a case file number the N.S.A. kept open. The other reporters in the gallery were shocked when the secretary of homeland security turned and walked out of the room without saying a word. The other reporters stood around the parking lot of the homeland security offices, talking about this new breach in the law. This law was written forbidding the U.S. government from spying on its own people. All wondered if the N.S.A. had a file on them and what those files might contain. Monday night, after a small party at the office, where everyone congratulated Wendy on her big scoop. Wendy took a cab to her apartment to find the D.C. police officers standing at her door. Concerned officers took her aside and explained her neighbor had called in a break and entered. When he and his partner arrived, they found the door open and her apartment destroyed.

"Miss, can you see if anything is missing and make a list so we can see if any of it is in local pawn shops." The officer said as he handed Wendy a notepad. After Wendy went through her smashed belongings, she found her files were missing, and her computer tower was gone. When she told this to the police officer, he frowned.

"Strange thing for some Junkie to take to sell for dope." He said to his partner.

"Hey, aren't you the reporter who asked about the N.S.A. having a file on her and some others today?" The second officer asked. When Wendy explained what happened, they asked her if there was someone she could stay with tonight.

"Yes, my boyfriend lives here in D.C. He works for the Canadian embassy; I've been drinking, and I can't drive." She told the two officers.

"Don't worry, we'll take you. Are you sure you're going to be safe with your boyfriend?" The first officer asked. Wendy just nodded and walked into her destroyed bedroom to gather some things she thought she would need. Both officers stopped at the main entrance to Wendy's building and then motioned to her it was safe to come forward. Directly in front of the entrance was a D.C. police car. It had been there when Wendy arrived home; now she knew why. The older cop held the back door open for Wendy, and without thinking, she got in, thanking the men for their help. It wasn't until they drove off she knew she was in trouble. The radio in this car was set to monitor federal frequencies'; also, the backup weapon looked like a machine gun. Though Wendy thought all automatic rifles were machine guns. This weapon was, in fact, an H&K MP5 used by federal enforcement agencies and the military for their rate of fire and accuracy.

"Who the hell are you guys, and where are you taking me?" Wendy asked. Neither man answered as they drove thru the streets of Washington. Soon they left the city. Wendy knew the route they were on was 267. If they stayed on it, they would go past Dulles international airport. She had never been past the airport before, she thought. As Wendy sat in the back of the fake police car, she watched the turnoff for Dulles pass by on the left of the car. Signs came and went, and soon the men slowed and turned into a farm; she was happy to be out of the car. She tried to make a run for the edge of the woods, only to be tripped and then dragged to the house.

Sitting in the house were the vice president and the new head of the Joint Chiefs of Staff. General Wyatt Whistler, and beside him was the Director of the C.I.A. C. Steven Wilson. Wendy looked at the men and thought they were going to tell her she had committed treason and have her shot. Instead, the Director of the C.I.A. stood and helped her back to her feet, then reprimanded the two who brought her here for being rough with her.

"I'm sorry, Miss Cameron; forgive these men; they are used to grabbing enemies, not friends." Director Wilson said. Then helped her to a chair and poured coffee for her.

"I don't understand; why was I brought here?" Wendy asked. Still looking at the two men who now stood guard. The Vice President stood and walked over to a table, then picked up a file.

"This is the file you were asking about this morning; it contains the e-mails you referred to during the press conference. I know to be a good reporter, you need to be nosey. You should hold a certain amount of distrust for the government in all its aspects. However, I'm going to be honest with you, Wendy...this file and others like it, information in these files was gathered and stored while you were outside the country. The information in it was not, I repeat not, gathered to monitor you or any of your colleagues. It had been gathered because terrorists around the world use the media now and talk openly to you. We were looking for faces for our recognition programs and voices for the same reason." The Vice President told her. The Director brought her over a sandwich, then he sat down and looked her in the eye.

"The reason is the same for your boyfriend; he travels around the world for the Canadians, he talks to all these people, and they let him into their homes. I know we should have dumped some of the e-mails, and this was a mistake I take responsibility for. As we speak, it is a mistake being alleviated right now. However, we wanted you brought here because of your apartment." The Director picked up a bottle of water and turned the cap.

"Yes, about my apartment, I loved that place. Paul and I decided when we were married, he would give up his, and we would live in mine. Now you've ruined it." She didn't want to cry, but she was scared, and all her keepsakes were smashed.

"We didn't do it. We don't know who did it; I give you my word; it wasn't us. We brought you here to see if you would be willing to work with us until we find out who breached our system?" The Director asked. Wendy knew even though it was a question and she had been asked, she didn't think there was any room for rejection, so she nodded.

"I knew we could count on you. Once a Marine's daughter, always a Marine's daughter." General Whistler said, smiling at her. Wendy turned and looked at the General, then smiled back; he reminded her of her father. When she saw the General smile, she knew she was safe.

The first time Jack had to make a run for freedom was in the occupied country of Tibet. Now he was trying to get into the Congo; there were roads in the African country. Some of them were good, however, out where they were. Roads were nothing more than two dirt ruts in the countryside. With the compass, Jack knew he was traveling north and east. Unlike the first time, Jack now had his passport and other documentation so he could cross the border legally. Although, like the first time, he now had weapons that would see him thrown so far in jail, his meals would have to be catapulted to him. Richard had switched seats with Joan, and he couldn't believe how rough the road was. Occasionally they would pass by some people walking on the rutted road. A man told them they would come to a small village called Amasunga, which was close to the Oso River.

"Once you cross the river, you will not see anybody for a day; then you may see hunters. If you see the hunters, you will know you are close to a place called Matalimbo. From there, it will take you another day to get to Butembo; in this place, you can find what you need." The older man said. Jack asked him if there was anything they had he could use. They all thanked the man when he smiled and shook his head.

Captain Zen Wong stood looking down at the bodies of the dead rebels.

"I think these men walked into the camp without looking around to see if they had a man outside the perimeter," Zen told his men. He knew whoever shot these men had snuck up from behind and killed them with a single shot to the back of the head. The dead man in the camp had been stabbed thru the heart while he bent over to grab something, probably a woman. It was the woman who sunk the knife into the man's heart. Zen couldn't help but smile as he thought about doing the same to Jack. When he reported the findings to the Group leader, Peng told him to find and kill all the people he had on the list and those with them. He also reported Jack and the others now had a vehicle in which they were traveling.

"We will try to establish where they are going; when we find out, we will try and get you there ahead of them so you can await their arrival," Zihao said before he ended the call. Turning to a smaller man who waited by the door, Zihao ordered all efforts be put into finding Jack and Richard.

"I don't care if you have to listen to every phone call out of the Republic of the Congo; I want them found *today*!" Zihao shouted.

All around them was green, and above them was nothing but a vast expanse of blue African sky. They stopped and boiled water to replace what they drank. Jack told the girls not to drink this water until they had no other choice. When he could get the battered old Land Rover above thirty kilometers an hour, the breeze would cool them off. For the most part, he could only keep his speed just above that of a jogging man. Jack could not shake the feeling this was too easy. He felt as if this was going too easy; it wasn't like the Group. They never let things slide this far out of their control when Jack told Richard about his concerns. Richard looked out the cracked windshield, then back at the dozing Tish and Tosh.

"I'm afraid I was thinking the same thing not an hour ago; I could try and call our friends in Langley and see if they can help?" Richard whispered and watched as Jack nodded his head. By the time Richard was finished explaining to Director Wilson about being shot down and his assumption the Group was behind it. The Director told him he would be Richard's eyes and ears and he would get back to him soon. As soon as the Director hung up with Richard, he called his long-time friend Wyatt Whistler and explained what was going on in the Congo.

"They have a sat phone, but the things got half a charge, and he doesn't have the charger for the phone." When Steven finished explaining the trouble in reaching Richard, he waited until Wyatt asked someone in his office what he thought.

"They are trying to get to a place called Butembo; I think we can get them out of there. I can't call Richard until eighteen hundred, Greenwich Mean Time." The Director explained. The time would allow them to try and get a real solution to the problem now facing the Unit. How to save its leader and keep its existence a secret from the world and other member nations of the U.N.

The man was helpful; he told the Group of Chinese men he had seen a smaller group on this very road late in the day. Now he was camped, and if they wanted, they could join him. The one who spoke thanked him and drove off into the night. Captain Zen Wong knew he and his men would have to drive all night to catch the others. The Group was working on finding out where they were going. He decided it would be better if he were to catch and kill Jack and the others out here.

At six o'clock on the dot, Richard turned on the phone and was surprised when it announced a call was incoming. The Director, along with the General, was calling to ask for an update. They told Richard what to expect from the Chinese. Richard explained when they got to the city of Butembo, he was going to try to find a charger for his phone.

"Don't bother. When you get there, go to the hotel Butembo, and there will be a package left for you. If they have room, check in; if not, there is only one other hotel in the city; check into it, and for god's sake, if you're traveling in a stolen car, ditch it." Director Willson told Richard. Both he and Jack laughed as Richard said he would and hung up. Richard looked at the battery display and was shocked to see the warning light flashing. Ten minutes left if they were lucky, and so far, luck hadn't been running in their favor.

"They are heading for the border with Uganda; there, we think the fat English man will go to a large ranch. His family has owned it, and now it is in the care of his sister. She has people who work for her and keep it ready in case she decides to visit. They grow coffee and tea on the property; if you can get there first, you will be successful in your mission." Zihao told Captain Wong. The Captain knew what he would do. He was going to pass his targets and then drive to the town of Masaka in Uganda. There he and his men would wait for

Jack and his friends. By the end of the week, he will be home, and the enemies of the Group will be dead.

The hotel was right where Steven said it would be. Going in, Richard found one of the local military officers had left a small package.

"Would you happen to have some rooms available for tonight?" Richard asked the young woman who was working behind the hotel's main desk.

"Yes, sir, we have four rooms free tonight. Would you like them?" The young woman asked.

"Oh yes, please, there are three men and three young ladies. Would those rooms have two beds in each?" Richard thought to ask.

"Three of the rooms have twin beds, and the last is a single occupancy room. Will this be all right?" The young desk clerk asked. Richard filled out the information card for his check-in. It had all the standard information requests. Name, home address, and vehicle information. It was the last part of the card he wondered how to fill in. Standing looking foolish, he thought about it and then smiled as a car drove slowly past. He quickly wrote the number of the plate down and handed the card back to the clerk.

Jack and Richard waited in the hall while the rest showered and changed into clothing Jack bought at a shop attached to the hotel. When the girls finished their preening, they all met in the hall. Richard said they should eat in their rooms while he charged the phone. Richard and the others were worried about the locals remembering them.

"I think we could probably get a plane into the local airstrip here and get going." When Richard finished telling them about a local company, it flew gold around the country. He said with the help of the C.I.A. director and the General, they would be out of the country, and they didn't need to go to Uganda. Jack drove the old Land Rover behind a dirt soccer field. He left the keys in the ignition, hoping whoever found the sturdy car would do better things with it other than fighting. That night Richard called his sister and told her there had been a change of plans, and he couldn't make it to Uganda. While Victoria was disappointed, she told Richard she understood. They spoke for a moment, then said their goodbyes. When Richard asked if there was anyone else who wanted to call family. He realized Jack had no one to contact other than Tran, and he didn't know if Tran would be in shape to take any calls. The girls only had each other and Eugene. As for Eugene, he had a sister from whom the girls called and had gotten some of his mother's recipes. He said he had no one other than the girls; Tish and Tosh never understood why he cut his sister out of his life. They knew it was painful for Eugene, so they never asked. Joan called home, telling her mother she was okay. She would be home for Christmas as they had planned. Joan told her mother to give Dad a kiss for her and to hug everyone else then she ended her call. Richards's next call was to the Director of the C.I.A.

"We got your package, and it works, so what now?" Richard asked.

"We were thinking about getting you guys the hell out of there. The only thing is we don't know where you would be the safest?" the Director said. When Richard asked the Director, what he meant when he needed clarification about the safest place the Director explained about the breaches in the N.S.A. and their networks.

"Now, I'm not saying it was the Group; I'm not saying it wasn't either. However, from now on, I'm working under the knowledge the Chinese know what we're up to shortly after we decide." Steven told Richard.

"Under the circumstances, can't the N.S.A. be left in the dark until they get their systems back from whoever is in it?" Richard asked.

"That order has to come from the President himself, and right now, Wyatt is telling the man himself. Of course, the Director of the

N.S.A. is in the meeting trying to tell the President it's all bullshit. He's bragging about how nobody could break his agency's code. However, Wyatt has a plan when the Director says their safe. Wyatt is going to drop the presidents' daughters' e-mails to her girlfriend in London on his desk. In them, she talks about her father being elected and how much she hates living in Washington. That should seal the deal for us." The Director said. Just as the General walked into his office.

"That was quick; what happened?" Richard asked as he heard the men talking. Then the Director laughed. When Richard asked what had happened, Steven told him Wyatt didn't bother to wait for the N.S.A.'s Director to object. He just went in with the file, and the President took the N.S.A. offline. Richard and the Director, along with General Whistler, talked for a few more minutes, then signed off with a time in the morning they would be in contact.

Looking at Jack, Richard held out the phone and asked.

"Do you think Tran's in shape to take a call?"

"No, I'll call Jaio. She said both she and Scott wouldn't leave his side." Jack said as he took the phone and left the room. When Jack returned a few minutes later, Richard noticed how the man seemed lighter for some reason.

"Well damn it, man, don't keep us in suspense; how is he doing?" Richard asked, leaning forward for the news of his friend.

"Jiao answered her cell, and she told me to call the house. The doctors are amazed at how fast he's healing, so they sent him home a week after the surgery." Everyone was happy to hear the good news. Now Jack had to worry about the Chinese going after Tran while he was convalescing at home in England.

"We are going to have to get the Captain and his men better transportation. It would be a crime if the fat English men and that bastard got away because the Captain and his men had poor transportation." Zihao said. He watched each member of the Group nod his head. He picked up a phone and called the Captain.

Zihao told him when he and his men reached the city of Butembo to get the best vehicle he could find.

Chapter 9

CAPTAIN ZEN WONG WAS sitting in the front seat of the eight-passenger Land Rover as he and his five men passed thru the city of Butembo. He took the time to study what they knew about Jack when the leader of the Group told him he was going to be sent to Africa. There he was going to hunt and kill the man who had escaped Tibet on foot after being tortured. The Captain knew Jack would stop and try to reach out of Africa to find help. Looking around, he knew his prey was in this city.

"Stop; if you were running and trying to find a way out of this country, wouldn't you go to the nearest city and see if there was an airport or some other kind of transportation?" Zen asked, not really expecting an answer. His driver turned and looked at him, then out the window.

"Find the biggest hotel this slum has to offer!" Zen ordered his driver. Zen sat smiling; if he was wrong, he would have wasted nothing but a bit of time. If he was right, and he killed the two men, he was sent here to kill in less time than the Group thought possible. Well, then, his next promotion was assured. Zen ordered the driver to stop where groups of men were standing and talking. When the driver stopped, the Captain asked if they could direct them to a good hotel. A young man turned and pointed down the street telling him if they were to go further, they would come to the hotel Butembo.

The hotel stood out in the city of dusty roads and poverty. Its white walls and painted metal doors would give travelers a false sense of security. The young woman behind the counter apologized when she told Zen there were no rooms left for him or his friends. She was kind enough to give him directions to the other hotel in the city. When Zen asked if the last person to check in was a heavy English man. The girl looked at him, then smiled and said yes, he was a touch on the portly side. Thanking the girl, Zen left, telling his driver to find a place where he could set up some men to watch for their targets.

Joan walked with Eugene to the front counter of the hotel; she asked if there was a restaurant in the area where they could get takeaway. While Joan received directions from the girl to a small place, her aunt owned around the block. Eugene was watching a group of Asian men driving off in an extended land rover. Smiling at the hotel clerk, Eugene told Joan he had forgotten something in the room, and he asked if she would help him. Knowing Eugene hadn't forgotten anything, Joan looked out the door into the bright African day. She wondered what Eugene saw outside to make him return to the rooms. Walking down the hall, Eugene looked out of the windows, trying to see if he could find the land rover. To see if he could follow the car and where the men inside were trying to hide.

"I think the Chinese have found us; I saw five, maybe six, in a Land Rover pulling out of the parking lot just as I was about to step outside," Eugene whispered in Joan's ear as she stood by him, looking out the hallway window. Without saying a word, she followed the broad back of the stocky man down the hallway to the room where they left Richard and the others. Standing in the room, Eugene explained what he had seen before stepping outside.

"Joan, go and see if there is a place where we can rent a car; if there is, see if they'll bring it to the hotel. I'll call Steven back and tell him we have to move and see if he can give us a direction to move in." Richard said as he picked up the phone. Joan hurried to the front desk. Standing at the front desk, Joan ensured she could watch the parking lot while talking to the girl.

"Oh yes, Mr. Bubanni has four-wheel drives; he leases them to people from national geographic. If he has one left, I think he would be happy to lease it to you." The desk clerk told Joan.

"Can you call Mr. Bubanni for me and see if he has a truck left. One big enough to fit our party, please?" Joan asked the clerk.

As Joan told Richard, the clerk had called someone who had a truck, and it would fit their needs. Richard was happy to meet Mr. Bubanni in the lobby of the hotel. Though Richard smiled through the process of filling out the paperwork for the rental of the truck. The price held a shock for the normally fiscal-minded head of the unit. Richard thought by the time, all the charges went through for the rental and insurance of the truck. He would have enough air miles built up that he could've flown everyone to England for free.

Jack couldn't believe what Richard had leased. Mr. Bubanni told them it was the only truck he had left that could fit all six people and their gear. It was a newer Unimog, a U4000 made by Mercedes-Benz. Its square cab boasted a high air intake called a snorkel on the right-hand corner. On the top of the cab was a bar holding six of the most impressive off-road lights Jack had ever seen; these lights would easily light their way through the night. A large bull bar protected the front of the truck; hidden inside the structure of the bull bar was a thirty thousand pound capacity Warn winch. Behind the lights on the roof was a rack to hold gear. The bed of the truck had been sprayed with a rubber coating so it could be hosed out. They had six people, with the front and back seats; four was the usual limit for this truck. Jack and Eugene added two milk crates, trying to create two extra seats; both men knew these seats would be hard on the girls.

"How did you find them?" Zihao asked the Captain as he stood in front of his desk. He stood listening to the Captain as he explained how he found Jack and the others.

"That is good, very good...this is what you will do." Captain Zen Wong listened as Zihao told him he was to follow Jack and Richard into the countryside. Then when the Captain felt it, they had gone far enough into the bush to kill everyone in the truck. The Group in Beijing wanted it to look like the fat English man and the others stumbled onto a gold smuggling operation. Everyone had been killed by the smugglers to keep their operation secret. Zihao liked this Captain Zen; he knew his job and his place. The man called in with reports when he was told to. Also, he didn't make rash decisions.

The Captain and his men watched as their targets finished loading their gear into the large German truck. One of the men behind the Captain commented how easy it would be to catch the others in the truck.

"It won't be easy if they stray off-road into the bush." The Captain said. Then he and his men watched the truck pull out of the hotel in a cloud of dust and diesel smoke. As the Captain told his men how their prey could get away, he knew this would be the only thing to keep him from killing the man who disgraced his country.

Jack watched for any vehicles following them; trying to catch sight of anything behind the Unimog was almost impossible. The large flotation tires caused so much dust to be lifted off the dirt roads. Jack soon realized the only way to see if they were being followed was to stop and wait for the dust to settle. Richard sat in the jump seat with Tish between them. Jack could tell the girl was uncomfortable; he had to give her credit. When he would ask her if she was good, she would smile and give him the typical *'no prob* .'This was her and Toshs usual answer. Joan sat behind Jack, Eugene was behind Richard with Tosh between them. Like her almost twin non-sister, Tosh sat on the other milk crate. She would smile and lean on Eugene. Jack felt terrible for Tish and Tosh, even though Mr. Bubanni brought pieces of foam with him for the crates. Jack knew their butts and backs would be sore as hell tonight. A warbling ring brought Jack back to the first time he and Tran ran from the Chinese; Richard answered and smiled.

"Yes, we are on our way and heading north on N2. It is what you might call a major route thru the D.R.C., though I don't think I would call it that." Richard stated. As Jack slowed to navigate, another axle-breaking hole washed out in the last rainy season. As the conversation continued, Jack thought he could catch the sun reflecting sporadically off another vehicle. Heading north, the sun had started to slip toward the horizon. It was now on their left as it faded through the evening. Jack had seen sunsets on many horizons in the world, and he thought the best sunset he had ever seen still had to be the one he had seen in Bhutan. Jack could still see the colors as the sun dipped behind the mountains of the happy little Asian country. Jack, Richard, and the others commented on how many other trucks and battered cars used the road. Once, Jack had to stop and help a man thru a large washed-out area. The kind man was using his Honda scooter to haul supplies to his village. The man thanked Jack, and the others, then continued down the rutted section of the road. While standing on the road, Jack had time to look back down the road. He couldn't see any other car or truck following them. Then Jack thought how easy it would be to hide behind them. As their Unimog grumbled thru the washed-out road. Jack tried to think of how long it would take them to reach the city of Bunia.

The five men, who made up the Chinese unit along with Captain Zen Wong, watched as Jack helped the man with the scooter through the water. They watched as the Unimog started through the water; Captain Wong ordered one of his men into the bush.

"Find a suitable place to shoot from and kill their leader, the fat one!" Wong ordered. The sniper of the Group was outfitted with a

QBU-88 rifle. It fired a 5.8x42 special sniper M.G. load. The man was one of the best to come out of the school the Chinese army had in the countryside of Outer Mongolia. The sniper lay down behind a log, taking his time; the sniper waited until his target moved into his scope. He could see the fat English man; his face was red, and sweat ran down his cheeks as he turned to look out his window. The truck started into the water and was crawling when the man took in a breath and let it out slowly, all the while taking up the slack in the trigger of his weapon.

Chapter 10

EUGENE LEANED OVER to ask Richard a question when it felt like he was hit by a sledgehammer in the shoulder. The impact of the round from the Chinese sniper was so fierce when it hit Eugene. The ex-marine forced Richard forward and to the left into Jack's lap. Eugene was thrown to the floor in front of Tish and Joan. They all heard the report of the heavy rifle. Jack knew they were sitting ducks if he didn't hurry and get them into the cover of the bush. Eugene was lying on the floor. Joan could hear his breathing, and from the sounds she heard, she was worried Eugene had been hit in the back. Jack drove the throttle to the floor and turned off the rutted road and into the bush. Richard sat up. He turned in his seat, trying to help Joan get Eugene off the floor and back onto the seat, where they could assess his wounds.

The sniper watched as the Unimog turned into the bush, trying to disappear. He sighted the back of the truck in his scope and fired two more shots trying to hit one of the fuel tanks. As the truck bounced into the bush. He watched as his shots did nothing more than break a mirror and smash a light on the back of the large German truck.

Once Jack felt he had put a couple of kilometers behind them, he stopped and jumped out. Joan, Richard, and the two girls helped Eugene out of the truck to the ground. Jack watched as Richard cut the old marines shirt off him and was shocked at the wound. The bullet hit Eugene in the right shoulder, passing through the deltoid muscle. The impact of the shot on the top of the humerus, where it enters the shoulder socket, caused the bone to break. The bullet then exited out of the top of the shoulder and traveled out into the African countryside. Jack knew the shot was meant for him or Richard. Eugene had simply gotten in the way; now, their friend and one of the only people with actual combat experience was down with a bullet wound and a busted shoulder.

Captain Wong had seen one of the people in the truck take the bullet from his sniper's rifle. He knew it had been a good solid hit; the person was either dead or dying. He didn't know that the training Eugene received from the Marines had saved his life.

The tough old marine did what came naturally when the bullet hit. He went with the force of the impact, and though he was hurt, he could still be helpful. Once Jack and Joan tended to Eugene, they secured his arm so the man wouldn't bleed to death. He and Richard managed to get Eugene back into the truck with as little jostling as possible.

"When we reach the next town, you have got to leave me there. I know I'm going to be a liability for ya'll, and I ain't going to be the reason them fucks kill my girls." Eugene stated through clenched teeth.

"Bullshit, I won't leave anybody behind, we all get the hell out, or we all stay and fight, got it." Jack returned. He turned and looked at the sweating face of the older marine.

The truck had headed east into the bush of Africa; this time, he was going to follow through and finish what the Group had started before. Almost two kilometers into the bush, the driver of the land rover found where Jack had stopped the Unimog. After some searching, Captain Wong was called over to a mound of piled branches. Under the small pile, they found what remained of a first aid kit. So the man who was hit was still alive. He knew this could

work in his favor. With a man wounded, the others would have to
help the man, which would slow the whole unit down. Unlike his
training, the Westerners were soft; they would take the wounded
man with them trying to save his life. If it was the Captain, he would
have shot the man in the head and carried on like nothing had
happened.

Jack knew they had been north of a village called Beni, and now
they were crawling thru the jungle of eastern D.R.C., trying to get to
an airport further north.

"You better call Steven and Wyatt and let them know what's
happened. Tell him we are now going east towards Uganda." Jack
told Richard. Joan watched Richard as he dialed a number into the
satellite phone. Once Richard finished explaining what happened.
He told them they were now heading into Uganda. The Director of
the C.I.A. and the head of the Joint Chiefs told Richard about one
of their satellite tracking stations picking up a signature of an F18
heading out over Madagascar. Richard listened for a moment while
Jack slowed down and read a faded bullet-riddled sign. The sign lay
in the long grass growing beside what served as a road in the bush.
Once Jack read the sign, he turned to Richard, who had gone silent.
The village of Murambi was as close to their path as any; it sat at the
foot of Mount Ruwenzori.

"At the rate we're going, we won't be there until morning," Jack
told Richard.

"I know; we have to keep going before we get to the village.
Steven will try to drop a package for us, but they don't have any air
assets in this part of Africa." Richard whispered. Then turned to see
if the Chinese were catching them. Jack hoped they would find some
sort of cover before they were forced to fight for their lives.

Zihao smiled as he listened to the conversation on the speaker.
The Captain told his leader of the shot that wounded one of the
party he was hunting. The Captain also informed the leader of the

Group in Beijing, Richard, the leader of the unit, was still alive for now. Captain Wong assured Zihao this would change shortly. The Captain apologized, saying he would pull the trigger on the unit leader himself.

"I know you will, Captain; keep up the hunt. You are doing a great duty for your country." Zihao said before he ended the call.

"Now, gentlemen, where do we stand on the Americans and destroying them?" He asked as he faced the rest of the Group.

"Our people in Washington have the reporter's computer and all her files. They have hacked into her P.D.A. and wiped it clean; we also have her boyfriend covered. If she tries to find out who her contact was or tries to get in contact again, our people will make it look as if she had a car accident." A tall, balding man in the back of the room said.

"Don't wait. Make sure the reporter's car accident looks suspicious. Make it look sloppy. This way, the American media will be overrun with conspiracy theories. They will start the call for an investigation into the N.S.A.," Zihao said. Before he left the room, the tall man was on the phone giving the order.

Jack watched as the sun fell below the horizon. The jungle darkened enough he was forced to turn on the powerful off-road lights. Stopping the truck, Jack got out and listened for the land rover the Chinese had been in. Cupping his hands around his ears, Jack turned in different directions. The sound of the suv failed to come to him. Jack could hear the sound of moving water. A river was nearby; he could hear it splashing over rocks.

Wendy smiled as her boyfriend walked down the steps of the Canadian Embassy. Wendy couldn't believe she had hooked what her best friend called a real catch. Wendy greeted Paul with a peck on the cheek and handed him the keys to her car. Paul smiled at her and laughed at how she always insisted he drove when they were together. Leaving the city, Paul looked forward to the drive. It took them through the country south to Georgia. He always looked forward to the visits with Wendy's mother and father. Once outside the city and on the interstate, Paul managed to bring the BMW up to eighty miles an hour and then set the cruise control. For the first part of the trip, Wendy and Paul talked about things they thought would look nice in the apartment. Like so many other young couples in love, the conversation turned to children and the future.

"We should get some gas at the next exit and something to eat," Paul said when he noticed a black suv behind him.

"Don't fill up on truck stop junk food; moms got a big celebration planned," Wendy warned Paul. She knew how Paul loved junk food.

Pulling off the highway, Paul thought the brakes felt spongy and reminded himself to check the fluid level when he was getting gas. When Paul tried to stop at the top of the exit ramp, the brake pedal dropped to the floor of the little sports car. Taking a quick look left then right, Paul slammed his foot down on the throttle. The BMW Z4 shot thru the intersection at the top of the ramp and down the entrance of Interstate 95. For a second, Wendy was caught off guard, then realized something was wrong with the car.

"Oh god, what's wrong?" She asked.

"Something's wrong with the brakes; I'm going to gear down when we are going slow enough. I'll ease the parking brake on slowly, so we don't lose control." Paul explained. In the mirror, he watched the black suv follow them down the ramp. Wendy was amazed at how calm Paul could be as he eased the car down thru its gears, then put it in neutral and slowly used the hand brake to stop. As Paul brought the BMW to a stop, the black suv stopped behind them, and a door opened. Getting ready for a fight, Paul jumped out of the car. He reached for a golf club, not knowing what he would do with the club if the men came out of the suv with a pistol.

Wendy recognized one of the men in the suv as one of the two who grabbed her out of her apartment.

"Paul, don't." That was all Wendy could say before the driver of the suv raised his hands.

"We didn't do this; in fact, we're here to help the two of you." The bigger of the two men said. He watched Paul slide the one wood out of the golf bag. His partner slowly brought his hand out from his sports jacket, holding a letter.

"The director thought we should keep an eye on you after what happened at your apartment." The second agent was saying as he handed Wendy the letter he was holding.

"He thought the Chinese might try something like this. He didn't want a friend getting hurt, so he sent us along to watch out for you two." The agent said.

"So what you're saying is you didn't mess with the breaks on the car?" Paul asked.

"No, we don't do that...anymore; all that black hat shit went out with J. Edgar and his lackeys." Agent Ted Boyles said. He stepped forward to shake Paul's hand. The second agent's name was Bill Clinton.

"Please, no tricky dickey jokes; I don't think I could take one more." Bill pleaded. Then he started to unload Wendy and Paul's luggage.

"What are you doing?" Wendy asked. She watched as Paul started to help the two-C.I.A. agents with their bags.

"Um, Wendy, if the Chinese did this because of something you saw or reported on, then it would make sense they are probably monitoring us now," Paul said. Looking around for something or someone who seemed out of place, the two agents looked at Paul, then at each other, and nodded as they carried the baggage.

"I'd be worried about going to your mom and dad's place just in case something happened to bring this to their doorstep," Paul said.

He was about to close the trunk of the car when a hole appeared beside his hand. Though Paul had never been shot at in his life, his training kicked in, and he grabbed Wendy and shouted for cover. Both Ted and Bill had been under fire before, and the shout for cover brought them to action. East of them was the truck stop; Paul couldn't see a vantage point for a sniper. To the west were woods and any number of points for a sniper to fire from. Grabbing Wendy by the arm, Paul crawled to the side of the suv and opened the door. He shoved Wendy into the rear seat. They all heard a bullet hit the suv and whine off into the sky. Smiling, Bill mouthed the words *armor plating*. Paul nodded and then slid into the back seat.

"Under the circumstances, I think we should get to your parent's house as soon as possible. Who knows what kind of shit these assholes are going to be up to." Ted was saying as another round hit the back of the suv.

"Well, at least the asshole is persistent." Bill quipped. He smiled at Wendy in the rearview mirror.

"I'll call the boss and tell him what we ran into. I think he'll get people to your mom and dad before we get there.

Standing on the bank of the Semliki River, Jack could tell, in some places, it would be deep. Before he stopped on the bank, he had come across what looked like a path. This path was worn deep into the ground. This told Jack it had been used daily for many years. Everyone held their breath as Jack eased the Unimog over the bank into the river. The slow-moving brown water of the river pushed against the side of the heavy German truck. Jack could feel the heavy tires of the truck slip in the muddy silt of the river bottom and then grab traction. Slowly the heavy truck started to plow its way through the water. Once the truck made it across the river, Jack urged it up the bank with a generous amount of fuel.

Captain Wong stood at the point where Jack rolled the large German-built truck into the river. Looking at his men and their land rover, he doubted it could cross the river with the ease the Unimog had. He was going to lose more time looking for a proper crossing. Standing at the bank of the river, the Captain listened as his targets made their way further out of his grasp and into the African bush.

"I can't know for sure; I think the Chinese will have to find a shallow point to get through the river," Jack said. Trying to reassure the others in the Unimog. Staring out the windshield of their truck, Jack wondered how he was going to get Richard over the mountains sitting beyond the trees. With his lack of exercise and a love of fine dining, his friend and leader was in terrible physical shape. Due to a Chinese bullet, Eugene would never be able to make it either, not with his wound. Jack forced the Unimog thru the night. He knew if they could reach the foot of the mountains, they would have a fighting chance of getting Joan and the girls to safety. However, what of Richard and Eugene? Jack didn't know if he could hold off the Chinese Group until help arrived.

"When we reach the mountains, I want you to take over for me, Joan. You'll have to get the girls along with Richard to Uganda," Jack ordered. Richard sat looking at his friend.

"I'll be damned; I am not going to sit here and watch you go off to fight the group wishing to see us dead by yourself!" Richard stated. He crossed his arms as a sign of defiance.

"He won't be alone," Eugene stated through gritted teeth. Joan knew why Jack needed to go off by himself though she didn't like it.

"Richard, you need to listen to me; I can't work when I have to worry about you and the girls. I need to be on my own, so I can stop these assholes, and as for you, Eugene, you're going with them." Jack told his friend, though he never took his eyes off Joan.

"The hell I am; I ain't gonna run out on a friend because of a boo-boo," Eugene answered as he tried to sit up straighter. Joan looked away; first, she wanted to check Eugene's wound. She couldn't believe the oldest of them was taking the pain of his injury without any medication.

The sun was starting to brighten the eastern sky over the mountains when Jack drove into the village of Murambi. Like most of the remote villages in Africa, children were happy and delighted in chasing the truck. When Jack stopped, and they got out, the children ran up to see the strangers. The small group of children stopped when they got their first sight of Tish and Tosh. Richard laughed when some of the small children turned and ran away. The girls looked hurt for a moment, then a little girl took Tish's hand and smiled at her. Even though the girls had taken some of their piercings out. Their faces still held enough metal to frighten off some of the children. One of the village elders walked out of a hut and introduced himself to Jack. Jack looked at the hand the older man offered; he could see the knotted scars showing the evidence of many hard-won battles in the past. When Jack shook the hand, he looked into the faded eyes of the weathered face. In the man's eyes, Jack saw wisdom also hard-won. The wisdom the old man held was earned from seeing his friends and family killed by rebels who ran in these mountains in years past.

"I'm afraid we might have brought trouble to your village," Jack explained.

"There are some men who follow us. They want to kill these people and me." Jack finished. He sat waiting to see what would be said. The village chief sat silent while a large woman brought in hot tea and some flatbread with a type of beans to eat. When she left, the old man looked up from his tea.

"Many have come here to kill and steal. All of them thought they had a good reason. What would be their reason?" The Chief asked. Then took a sip of his tea.

"A couple years ago, I escaped from a cruel and evil man. I was hurt badly. I was found by some holy men who live in the mountains in a country far from here. They healed me and saved my life. Then I found a man. It turned out he and I shared the same enemies. I made good my escape. We found four men and helped them bring the news of these evil men and their deeds to the world. Now they wish to kill me for what they perceive as a great dishonor." Jack told the village elder.

"Even here, I have heard of this; you were in a land called Tibet. I remember some men and a woman with national geographic had a newspaper and a radio. One of them knew a reporter you saved from the Chinese." The Chief said. It seemed the Chief had made up his mind. He would trust Jack and the rest of them when he guessed who Jack was.

"You would make it over the mountains, but I don't think the rest of your group will." The Chief told Jack as he stood.

"I mean no disrespect; I just wish to be honest with you." The older man said. Before anyone could say anything, the old Chief continued.

"Some of our young men go to the mountains with scientists and photographers as porters; even for them, it is hard...." When the Chief stopped. He looked at Richard, not wanting to say what could be seen. Richard looked down at his belly and knew he was going to be a burden; he thought, what if one of his friends died because of him. Even when he was younger and at school, sports had never been his thing. While the others were out running and having a good time, Richard kept to his studies, and it showed he finished at the top of his class in all academic studies. He was almost at the bottom of his class in physical education.

Richard always laughed to himself at the word, almost in the statement. He finished just ahead of a classmate who broke both his legs in a horse riding incident. The poor bastard had been wheelchair-bound for the second half of the year. At Eaton, that was no excuse, hip hip hoorah and all that bullshit, Richard thought.

"Well, that tears it. If I'm going to be a danger to the rest of you, then I'll have to go it on my own." Richard stated.

"The hell you say!" Jack responded.

"And before you get all British on us and say it's for the safety of the girls or some shit like that. I will point out *you* are not equipped for a fight in the jungle." Before Jack could carry on with his argument, Richard spoke.

"I don't want to be the reason my friends are caught and murdered. I'm not in the same physical shape you are in. I'll slow you down and help the bastards following us to catch us that much quicker. I can not be responsible for that." Richard said. Jack looked at his friend and smiled. For some reason, Jack's smile did nothing to reassure Richard; it had the opposite effect.

"Well, you and Eugene can team up and help each other along; as for going out on your own, it's not that cold in hell yet, and I have a plan. I was going to say Joan could take the girls over the mountains into Uganda to your sister's place. You and Eugene in tow." Joan and Richard started to speak at the same time. Jack knew what they were going to say. He had had the same argument with himself.

Richard was a good man, but he had never been in the field before. He was terribly out of shape, Richards, only experienced in the jungle, was at the bases he helped set up around the world. Along with Richard was Eugene, whose right side was useless from a busted shoulder. Jack knew all the arguments; he had the same fight with himself just a little while ago. Now he was going to have it again with Joan and Richard.

"Now hold on, Jack, if I...." Before Joan could finish, Jack cut her off by making it an order. Joan didn't like it, but she would follow orders.

"I don't like it; that being said, I can see your logic. Your ass better finds its way to the house." Joan said as she watched a buzzard circle overhead.

"Well, old man, you might be able to give Joan orders, but as for me, you don't have a leg to stand on...." Richard was going to add that he outranked him. Jack turned and smiled at him again...damn that smile. How it worked, Richard didn't know. Of all the weapons Jack could use, it was the worst. Unlike most people who smiled at others, they did so to comfort or when they were having a good time. Love... friends, family, all the reasons one could think of. Then there is Jack. He could use his smile to turn your blood to ice in your veins. The smile he gave Richard did just that. It also had the added ability to cause millipedes to run up his spine, giving Richard goosebumps over most of his body.

"You wanted to say something?" Jack asked Richard, still smiling. "No, good; now, as for Eugene, you're going to have to find some way to eat the pain and fatigue from the blood loss and altitude." Jack started. Before he could go on, the village Chief cleared his throat.

"I'll send enough strong young men to help your injured friend, and they know a way through the mountains;." The Chief told Jack.

"Thank you, I am sorry we have brought this to your village," Jack said as he looked into the sad brown eyes of the Chief.

Chapter 11

CAPTAIN WONG SMILED as he watched Jack talk to the others. If it were up to him, he would have attacked when they were eating in the village. Captain Wong was under orders not to have too much collateral damage. China still wanted places around the world where she could go and have a place to hide some toys. The Captain thought Jack would send the rest of his Group on without him. Then Jack would try to lead him and his men on a wild goose chase, as they say. The Captain knew Jack would send the three women, the fat man, and the injured one to the mountain. If this is what Jack did, he will send two of his men to follow the women and the two men. The men had orders not to kill the fat man until he arrived. The Captain didn't care about the others they chased. First, he and the three men with him would follow Jack into the bush and kill him.

Richard couldn't believe he was letting Jack go alone into the bush with six Chinese soldiers hunting him. Jack had a hunch the leader of the Chinese would follow him. He would want to be there when his men killed him, so he could claim the action as his. The Chinese officer would send one, maybe two men to follow Richard, Joan, and the girls. This was his gamble. Jack was hoping the Chinese leader would want all the credit for himself. This being so, Jack hoped the leader would order his men to hold the others until he arrived. Standing in front of Joan and Eugene, Jack told her what he thought the Chinese would do and that she should watch her back trail.

"I don't know for sure it's what their leader will do; it wouldn't hurt to go under the assumption they want Richard dead too. You and the girls would be guilty by associations." Jack told her. He turned away to make his way into the bush. Joan grabbed his hand, kissing him on the cheek and then on the lips.

"Like I told you before, this is an order. You get your ass to that house, mister." Joan told him. Then let go of Jack's hand and walked to the others to start her Group into the mountains.

Both the Director of the C.I.A. and the head of the Joint Chiefs listen to a man standing at a large map. The man they listened to was in charge of central African intelligence gathering. He spelled out the assets they could use to help Jack and Richard in their run from the Chinese.

"Well, it ain't much." The man drawled in his heavy South Carolina speech.

"I know it isn't much." The Director returned, trying to correct his man's grammar.

"However, anything is better than what they have now." The worried-looking C. Steven Wilson said. He leaned over a large map of the country his friends were trapped in.

"Here's a question, I know there are two aircraft carriers, and their groups just left Guam; they are heading to the Sea of Oman?" The tall General Whistler asked as he looked at the world map on one wall of the Director's office.

"Um, yes, sir General, they are heading to the Sea of Oman, and then they are going to split and start their respective missions." Stated the C.I.A. analyst.

"Good, I know when I was a young marine, some of the carrier groups kept a unit of Seals on board, right." The General said. To the analyst, it didn't sound like the General was asking for confirmation.

To the analyst, it sounded like he should pick up the phone and ensure there were seals on one of the carriers.

"Ok, the carrier group Enterprise has a unit of seals on board, and they are outfitted for insertion into Afghanistan." Bob Knitter said as he hung up the phone.

"Afghanistan or Africa both start with the letter "A" so I don't see a problem, do you, Steve." The General asked with a sardonic smile on his lips; the General could see the same smile on his old friend's face.

"Not from where I stand; how about you, Bob? Do you see a problem?" Director Wilson of the C.I.A. asked his man.

"Problem, with what, sir?" Bob Knitter answered.

Bob Knitter watched as his boss and the head of the joint chiefs smiled at him. Now to get the seals from the carriers to the mountains separating D.R.C. from Uganda. It would be too hard to hide the jets taking off from the carriers' especially one large enough to fit the seals and their gear. Therefore, they had to find a fast plane that could land and take off on an aircraft carrier and still carry six men with their equipment.

"I think we have just the thing in Pearl Harbor. It's the Citation we outfitted and never had the chance to try out for landing and take-off from a carrier." Director Wilson said as he turned to the phone.

"With the belly full of fuel and only the pilot and copilot on board, they should be able to make it in hours, as long as the group sits still." Before the Director could finish telling the general about his plan. Whistler had placed his own call to the Commander of the carrier group and ordered him to keep station where he was. He was told to have his seals ready to go at a moment's notice.

"Sir, can I ask what this is about?" The Commander asked.

"We are going to try to land a business jet on your deck. When it gets there, if it doesn't fall off, then you're going to refuel it, place your seals on it, then carry on with your mission as if nothing happened," Whistler told the Captain.

"Yes, sir, we'll wait until the jet lands." The man stated as he ended the call, then turned and shook his head. This Commander wasn't in the habit of questioning his orders, even if the damn things didn't make any sense. If his bosses thought trying to land a small jet on his deck was a good idea, he would go along until the shit hit the fan.

Twenty-five minutes later, a blue and white citation X lifted off from Honolulu airport. Its clearance came down from the top of the F.A.A. The tower had been told to hold all other traffic to get this private jet in the air and headed west now. They were also told to clear a one-hundred-mile-wide path along its route; no reason was given. All the controllers knew a black ops flight when one entered or left their airspace. The speed of the clearance and the wide corridors the flight required gave it away. One of the controllers turned to his friend and commented that if the government wanted to hide the flight, they wouldn't go through the trouble of hiding and trying to keep people from seeing the plane.

"What they should do is just take off and land, like the rest of the fuck'n world. But no, these dumb bastards make a grand spectacle about it, calling more attention to their movements." The air traffic controller said to his friend.

Captain Wong couldn't believe his luck. He and his men watched as the man he was here to kill and the others split up. Jack headed back into the bush. Joan led up the mountain with Richard, the two girls, and the wounded man. The only thing they had with them was the food they bought at the village, two teenage boys for porters and two men in their twenties for protection, and an older man in his forties. Wong smiled as he thought about how easy it would be for his highly trained men to hunt and kill this Group. Then he thought about his prey, and his smile grew. He would be a hero when he returned home.

The heat of the day started to burn through the light wispy clouds high in the African sky. It wasn't long before Richard promised himself he would spend more time in a gym if he made it out of this alive. Two of the young men and the older man from the village stayed behind to make sure Richard and Eugene did not fall too far behind. One young man would smile at Richard and, in his broken English, tell him he was doing fine. While the older man would silently encourage Eugene to keep moving forward. The second young man would smile as he carried some water.

"Mister Richard, a bit further than we rest, you to Mister Eugene, rest is just up there." Their young protector would say as he pointed to a clump of trees. Richard and Eugene would nod their heads, and neither man would look to where the young man pointed. Richard didn't look up because he feared he would stop and then couldn't get going again. For Eugene, it was he couldn't lift his head, the swelling had worsened, and he wasn't able to move his neck. Also, Eugene thought if he lifted his head, he might pass out. So like the old bull, Eugene kept his head down and pushed on. The older native man quietly kept pace with the wounded Eugene.

Jack knew his body and limits, so when he left the village, Jack knew how long he could go for. He set a pace he could comfortably keep for the rest of the day and into the night. He wanted to get the hunt started and over with. However, Jack wanted it on his timetable at a location where he had the upper hand. Jack was giving up numbers to the Chinese. He thought he'd be damned if he was about to give up the rest of the fight.

Major Steve "Dodo" Duncan looked at the deck of the aircraft carrier. He turned to his copilot and noticed the man was smiling.

"Well, I'm tickled pink you're having such a good time," Steve said. Steve didn't want to smile at his friend and copilot. He just couldn't stop it and smiled. His friend and copilot had one of those smiles when he walked into a room with it pasted on his face; before you knew it, the whole room was smiling. The only person who could resist the smile was the Chief of the Joint Chiefs. At times he thought the old bastard was born with the marine scowl on his face. During his years, he came to believe the old hard-ass just couldn't smile.

"Hell, I'm just along for the ride. If this all goes wrong, you're the one in shit, not me." Alex "A train," Knitter said. Most men and women of the air force received their call signs from their personality quirks. Things that happened while at the air force academy. This fact holds true for the Major, who, while on a Christmas ski trip to Colorado with some of his classmates from the academy, had on countless times crashed. During one of the majors, more flamboyant fowl ups. One classmate commented Steve looked like a dodo bird trying to land with a brick tied to his ass. Thus one call sign was born, at six foot two inches and with a head of wavy black hair and eyes the same blue as icebergs. The Major was what some women swooned over, though he never seemed to notice. Steve Duncan gave up skiing that weekend and decided to sit in the lodge and prove the Dodo was the best lover of all the fowl. To his friend's dismay, he was proved right when he had three of the most beautiful women on the mountain chasing him for the rest of the trip.

With "A train," receiving his call sign was less painful; Alex is a farm kid, a white farm kid from Nebraska. A farm kid who has an undying love of soul music. It has to be from the sixties and seventies, or in his own words, "It ain't worth the ear time." One of his instructors, who also had a love of soul music, gave him his call sign at the academy. Each loved soul music. The difference between them was the instructor was from Detroit and was a six-foot-five-inch African-American man. While Alex is a five-foot-ten-inch red-haired farm boy with a killer smile and freckles. Their difference started and ended with their love of music.

"Shit, that deck doesn't look big enough to land a toy plane on, let alone this thing," Dodo said as he lined his nose up with a strip of lights running down the deck.

"Well, for god sake, don't miss." Was all A-train could think to say before they started to go through the checklist for the landing.

"Ok, that's it; drop the hook and pray it holds, or we're going for a swim," Dodo said as he started his final approach. Dodo could hear the flight control of the carrier calling out the distance and height of the Citation. Dodo could only hear the controller half the time. All at once the controller said the words, "ok, call the ball," which got Both Dodo and A-train's attention. Both Dodo and A-train could see the catch net at the other end of the deck. For a second, A-train thought something had gone wrong, then they hit the deck and felt the hook catch the cable stretching across the deck behind them. Both men were hurled into their harnesses as the plane was caught and dragged to a stop.

"Holy shit, boss, I'm glad that worked. I can't swim; I'm from Nebraska." Alex said. Then both men started to laugh, not relishing they were still transmitting to the control room.

"Hell, they made it down and are on the deck." Bob Knitter, who at the time had no idea his youngest sister's son and his favorite nephew, was the copilot on this mission.

"Yea, they made it onto the deck; now let's keep our fingers crossed they can get back into the air where it belongs." Said the Director of the C.I.A., a highly decorated retired fighter pilot. A pilot who knew how hard it would be to try to get the small jet back into the air.

Both Steve and Alex, along with a team of navy airframe technicians, combed the Citation looking for any damage from landing the plane on the deck of the aircraft carrier. Both men stood by the jet and watched the seal team start across the deck. The leader of the seal team was a quiet, heavily muscled six-foot Texan. His dark skin might have fooled some into thinking he had Mexican blood. They would have been wrong, and he would have told them quietly. His people were the traditional Kickapoo tribes of Texas. His mother named him for the month he was born, August. Both his grandfather and father had served in the U.S. military. This caused them no end of grief when they returned home. He was proud of their actions. He followed in their footsteps, joining the navy and entering the Seals when he was twenty. As the seals reached the stairs of the jet, August turned to the shorter of the two airforce pilots standing waiting for them.

"The captain asked me to give this to the farm hand," August said, handing A-train an old fashion flotation ring like they used during the Second World War. Looking at the ring, Dodo started to laugh. To his credit, A-train turned and thanked August for the ring.

"I'm going to mount this in my game room, and every time I look at it, I'll have a drink for you and your men." Once August told his men about the two men in the front of the plane, the level of trepidation dropped a notch or two. It would never go completely away. Steve and Alex sat in the cockpit of the Citation X, looking down the deck to the point where it ended. All that was left was the ocean. Both men looked at each other and then at their cockpit dash. Both hoped not to see any red lights or wavering gages. Everything looked good; Steve and Alex looked at each other when they were cleared for take-off.

Steve started to push the throttles forward. Both he and Alex scanned the gauges to see if any wavered. Sitting in the cabin of the Citation X, August and the rest of his men gripped the armrests of their seats. They sat and waited for the gut-wrenching drop at the end of the deck. They hoped the inevitable crash into the sea wouldn't come. The seals knew this stunt had never been tried before. Before that happened, the jet's engines went from a high-pitched whistle to a banshee scream. The men started to wince from the sound, trying to cut through their heads. It was almost unbearable as the two Rolls Royce jet turbine engines fought the block holding the jet in place.

"Holy shit, it sounds like the fuck'n things going to come apart!" One of the seals shouted from one of the back seats. One of his teammates turned and looked at August and asked if this was normal.

"If you wanted normal, you should have joined the fuck'n Coast Guard!" Another shouted, smiling as if he had found the best roller coaster in the world. Then the block holding the screaming jet back was released, and the men were slammed back into their seats. The plane jumped forward, and both Dodo and A-train were launched back into their seats. The Citation X raced down the deck, being helped toward sure destruction by the catapult and its engines. Both men watched as the end of the deck raced to meet them. Then in what seemed like slow motion, the front of the Citation lifted from the short runway of the aircraft carrier, then the rear of the plane dropped off the deck.

Every person on the bridge and on the deck held their breath as the plane raced toward the end of the aircraft carrier. All the men and women on the bridge were putting all their combined will into helping the plane and the men in it off the deck safely. They watched as the front landing gear started to lift then the plane dropped off the end of the deck. The Commander began to shout for the rescue team to get going. Relieved, the Commander, along with the crew, watched as the Citation reappeared, clawing its way into the blue sky. The Commander and the rest of the crew let out their breath as one collective sigh of relief. The old man placed both hands on his hips and lowered his head; looking at his executive officer, he said.

"Remind me to tell whatever dumb ass came up with this idea that he is, *indeed,* a dumb ass."

"Um, well, I think it was the Joint Chiefs who came up with this one, sir." The First Mate answered.

"Yep, sounds about right." The Commander smiled.

Chapter 12

"ARE WE DEAD YET?" ONE of the seals yelled from somewhere in the cabin, and without missing a beat, A-train yelled back.

"Almost; just give us a second." Both the Major and Captain could hear the sound of laughter. They knew it was from the relief of being in the air and not trying to get out of a sinking airplane. Getting out of his copilot's chair, A-train walked into the cabin and addressed the seals.

"We were told, once we got into the air, we would be receiving orders. As to where the hell we're going, don't suppose you might know, would you?" The young Captain asked August.

"Sorry, sir, we were hoping you or the Major might know," August answered. Steve shouted back. There was a video call coming in. As A-train turned on the plasma screen, the image of Wyatt Whistler, the Chief of the Joint Chiefs, looked back at A-train. The General started to give the briefing without any greeting.

"I know this is anything but s.o.p, and I know it's less than short notice, but here it is no bullshit." Each man listened as the General laid out what was going on in Africa and who they were going to rescue. When he was finished, the General took the time to look into each face staring back at him from a large screen in the situation room of the white house.

"If you have questions, now's the time." The General told the men.

"I have a couple, sir," August said.

"How are we to find our targets, and what kind of resistance should we expect from local assets of the Chinese?" Augusts asked.

"Well, Lieutenant, I can tell exactly nothing that will be of any help to you. Except there are six men chasing friends of ours, and they have injured an American. This man is a highly decorated retired Marine; I know him personally. He's saved my life more than once, and the Director of the C.I.A. Now the man you're going to help has dealt with the Chinese before and is, what you might say, high on their to-kill list." When the General finished, August smiled and asked his next question.

"Would this be the man who escaped along with a Tibetan and the B.B.C. reporters from China and Tibet a couple of years ago? The man who left the Chinese holding the short end, sir?" The seals and A-train watched as a near smile tugged at the corners of the General's mouth.

"You got it, son. Now we know they were forced to split their Group. Jack has gone into the bush on his own. He is hoping the Chinese will follow him and leave the rest to escape. However, I can't see it; one of our Group is a member of the royal family and is of vast importance to the peace and stability of many different areas around the world. He was instrumental in Jack getting the B.B.C. men out of Tibet. Now I know our man Jack can handle just about anything thrown at him. So what I'm tasking you men with is getting Richard and the others out safely. Remember, except for the wounded retired marine and the Chief Warrant officer, none are what you could even remotely call the military. This won't be a walk in the park, gentlemen, be safe and get those people the hell out of there." When the General finished his briefing of the seals, August nodded at the screen and gave a crisp *Yes, sir!* As each man took in what he had just heard, a light blinked on the overhead monitor.

A-train told the seals there were meals and drinks ready for them in the rear storage compartment then he ducked back into the cockpit.

"Running at full throttle like this, we're eating our fuel fast. I just called the Philippines and told them we're going to need a fill-up just as we scream over the tip of the island." Steve said as he watched the altimeter climb to the forty-five thousand mark and level off.

"You want me to go and tell the seals what's up?" A-train asked as he looked at the fuel gauge.

"No, they'll have enough to worry about. Let's not add to it. If we miss our stop, we'll have enough for an emergency landing in Jakarta. If it comes to that, we'll tell them what's going on." When Steve finished, Alex looked back at the seals huddled over water bottles and sandwiches, talking over their plan.

Alex nodded to Steve; he knew his friend was right. The men in the rear of the plane did indeed have enough to worry about. He heard the briefing the men received from the General. He also knew there was a good chance one or more of these men might not make it back home.

At its maximum speed, the Citation screamed through the blue sky at nine hundred kilometers an hour, or just short of breaking the sound barrier. At that speed, the distance the plane could fly was significantly shortened. Steve and Alex checked each other's math, and they confirmed their jet would indeed have enough fuel to just make it back to Jakarta. If they missed the KC135 stratotanker taking off from Clark air force base in Luzon, Philippines. They would barely have enough fuel to land.

"Well, let's not miss that meeting," Alex commented as they both looked out the windshield of their little jet to the light cloud cover below them. Though neither of the men could see the blue ocean below them. They both knew if they somehow managed to miss their refueling, not only would they be in serious trouble, but also some people in Africa could lose their lives.

The rain had been falling in Beijing for the last few hours, and with it, the city seemed to turn in on itself, trying to hide from the clouds. In the military information gathering offices, Zihao turned and stared at the face of a technician in charge of a spy ship in the sea near the Philippines.

"What do you mean a small business jet has appeared out of nowhere?" Zihao questioned.

"As far as we can tell, it came out of the ocean around Guam. It is now flying on a course that will bring it in close contact with a flying tanker the Americans keep in Luzon." An analyst told him.

"Get the Captain of the Bogon on the line. He will be of some use." Zihao ordered.

"God damn busy bodies, the Americans are up to something. I know whatever is on that plane is important. It will help their people get away from Captain Wong and his team." Zihao cursed.

"Does the trawler have any type of offensive weapons on board?" One of the Group asked from the darkened room.

The Captain of the fake fishing trawler answered a torpedo was for submarines only. Zihao tented his fingers in front of his eyes and desperately thought of a way to take the westbound jet out of the sky.

"If the Americans wish to stick their noses in further, then we'll have to cut it off for them. Monitor the Americans as long as possible. We will be sending something to knock them out of the game." Zihao informed the Captain of the trawler.

Ending the call, Zihao turned and smiled at the General in charge of China's only truly hypersonic aircraft. Though the rest of the world was still trying to get past Mach 5, the Chinese had defeated the problem. With the invention of a new alloy, China beat the problem of overheating.

Their creation had never been tested in a real-world application. The Group had no doubt it would work. The General smiled as he picked up the phone and made the call to put the world's first hypersonic aircraft into military service.

A small man answered the red phone in the hanger housing the ninth dragon. There had been eight failures before the success of this masterpiece of technology. None of the Group except the General thought anything about the number of the craft. The General wasn't about to tell the others in the Group; he felt it was the number of the craft that made it work. However, the General knew the number 9 was one of the best numbers to have on you. It meant long-lasting and stood to the nine dragons adorning the emperor's robes. In addition, he wouldn't tell the rest of the Group he wished to be free of them, and he longed for the freedom the west offered.

"Yes, sir!" The small man said into the receiver of the telephone before hanging up. As the small man turned, he looked at the officer standing behind him and smiled.

"They have ordered you into the sky, sir. You will get to test the weapons after all." A taller, younger version of the General smiled, unlike his father, the General. Colonel Vi Lee loved his homeland. He thought the rest of the world should bow to China's will and domination.

"Now the world will know we can go anywhere and strike." Lee smiled as he turned and looked at what his government called a low-orbit hypersonic craft. He thought of it as beautiful, and he was about to take it on its first flight and kill some Americans. The base housing China's newest marvel, Jiutia Long, sat in the middle of the Takla Makan desert the base sat north of the Kunlun mountains. Looking out at the vast wasteland, Lee thought about the people who used to call this place home. The colonel smiled at how they felt they had the right to stay.

Those people were now part of the landscape once they were told jobs awaited them in the town of Urumqi. They gladly picked up their scraps of belongings and started towards the city with his note in their chiefs pocket. The only thing awaiting them was a small contingent of Zhongguo tezhong budui; this is the Special Forces branch of the P.L.A. When the Chief of the desert people was asked for his papers, he obediently handed the Captain the note Colonel Lee gave him. The nomad proudly stated he and his family were going to the town of Urumqi for the jobs promised. Smiling, the leader of the special team congratulated the Chief, then, while still smiling, shot the man in the stomach. In a matter of seconds, the small group of nomads were all killed, and no one was spared. A trench was dug deep enough so the bodies, along with everything they and their pack animals carried, could be thrown in. Soon after, the small village of nomads was forgotten. Just another of many groups to disappear into the wasteland of the desert.

They had made their first refueling right in the nick of time. When Steve and Alex reached the area, they were to meet the stratotanker. The pilots found themselves alone, looking into the empty sky.

"Well, that shaves it. We're going to have to turn back and go to Jakarta." The Major was saying when his headset crackled, and the pilot's voice of the stratotanker came through.

"Whiskey special one one." The pilot gave the call sign and waited for the return.

"This is whiskey special one one." Steve returned and then smiled at Alex.

"See told you I wouldn't miss our fuel stop," Steve said. Rolling his eyes, Alex shook his head, knowing he would be hearing about this for the whole ride home.

The second refueling took place north of Malaysia, and like the first refuel, it went off with no problems. By the time the third refueling came south of Sri Lanka, a heavy storm had developed over the Indian Ocean. It wreaked havoc on Steve and Alex as they tried to couple the Citation with the flying tanker.

"Holy shit, we're down to fumes in the tanks," Alex said as the tanker's umbilical missed the nozzle and brushed the side of the cockpit for the second time. On the third attempt, the umbilical thumped hard on the roof of the cockpit. The seals in the back started to look at each other. They knew the men up in the cockpit could fly. The seals wondered if Steve and Alex had ever been through the process of jumping out of a jet. The men looked out the cockpit windshield and watched as the umbilical from the tanker stopped whipping around their view and settled into a steady flight. With one last attempt at placing the fuel nozzle into the shuttle end of the tanker's umbilical, Major Steve "Dodo" Duncan eased the throttle up a notch. He was surprised to find he could connect and heard A-train call to the operator of the tanker.

"We have a green light for fuel."

"Yes, sir, we are showing green; fuel is on the way." The operator at the rear of the tanker called back. In seconds A-train watched as the fuel gages started to rise off the empty marks. Within minutes, the tanks onboard were reading full. A train called; they were ready to break the connection. Once the connection was broken, they watched as the tanker banked away to the north. The pilots and the passengers of the Citation had no idea the first hypersonic jet had taken off from deep within China. It was at this time screaming its way through the inner atmosphere hunting them.

A small man with thick horn-rimmed glasses ran through the corridors of the C.I.A. building in Langley. Shouting at people to move before he would race by heading to the Director's office. People moved out of his way, not from his orders. They move because of the panicked look on his sweating face.

"What the hell do you mean something took off from China and is now in the inner atmosphere?" The Director of the C.I.A. asked as he looked at his Asia deskman.

"The call came in from our asset we have over in Beijing. I called the Russians. They confirmed something did take off; it soon reached the speed of Mach 5 plus, then entered the lower atmosphere. We are using our satellites as well as NASA to track it." The man in charge of the Asian area said. He sat down in the Director's office, sweat running in streams off his balding head.

"Hey boys, now it's not like you're talking to a dumb ass. I fly and have flown; hell, I even flew test planes. So I know at Mach 5, and faster, the friction from the air causes the surface of any aircraft to heat fast." The Director said. Another man with an armload of papers entered the office and stood by the door. The agent in charge of the Asian desk of the C.I.A. turned and introduced the new man.

"Sir, this is Chris Richards. He's new to us from M.I.T. and has some letters behind his name. Something to do with physics as it applies to aerospace or something like that. Sorry, Chris, I just can't keep it straight."

"That's all right, sir, Director, General, from the information gathered and the speed the craft is traveling at. I would have to say the Chinese have built a hypersonic jet." Chris was about to go on when the Director of the C.I.A. interrupted him.

"How could the thing travel at Mach 5 plus in the atmosphere and not cook?" Was the question that C Steven Wilson wanted to be answered.

"Well, for them to do it, they had to find a mineral like diamonds; this mineral could absorb heat. Unlike diamonds, this mineral won't hold the heat; it would have to release it. Now, as far as we know, they have found such a mineral, of all places, right in their own backyard. About five years ago, we started to get suspicious of an area out in the middle of nowhere; it's called the Takla Makan desert. We could see from our satellites the Chinese had been doing something out there with large mining equipment for years then all activity stopped. Nothing for two years, then on one photo, you could see a spectacular fireball and then debris; this happened numerous times. Then nothing for quite some time; we thought they were testing some kind of shuttle craft like ours. Our best guess was they were having trouble. I guess we know now what they were up to." Chris finished.

"Ok, I understand that much, but how in the hell does this new mineral get around the heating problem?" The Director asked.

"Well, I think it would have to be some sort of carbon-based mineral. It would look like glass when applied to the skin of the craft. As for how it works, I would need a sample of it to give you an answer you could take as real." Chris told the Director.

"Well, now someone who can finally say I don't know, well, when this is over, that's our top priority. For now, let's keep an eye on that thing. I don't like that it took off when we have assets overhead. I think they know we're trying to get our friends out of Africa." Director Wilson said.

Chapter 13

AUGUST STOOD IN FRONT of his team. He looked each of his team in the eyes for a moment, then explained how he wanted the caper to go down.

"We know how important these people are. We also know they have one man hurt and three females. Now one of the ladies is a Chief Warrant Officer in the British army, so she has training. She also has a wounded man and two civilian girls with her. The only warrior they have is trying to lead the Chinese away from them. Our task is to get the ones going over the mountains into Uganda safely to this plane and kill any Chinese after them. I can't bring myself to leave the lone man on his own. The only thing is, I don't know what to do about it yet." When August finished, he looked at the floor and waited. He had a good bunch, and they worked well together. His second-in-command came up with a working scenario.

"If we find the ones coming over the mountains and kill whatever is following them, we know they have guides helping them and local fighters from the village the Chief sent for security. What we do is go around the Group heading up the mountain; once we pass them, we see if any Chinese show up, and if they do, then Bobs, your uncle." When Petty Officer John Bowen finished, August nodded.

"We'll then catch the Group, and then we'll see if they need us to continue with them. If not, then we make a fast run down the mountain. Once we see the Chinese, we will see if we can interfere with the rest of their plans. We can tweak the plan as we go, recheck the gear and weapons, check each other, then get some grub and sleep." August ordered.

Richard sat on a rock and tried to massage the cramps out of his calf muscles; it was hard for him. Then he thought about Eugene. Richard watched as Joan checked his friend's bandage for the third time. Though he wanted to, Richard couldn't find it in himself to complain.

"How are you doing, Richard? Do you think you can go on?" Joan asked as she turned from Eugene.

"Me, oh, I'm right as rain, just getting my second wind." Richard lied. He hadn't wanted to tell anyone he had been going on sheer willpower for the last hour.

"It's Eugene I'm worried about," Richard said, trying to be stoic.

"Hey don't you worry over me, old boy; I'll out hike you with or without a bullet wound," Eugene said as he forced a brave smile for his girls. Tish and Tosh refused to leave his side as Joan checked his wound. The oldest native man who came with Joan and the others smiled when he heard the two men trying to get each other going. Even now, he had doubts about whether either man would make it to the top, though he was surprised both had made it this far.

"Well, let's get to it; the sooner we start then, the sooner the girls can have a bubble bath," Eugene said to Richard, who smiled and nodded his head. Joan looked at the oldest man and then up the mountain.

"Can we make it to the cabin before dark?" Joan asked.

"I think we can if we shorten our breaks," Janto said as he looked up the mountain. Joan knew what he was telling her; he wouldn't come out and say it. Richard was the first to head up the trail, the two young porters behind him.

The Chinese who were sent by Captain Wong to kill Richard and the others on the mountain had gotten lost more than once.

These men were forced to backtrack to find the trail of their target. Each time this happened, they lost time. Even with the rest breaks their targets were forced to take, the Chinese fell further and further behind. The sun started to set behind the western mountains when the Chinese found the trail for the third time.

Looking back at the two men struggling up the trail, Joan looked at her friend and boss. Richard lost all color in his face, and he started to fall further behind. Eugene fought the pain and loss of blood; now he, too, was running out of strength. She thought the only reason he was on his feet was the two Goth girls on either side of him. When he would slow down, either Tish or Tosh would whisper to him. Eugene would smile and wink at the girl, then push on. Janto looked up to where Joan stood. As Richard trudged past, he smiled at her. Joan was shocked to see the color had drained even from Richard's lips and gums.

"I want you to drink more water, Richard," Joan told him.

"If I drink any more water, I'm afraid I may drown," Richard said. Joan just smiled. She knew Richard was lying to her. He was trying to save water so Eugene and the girls could have more. She admired him for his thoughts of the welfare of the other before his own. Joan worried Richard's selfless act might put them in danger. Turning, Joan caught Richard by the sleeve; she forced him to turn and look at her.

"Ok, Richard, that's enough of your huff and bull; I know you've passed on the water twice now. I'm going to tell you this once you are getting dangerously dehydrated. If Jack were here, you would drink when he told you to; well, mister, I'm telling you to drink." Joan ordered. Richard felt her push a canteen into his hands. Thanking her, Richard started to sip the warm water. Joan smiled as she watched him drink.

Joan thought it looked better than Buckingham Palace and told Richard this.

"You know, I think you may be right, now, if only someone would go and tell those bastards following us to sod off. This would be a nice place to sleep for a week." Richard said, and Eugene gave him a 'here here.' As the sun started to slip below the horizon, the leader of the two-man kill squad Captain Wong sent up the mountain decided to stop. They wanted to wait until night settled around them. This way, they could use their night vision goggles and sneak up on the Group going over the mountain.

Jack watched as Captain Wong and two other men followed the tracks of the Unimog into the African bush. Smiling to himself, he thought of taking them to the foot of the mountain and then killing them before going up and killing the others. Then fate or just sheer Mr. Murphy showed up, and the Unimog started to miss on one cylinder. Jack knew it wouldn't be long before the thing broke down for good, plans change, and a good warrior changed with them. Jack rammed the Unimog through a heavily bushed area, then grabbed his pack and the lapua sniper rifle. He had an A2 in the pack and two of the sig P6 pistols with extra clips and loose ammunition in combat holsters on him. Jack headed into the bush as the sun started to set. He couldn't hear the Land Rover; he knew the Unimog wasn't hard to follow. Jack also knew the Chinese would be behind him. He knew it was time to head to high ground and see what he could see.

It was the one thing Jack knew as an absolute, get to the high ground and watch your enemy see how they move. This will tell you if they are a unit that has trained and worked together for some time. Or they had been thrown together for this assignment. If they have been together for some time, your job will be more challenging, not impossible, just harder. If they have to constantly look back for the other man, it's a good bet they haven't been together for long. It shows they don't know the others or how they move through a combat area.

Climbing to the top of a ridge, Jack watched through a pair of binoculars, making sure the sun wouldn't reflect off the lenses and give his position away. As Jack watched, it didn't take long for him to see this Group was highly trained and led by an excellent solid officer. Putting the binoculars away, Jack checked his lapua rifle. Looking through the scope, Jack waited for the last Chinese soldier to enter his scope. He watched as the man moved from cover to cover. As Jack watched, he found what he was looking for, a pattern to the man's movement. The one Jack watched would break cover, sprint for three seconds, then grab cover again. As Jack watched, this pattern never altered. On the fourth time the man broke cover, Jack was ready and had already taken up the trigger slack on the lapua.

Wong heard the shot; it sounded like it came from a heavy-caliber rifle. He heard the sound of a man gasping in pain. When the Captain turned to see which of his men had been hit, he could see it had been his driver. Pulling his sidearm out of its holster, he looked at the man and then, without a word, shot the driver in the head. None of the other men turned and gave their dead comrade a parting look.

Jack watched as the Captain pulled his pistol out and shot the man in the head. Jack knew where his shot went, and he knew the man only suffered a wound and a busted leg. He continued to watch as the rest of the Chinese team moved out into the bush. The team leader stayed and walked over to the corps of his man. Jacked watched as the Captain pulled three bags with some kind of powder in them out of his pack. He then placed each of the dead man's hands into a bag. Once the hands were in the bags, the Captain retrieved three vials with a blue liquid in them. He placed the vials in the bags he used plastic zip ties to close the bags over the dead man's hands. The Captain then repeated the same procedure with the man's head. Once this task was completed, the Captain pulled his pistol out and smashed the vials holding the blue liquid. Captain Wong then turned and walked off into the bush. Jack watched as the power absorbed the liquid and then started to bubble. As Jack watched the mixture turn pink, the bag began to inflate and dissolve. Once the bags had dissolved, the only thing left of the hands and face was yellowed bone.

Chapter 14

WENDY AND PAUL WATCHED the countryside as they crossed the Georgia state line. The picture of a beautiful young woman dressed in a quaint antebellum evening gowned. She was holding a basket of peaches, greeting travelers to the finer things the peach stated had to offer. Agent Clinton and Boyles smiled at the state line. Paul didn't even look at the billboard. He knew Wendy hated the thing. When they started their relationship, he had asked her about it. Paul had sat astonished as Wendy had gone on a rant about how it depicted southern women. Wendy told Paul how it gave a false notion her gender was only used for staying at home and waiting hand and foot on their husbands. Wendy hated anything that stereotyped women.

"I suppose you men think that picture is the way things should be?" Wendy asked. She was trying to bait one of the agents into a battle over gender roles in the modern world. Paul inwardly groaned. He had seen this before. Paul never let her bait him; he saw Wendy do it to a truck driver and then watched as she verbally tore the poor bastard to ribbons. The only thing to stop her that day, and for the first and only time Paul had known Wendy to be at a loss for words, was when the driver stood up. Paul watched as the driver smiled at Wendy and then said.

"Miss arguing with a truck driver is like wrestling with a pig in the mud. Eventually, you're going to realize the pigs enjoying themselves." When it was over, the driver thanked Wendy for the chat, excused himself, and went to pay for his meal. That driver paid for Paul, and Wendy's coffees, then drove off to a destination unknown. It had become a private joke between them; when Wendy would start, Paul would say free coffee, and they would laugh. Both of them wondered how the driver was doing and whom he was arguing with now. Wendy often wondered how that driver was and, better yet, who he was. She thought of all the power brokers in Washington she knew and interviewed. Wendy often thought he would give her the most honest and straightforward answer to any questions she needed to ask. Whether the politicians or anyone for that matter liked it or not.

"I think times were better back then." Wendy heard Agent Clinton say as she came out of her remembrances of the driver. Before she could get a head of steam worked up, Paul was saying something about free coffee.

"Sir, how are you going to get any coffee? We're twenty miles from anywhere?" Boyles said. Paul and Wendy had started to laugh when Clinton turned and shouted for them to hit the floor. Paul grabbed Wendy and shoved her off the back seat and down onto the floor of the suv; climbing on top of her, Paul shouted back to the two agents to go. Looking around, Agent Boyles found the reason for Clinton's warning; another black suv was passing them, and a man was pointing a sig 9mm out the window at him.

The first shot snapped against the bullet-resistant window of the armored suv. Boyles knew the window wasn't bulletproof; it was only resistant. Eventually, the window would give, and the rounds would find their way into the cab of their vehicle. Agent Clinton looked at his partner, then turned into the other suv. The sound of tearing sheet metal told Boyles the other suv wasn't armored. The Chinese suv gave into physics, and the will of gravity, and the suv started to slide into the left-hand ditch. Once enough friction built up from the sliding tires, the second suv started to roll and break apart. Wendy watched as they left the second suv rolling into the Georgia pines lining Interstate 95.

The Director of the C.I.A. sat behind his desk and listened to Chris Richards finish his debriefing on how this new weapon would work.

"We know the Chinese, everyone in this room knows they would never build this without weapons on it. Now, for the most part, conventional guns and short-range missiles won't work on this thing." Chris was saying as General Whistler interrupted.

"Why won't guns work on this?" The General asked.

When the General finished his question, the young M.I.T. educated scientist opened a laptop. Chris turned the computer so the five men and two women sitting at the table could see the screen.

"If you watch this program, it will answer your question, sir." The program showed an arrow-like plane racing across the sky.

"As you can see with conventional rounds, like on a normal fighter, the bullet speeds away from the plane, going out and hitting its target. Not so with this baby," Chris said as he pointed to the arrow-like plane.

"The bullets, when first fired from this craft, will outrace the plane. Then as the air acts to slow down the round, the aircraft will catch its own bullets." Chris finished as the program ended on the laptop.

"So whatever is fired from the plane, it and the plane will, in theory, get to the target at the same time." Director Willson said, looking at the younger man.

"Well, how the hell do we stop this thing?" The Vice President asked, looking at Chris. The second in command of the U.S. was hoping like hell the young man standing at the front of the room. A young man who looked like he had stepped off a bus at the wrong stop would have the answer to get all their asses out of the fire.

"Well, that's the thing, sir, it's not like I can give you the magic answer. God, I wish I could; the only answer I can give sounds so dumb. I think you would throw me in the loony bin and throw away the key." Chris answered the vice president.

"Well, son, I hang around with politicians all day. You wouldn't believe the dumb things I hear." The V.P. said as the rest of the room laughed.

"Well, sir, I can knock it out of the sky, but it's going to cost the taxpayers one of the Air Force's newest drones and about eight hours to reconfigure its engines." Before Chris could finish, the General told him he could have whatever it took to kill whatever the Chinese had in the air.

"Well, I'm glad you said that, sir; what we need is the new X60R, the ones at global strike command in Louisiana," Chris told the General. The Vice President stood and nodded to the others around the table. Then followed his secret service team out of the room.

Chapter 15

COLONEL VI LEE WATCHED as his global position tracking system told him he was traveling at Mach 6.9. He smiled as he was about to break the sound barrier for the seventh time on this first combat flight of the ninth dragon. He wished the people of his country could know he was about to knock the Americans back to where they belonged.

Chris watched as NASA's brand new X43-B hypersonic scramjet-powered creation landed at Andrews air force base in the dead of night. Chris heard about the X43-B. He couldn't believe NASA fixed the problems with the skin heating and failing. If people knew about this aircraft and how it was responsible for the reported U.F.O. sightings. All the way from the Canadian border to Mexico, from California to Kansas. Walking around the odd-looking aircraft, Chris couldn't get over how it looked. He thought the best description was it resembled a chisel lying flat. Both he and the pilot talked about the plane while they waited for the ground crew to lower the secret drone from under the X-43. As soon as the drone was on the ground, work on the engines started. Chris would oversee the modifications until it was ready to be deployed; then, as ordered, he would fly it to Africa. There Chris was to intercept the Chinese before their pilot could intercept the seal team.

Captain Alex Knitter listened as General Wyatt Whistler told both he and Major Steve Duncan. The Chinese and their hypersonic aircraft were suspected to be heading their way. When the General finished, the two men looked at each other and then back to where the seals sat napping. August caught the pilot and copilot looking back at his men. August was curious, what had two pilots who joked about taking off from an aircraft carrier, then refueled during a force 12 storm worried. Alex looked at Steve and nodded; he would go and tell the seals what the General told him and the Major about. He didn't want to; however, both he and the Major knew these men needed to know. Standing in the front of the citation 'A train' laid it all out for the seals.

"Ok, what have the desk jockeys back in the world say we should do when the bastard shows his intentions?" Petty John Bowen asked. He asked the question the rest of the men in the passenger compartment wanted to know.

"Well, as far as the conversation went, they have a plan. They couldn't let us into the loop. The bosses are worried the Chinese would somehow get wind. Then we'd be in the same place we are now." Alex said.

"Yea, up shit creek, and the fuck'n paddle took a hike." Bowen finished.

"Not quite yet; the Major and I have an idea. We finished our last mid-flight fuel grabs. We are three hundred miles southeast of Mogadishu. We have more than enough to get us to your target. If the Chinese show up, then we go low. Both the Major and I don't think this hypersonic plane can use its great speed at low altitudes. If it can, then the thing sure as shit can't turn as fast as we can." When Alex finished explaining what the plan was. August just nodded his head, then leaned back and closed his eyes.

Chapter 16

JACK WATCHED AS THE Captain, along with his remaining man, searched the ground looking for his trail. The Sergeant stopped and pointed to something on the ground, then up the mountain in the direction Jack had traveled. Jack didn't want to kill this man. He knew the Sergeant was better than his Captain at tracking. The Sergeant would be able to find him if given enough time. Jack sighed the man through his scope; he waited for the man to turn his head and look up the mountain. Measuring his breathing and listening to his heartbeat, Jack waited as the Sargent looked up the side of the mountain as he took up the last of the trigger slack. Then the rifle jumped back into his shoulder, and most of the Sergeant's head exploded into a mist of brains and blood.

Captain Zen Wong felt the brains of his faithful Sergeant splash across the side of his face. Years of training served the Captain well as he never thought about his action; he just reacted and dove for cover in a nearby bush. The Captain leaped into a large brush, trying to gain some cover. Jack kept an eye out, watching to see what direction his target would run. Knowing his target was used to having underlings do the grunt work for him. Jack thought his latest target would run back to where he had left his transportation. Once there, the Captain would call in and wait for reinforcements.

Wong knew he couldn't sit under this bush for long. The time he took to decide which way to run would be the time he would need to make his getaway. Sitting, trying to hide from a bullet, gave Wong time to wonder how things could go so wrong. When this all started, he had the best men to lead, now they were all dead, and he was alone. Zihao assured him he would be a hero; now, his men were food for vermin.

A man picked up his encrypted cell phone; he hit the speed dial and waited for the Group to pick up the other end. As the dust settled around the black suv, he heard a click telling him the Group answered.

"Our men in Georgia were not successful. I fear they may be beyond our help." The man said into his phone. He waited for what seemed an eternity before Zihao spoke.

"Follow the reporter. When they arrive at their destination, call us back. In addition, if any of your men survive the crash, then you must be sure the Americans never get a chance to question them. Do you understand?" Zihao asked. No answer came; the man in Georgia ended the call. Watching one of the front tires on the upside-down suv slowly turn. The small Asian man caught movement in the truck, telling him at least one man was still alive. As he watched the man struggle to free himself from the wreckage, this lone survivor thought of his own son. He wondered if his boy would be safe at home in Beijing tonight. The slight Asian man stepped out of his car and ran to the suv. Getting down on his knees, he looked into the eyes of the lone survivor and tossed in two hand grenades, then sprinted back to his car. The double blasts from the grenades threw him into the door of his rented Crown Victoria. In less than a second, he recovered and was heading south, trying to catch up to Wendy and Paul.

Agent Clinton looked back behind their black government-issue suv. Looking back, he watched Interstate 95 disappear around one of a hundred turns as it ran south through the state of Georgia.

"I think we're in the clear, but for Christ's sake, don't take your foot off the floor, partner," Clinton said. His partner and best friend, Ted Boyals, just nodded and pushed the suv harder.

"We should be at Wendy's mother and father's place within the hour," Paul said. He thought he saw the glint of sunlight off a windshield. It was just a glint, then nothing. He told himself not to get paranoid. After the afternoon they were going through, it was hard not to let a little paranoia creep in.

Chapter 17

JACK WAS GETTING TIRED of waiting for the Captain to do anything. Watching the bush through the scope of his rifle, Jack could make out a patch of green that didn't quite match the green of the brush. Taking his time, Jack watched as the off-green patch moved. In a short second, it came back into his field of vision. Jack started taking up the trigger slack as the odd patch of green moved again and reappeared. He fired a round into the green patch. Jack was surprised when the figure of the Captain crawled halfway out of the bush and then laid still. Watching the prone figure of the Chinese officer, Jack thought about going to the body. Jack decided to make sure the man was dead. His second bullet smashed most of Captain Wong's head into the African soil. Jack stood from his position and looked back at the mountain Joan and the others were trying to climb over. Then he thought of the distance and knew he could not catch up with them without a truck. Looking back at the body of the dead Captain, Jack knew what he had to do. He needed to get back to the Land Rover the Chinese had followed him in, then use it to get back to the others. Stopping at the body of the dead Chinese man, Jack looked for any kind of identification, but not finding any, he wasn't surprised. It would be stupid for any of the men to carry I.D. just in case they were killed or captured.

Joan watched as Richard and Eugene slowly made their way up the last two hundred meters of the mountain. She and the others encouraged the men, telling them they could do it. The sun had set an hour ago, and they were now in total darkness; neither man cared about the time; they had made it. Looking back at the small building, she silently urged the two men to hurry just a little bit one hundred and fifty meters.

Jack watched the Land Rover for a few minutes before he approached it. Looking around the truck, he watched for any signs the former owners of the suv might have set some explosives. After a quick search, Jack was satisfied all was good. He found the keys to the Land Rover under the floor mat on the driver's side. Soon he was tearing through the African bush. Trying to get back to the mountain, Joan and the others had started up before it was too late.

Fifty meters, just fifty meters left, Joan was now cheering the men on, along with Tish and Tosh. Both men were still going to say that, for Eugene told of how tough the man was. After being shot and fighting his way through, the shock and pain to be this close to the top was incredible. Joan never thought about herself or how, not long ago, she had to undergo surgery for a bullet wound suffered on Smith Island. Her shoulder still hurt, and the surgeon had told her she would suffer some discomfort, along with lost strength in the shoulder for some time. Her wound was nothing compared to Eugene's, and she didn't want to complain. Richard was watching Eugene's back as the wounded man marched up the last bit of the hill. Richard wanted to have another break some time ago; he just could not bring himself to ask for one. If Eugene, with his smashed shoulder, did not need to stop, how could he ask for a break? Once again, Richard promised himself if he got through this, he would start whatever health regiment Jack and Tran planned for him.

Chapter 18

THE CITATION X CARRYING August's seal team screamed over the shore of Kenya. Both Steve and Alex knew pushing the Citation at full speed was going through their fuel at an astounding rate. It also meant they more than likely would not be able to make it to their fuel stop after the seals deployed. Both men had talked it over and decided they were not going to be the reason the Chinese finally got their revenge.

"You had better go and tell the team leader of our situation Alex," Steve said as he finished the calculations on fuel for the third time.

"Ok, let's hope some ass hasn't removed the chutes from this thing," Alex said as he climbed out of his seat.

August watched as the Captain climbed out of his seat and stood at the door of the cockpit. He could tell the man was trying to collect his thoughts. August was just about to get up and meet Alex halfway when the young pilot started to move. Watching Alex, August was sure he had bad news, and he was about to get it.

"I don't know how to tell you, men, this; we have a bit of a problem." Alex started. To his surprise, August smiled and said

"No problem is so bad that you can't tell friends." When August finished, Alex chuckled and shrugged his shoulders.

"Ok, well, gentlemen, we have enough fuel to get you to your target site. However, we've been battling a strong headwind ever since our last fueling. The pace we've kept up has gone through our fuel faster than predicted. So when you jump, we will have to join you." Alex stood in front of the seal team and waited for the spec ops warriors to react angrily. He didn't expect Bowen to pat him on the shoulder.

"Well, that's great, Captain; I could use some better company than this crowd." When Bowen finished, a muffin hit him in the side of the head. It brought a laugh from the seated men and a smile from Alex. Then August stood, and the men, along with Bowen, became serious.

"You and the Major need to be aware of one thing. Once we are out of this plane, you will do as I say. Your ranks do not enter into the equation; my men and I have been together for years. We know what the other is going to do under fire. You and the Major will be an unknown factor in our unit." August said as he walked up to Alex.

"I can tell you, Major Duncan and I will do anything we have to do to see everyone gets home safe," Alex said as he shook August's hand.

"Oh, I don't doubt that A-train, we'll have camouflage and weapons for both of you. Once on the ground, I will give you a man to shadow." When he was finished, August patted Alex on the shoulder. He knew the young Captain was afraid he or Steve would be the cause of someone getting hurt.

Colonel Vi Lee knew he was screaming over the Indian Ocean and was catching his target fast. He smiled to himself; he knew by now the Americans had to know he was hunting their rescue party. He would kill the smaller plane and all those in it, then go back to China as a hero. Soon they would be calling him General Lee. Vi Lee didn't know that at that very second, the newest hypersonic stealth drone was making landfall after leaving Andrews air force base in Maryland. Chris Richards sat at the control center and flew the ultra-top secret plane over the coast of Senegal. It was heading east to catch Colonel Lee before he could kill the Citation and the men who flew in it.

Chapter 19

WENDY'S FATHER STOOD on the bottom stair of his and his wife's two-story Victorian-era home. He knew something was wrong as he watched the black suv pull up his drive. Wendy's father watched as the Asian man stepped out of the passenger door and smiled at him. Holding his hands behind his back, retired first strike Marine Colonel Benjamin "Big Ben" Cameron raised his left hand to wave friendly. Then shot the Asian man with a Berretta 9mm he held in his right. Side-stepping fast, Ben Cameron took aim at the driver and fired two rounds through the windshield. Both rounds found the driver, the first hitting the man in the throat and the second punching a neat round hole just above his right eye. The third man in the suv tried to leap out the back door. As his feet hit the Georgia clay, a round from the Berretta found his hip and spun him around. The second round hit the Asian man in the shoulder, slamming him against the side of the suv. Trying to get his weapon out of the shoulder holster took time. As the third Chinese agent pulled his pistol free of the holster. The third round from Wendy's father's Berretta entered his skull just above his left ear and exited below his right ear.

Turning and running up the steps of the porch to the house, Ben found his wife coming out the front door of their home. She handed him his Remington 870 tactical shotgun with a box of SSG buckshot.

"It's loaded, be careful." Mrs. Cameron said as she kissed Ben's cheek. Nodding to his wife, he started to head to the idling suv when he heard another vehicle turn off the road onto his driveway.

"Get in the house, May," Ben shouted as he chambered a round in the shotgun. Big Ben started to run to the first suv taking cover behind it. Agent Bill Clinton was the first to see Wendy's father step out from the front of the suv with the shotgun held to his shoulder.

"Um, Wendy tell me this is your father," Bill said as he and Agent Ted Boyles raised their hands so the man who approached them could see they meant no harm.

"That's my dad; for god, sakes don't put your hands down; I've seen him cut the head off a turkey with that cannon," Wendy said as she waved to her father through the windshield of the suv. She watched as her father shouted something. Paul told Wendy that she should get out of the truck to let her dad know what was happening.

"That would be an excellent idea. The barrel of that shotgun is looking like death's left eye right now." Ted said as Bill nodded his head in agreement. Opening the back door of the suv, Paul called out to Ben Cameron.

"Sir, it's Paul, don't shoot! Wendy is with me, and these men were sent to us as protection." As Paul told Ben Cameron, Wendy peeked over his shoulder.

"Alright, tell them to get out of the truck; we'll go inside to get some tea," Ben said. Both CIA agents noticed how the retired marine officer never lowered his shotgun.

As Agent Bill Clinton stepped from the suv, he smiled and opened his sports coat to show his weapon was still in the holster. As Agent Ted Boyles stepped out of the suv, he did the same, revealing his gun to Wendy's father. The older man smiled, then holding the Remington in his left hand, he hugged Wendy and shook Paul's hand, then nodded to both Ted and Bill.

"Wyatt Whistler gave me a call and told me to be ready for these bastards." Ben Cameron said as he pointed the barrel of his shotgun at the dead Asian men around the first suv.

"He also told me you were in good hands with Stevens men here." He smiled at the two agents.

"I knew Paul wouldn't let you come to harm while he was around." Ben finished as he clapped a hand on Paul's shoulder.

Jack had to give credit to the people who designed the Land Rover discovery. He had been driving the suv wide open since he found it. Jack had, on more than one occasion, had all four wheels airborne. Now Jack could see the mountain he had left Joan and the others to climb. He knew his friends only had two young men for porters and three older men as protection. Jack knew these men would do their best, but he also knew they were not up to the standards of a professional soldier. If it came down to a tactical move, Jack knew the soldier would wait and watch for a mistake on the native fighters' part. This was the biggest downfall to the native warrior the world over. It was the same for the native North American people, the Aborigines in Australia. Jack feared it would be the same on this mountain, on the border with the Democratic Republic of the Congo and Uganda.

Richard could not believe he had made it; he was at the top of the mountain. He was sitting on a chair, trying to massage the cramps out of his calf muscles. Joan was looking at Eugene's shoulder; after she satisfied herself, it wasn't bleeding. She asked Tish and Tosh to hold Eugene while she tightened the arm wrap. After Eugene was looked after, the girls helped their wounded adopted father to lie down.

"How are you doing, Richard?" Joan asked. Kneeling down and looking at his calves.

"Oh me, well, I'm as right as rain; I'm more worried about our boy out there all by himself," Richard said as he held Joan's hand. Joan looked around the cabin while she was worried about Jack. Joan was more concerned about the exhausted people in this room. The only people who looked like they could go on when the sun rose were the porters and fighters the chief of the village sent with them.

Jack drove the Land Rover onto an old path he spotted as he approached the mountain. After plowing through some brush, Jack found he was on an old two-rut road of sorts. Though he did have to slow his pace down, it was still a hell of a lot faster than walking or trying to run up this mountain.

Chris couldn't believe the hypersonic drone he piloted was now screaming its way over the border between Congo and the DRC. He was in the control room at Andrews Air Force Base in Maryland. His wrap-around screens showed him an African plain. General Wyatt Whistler was standing behind him, with the Director of the CIA. Both men had good friends on the ground and were in real danger. A satellite tracking technician watched his target. The Chinese built a hypersonic jet and the Citation; the technician called out how close the Chinese were to the Citation and their rescue team.

"We are fifteen minutes from the drop area." Captain Alex Knitter told August as he and his men checked and rechecked their gear.

"OK, I was thinking we might go a minute early because it will take extra time to get you two out of the plane," August said as he looked out the cockpit windows. Both Alex and Steve just nodded and gave their authority over to the seal team leader. Setting the autopilot, Steve and Alex stepped out of the cockpit, and the seals helped the pilots into their parachutes. Augusts told Alex and Steve who they were to team up with once they were on the ground. Steve was teamed with August, and Alex was to be teamed up with Petty Bowen. August looked at his watch and signaled five minutes.

"I'll make one last check on the flight instruments then. We should be free and clear," Alex said, then he headed to the cockpit.

Opening a special hatch built in this plane by the air force. August then released a panel and watched as it dropped away from the bottom of the aircraft. A telescopic pole dropped out of the hatch, rungs locked in place for foot and hand holds. Alex turned and, with a look of panic on his face, yelled over the sound of the rushing air.

Chapter 20

"**We have got to go now, right fucking now!**" As he ran up the short aisle.

"That Chinese jet we've been worried about just popped up on our radar. It's within fifty miles of us and coming fast. By the look on the two pilots' faces, August didn't think this was the best time for twenty questions, so he ordered his men to fast deploy. Grabbing Alex by his shoulder, Bowen almost pushed him down the pole and followed, going headfirst. The rest of the seals followed in rapid secession. The last to leave the Citation was Major Duncan and team leader Lt. August Hawks.

Colonel VI Lee could see by his radar he was within fifty miles of the Americans. He slowed the ninth dragon down. Colonel VI Lee watched as his speed dropped from Mach 7 down to Mach 2. He could see the plane. It was nothing more than a tiny speck in his field of vision. Colonel Lee knew this speck was the thing that would make him a hero.

Bowen watched as Alex tried to scan the sky from under his parachute. The man was twisting around, trying to see the plane they had just left. All at once, Alex started to point to the north and waved his arms like he was trying to fly back up to the Citation. When Bowen turned to look at what had Alex so excited, he saw what looked like a needle with stubby wings fly out of the blue sky.

Colonel VI Lee watched as his weapons radar locked onto the American plane. A smile spread across the Colonel's face as he fired the special missile designed for this marvel of Chinese superiority. His smile faded, and a white-hot rage took over as Vi Lee watched two parachutes blossom as the plane flew on. The Americans had cheated him of his glory. They knew he was coming and jumped at the last minute. Looking around below his plane VI Lee could now see seven parachutes floating down and away from him. Looking back to where his missile and the Citation met. All he could do was watch as burning parts of the plane fell out of the African sky, knowing he had failed.

"I have the Chinese hyper jet on my screen." The radar tech called out.

"I have the coordinates," Chris called out. He watched a fireball blossom in the sky. Just before Chris could call out, a plane just exploded mid-flight. The image of a long thin aircraft came into view. Chris knew this had to be the Chinese hypersonic plane. The tactical display went from green to red, and all the weapons on this X60R drone became highlighted. Chris waited until he was sure this plane had just shot down their rescue team. The men in the control room watched as the Chinese plane started to climb and turn.

"Just as I thought." Chris started to say, then stopped. Director Steven Wilson looked at his friend and head of the Joint Chiefs.

"Well, just as you thought what, son." The General asked.

"Sorry, sirs, I was thinking in their rush to build something like this, the Chinese would have cut corners. By the look of that turn, it was maneuverability they sacrificed to get it in the air." Chris told the two men. They all watched the ninth dragon continue its turn to the northeast.

"Glad to hear they haven't figured it all out yet, so let's catch it and kill It." The Director of the CIA said as he watched the tactical screens.

"Call coming in from the rescue team...." A communication tech said as he stood to attention beside the General.

"They have deployed and are safe on the ground, starting their search for our people." Chris heard the men behind him. They all gave off a collective sigh of relief.

The men in the room watched; Chris gained on the Chinese plane. Then as two circles slowly came together, Chris squeezed the trigger on his right-hand joystick. He, along with the other men in the room, watched as the missile raced away from their drone. Everyone in the control room held their breath and watched as the missile raced toward the Chinese hyper jet.

Colonel VI Lee couldn't understand what was happening. Nothing on this earth could catch his plane. He was finishing his turn to go back home when his threat warning started to scream its alarm. He straightened his plane out and slammed the throttles to the maximum they would give. Just before his twin, solid fuel engines kicked in, VI Lee felt the hammer blow of an explosion knock his beautiful plane sideways. Before the solid fuel ignited, he caught a glimpse of another odd-looking craft. His last thought, before he was a ball of fire, was of how much he hated Americans. Because of the solid fuel the Chinese used to power their plane. No piece larger than a household dustpan would ever be found of the ninth dragon.

Chapter 21

THE ASIAN MAN IN THE Crown Victoria watched as the reporter's father killed the second team. A highly decorated Marine Vet who kept himself in top shape. He wasn't looking forward to calling the Group with this news.

"Our second team sent to kill the parents and wait for the daughter and her protectors; they have failed. They underestimated the reporter's father and paid the price." The lone Asian man said into his phone. Sitting in his car, the spy for the Chinese intelligence service was shocked at what he was told.

The Group wanted him to try to kill the reporter by himself and then return home. The spy knew this was a death sentence. Besides, he planned to desert his country. The plan was to wait until he had something the Americans could use; then, he would go to them and ask for asylum. Pulling the sim card and battery from his encrypted phone, the spy placed them in an envelope. Turning the car around, the man drove north, knowing what he was doing would end his chance of ever going home to see his father again.

Jack watched the cabin from the Ugandan side of the mountain. He watched as one Chinese soldier changed position. Now he waited for the other to show himself. As the moon started its descent, Jack sat in the darkness and watched as the last of the two-man kill squad moved closer to the cabin. Fitting the silencer to his A2, Jack started his way around the Chinese to get them from behind.

August watched as the big white man, whom he and his team only knew as Jack, stalked the Chinese. Bowen was at his side with the rest of the men spread out in picket line fashion.

"I rather feel bad for the Chinese dudes; they ain't got a clue death is behind them," Bowen said. They watched as Jack killed the rearmost Chinese soldier with his knife. The lead Chinese soldier never knew his friend and squad mate had been killed. If the seals, along with Alex and Steve, hadn't seen it happen, they would have never known.

"This fucking guy is a real pro...who is he?" Bowen asks August.

"All I know is he is a friend of the Whisper and the Director of the CIA," August answered. Then they watched as Jack disappeared into the darkness again.

Jack knew someone else was near the cabin. He didn't think they were here to harm anyone. Just the opposite, he thought they might be friends. He would find out once he was finished with the Chinese. As Jack finished his thought, he heard the cabin door open. The last Chinese soldier listened to the door of the cabin open and close. This would be their time to move, to kill one of the men who helped their targets. Jack was ready for the final Chinese soldier when he started to move. The last of Captain Wong's men died from a single bullet to the back of his head. Once Jack was moving, he never stopped.

Walking up to the cabin, Jack called out to the local fighters he was coming into the light, not to shoot him. When the man sent with Joan and the others saw Jack, he smiled and shook his hand. Joan was standing in the middle of the room, looking even more beautiful than Jack remembered. Tish and Tosh ran to him and wrapped their arms around him, one on each side. This made Jack uncomfortable. Joan could see it in his face, but he let the girls hug him.

"Hey, now what's this about?" Jack asked. Tosh looked up at Jack; she looked like she was going to cry.

"We thought they might have got you." She told Jack.

"Not a chance, not a chance," Jack answered. Then the girls let him go and returned to Eugene, who smiled and gave Jack a thumbs up. Smiling at the wounded man, Jack nodded and then went to Joan and Richard.

"We have friends out in the bush...I think." Jack told Richard. Turning, Richard looked at the door and then at Jack.

"Well, we should invite them in." Nodding, Jack stood and kissed Joan on the cheek, then went to the door.

"Well, you seals should come out of the dark... it's getting cold out." Jack called from the doorway. He could hear someone chuckle in the dark.

"Well, now he's just showing off," Bowen whispered.

"But he's got style." August smiled as he stood up and waved to the man they watched kill two Chinese specs ops soldiers.

Chapter 22

EVERYTHING HAD GONE wrong; their men in the Democratic Republic of the Congo missed their last two call-in times. It must be assumed they are dead. That was bad enough. Now they have lost all communications with Colonel VI Lee and their newest hypersonic jet. The scientists cannot tell the Group if it is the radios or if the plane has been destroyed. Now they would have to wait until one of their satellites flew over the area to see anything. Even more worrisome is the phone their spy, has in America is no longer working. These three things cannot be a coincidence.

Driving north on I95, the former Chinese spy Bai Xu ensured he kept to the posted speed limits. His paperwork was all in order, and it would pass the inspection of a highway patrol officer. He didn't want to leave a trail of his movements, which his former handlers could find.

Wendy stood with her mother at the kitchen counter, making sandwiches. Both women looked at each other and shared a smile.

"You know it was Dad who said he never wanted me in the military, said it wasn't safe," Wendy said as she raised an eyebrow. Then both women laughed.

"I know, but you know your father, right is right." May Cameron said, mimicking her husband. Both she and Wendy laughed harder. The four men sitting in the dining room looked at the kitchen door and wondered what the two women were laughing at.

"I think we should go to the hunting cabin. I don't think anyone will find us there." Ben Cameron said as he unfolded a map showing the area of Boone, North Carolina. Looking around the table, he could see the rest of the men nodding their heads.

Wendy loved the hunting cabin when she was told this was where they were going to hide. Wendy and her mother thought it was an excellent idea. She had always wanted to take Paul to the cabin in the woods. Both Ted and Bill were glad this rough old man was a former Marine Colonel. He showed the men his gun room once they packed clothing and food for the cabin. The men started to take out rifles and shotguns as well as extra pistols, all the ammunition they could handle. Wendy's father had been reloading his own rounds for years. When a batch became too old, he would shoot it off at a target range he built on the back side of their Georgia property.

Standing in the one-room cabin, Richard stood and shook August's hand, then made introductions all around. The Seal team's medic didn't wait for introductions when they entered the cabin. He went straight to Eugene. Petty Officer DeRoue was surprised when he found Eugene sleeping. He didn't want to wake the wounded man, so he looked at the wrappings and then decided to wait until Eugene woke on his own to look at the wound.

Richard was now telling the team what had happened to them since being shot down by the Chinese. Once he was finished, the two American air force pilots looked at each other and nodded.

"If Alex here hadn't gone back to the cockpit to check our instruments and saw the radar become active. We would have suffered the same fate as your pilots did." Major Steve Duncan told Richard.

"The last thing I saw was a large fireball before our chutes opened," August said as he sat down.

"Well, what do you think, Jack? Should we change plans, or do we carry on?" Watching Jack, the others knew when it came to the fighting end of things, Richard always respected Jack's skill and training.

"We'll change our planes a little; now we have two pilots," Jack said, smiling at Steve and Alex. Once again, Jack's best death head smile did its trick and chilled both men to the bone.

"We are going to Uganda. Our main priority will be to find a plane large enough for everyone. Then we fly our way out to a friendly country." Jack said. Richard liked the idea of a friendly country. He also liked the idea of not walking out of Africa better.

Richard turned and smiled at the oldest of the four men from the village.

"You have helped so much; I wouldn't want you to get hurt. Thank you, and give this to your chief; it's for your village. I hope it's enough." Richard said as he handed the older fighter a neatly folded wad of American cash.

"It is too much. The chief says no pay." The older man was about to protest when Richard placed the money in his hand and smiled.

"I would feel bad if you didn't take it; please, it is for everyone in your village, please." Richard pleaded.

"Thank you, I will tell the chief; you give to everyone." The oldest fighter said. With that, the two porters and the other fighters stepped out into the night and started down the mountain.

Bai Xu was going by the first exit for Sumter, South Carolina. He was just starting to think of his life after he told the Americans everything he knew of China's espionage in their country. Bai thought he might like to live in the South. The country he had seen while here was beautiful; it was warm all year. Sumter, he recalled a great battle during the American civil war here. Bai Xu made a note to come back and learn about that battle when a bullet smashed the driver's side window hitting Bai in the left temple and killing him instantly.

Dead at the wheel of the Crown, Victoria Bai swerved into oncoming traffic. His car hit a southbound tractor-trailer head-on. The driver of the tractor-trailer managed to keep his rig upright. The driver knew with the impact of his rig, and the car, no one in the crown vic would have survived the crash. The shooter watched through her scope as her target crossed the median. Crashing into a big Peterbilt truck heading south. She smiled; this was her first assignment. She had been where the Group told her to be. Her target was dead; this would mean more assignments for her.

After everything was packed, Wendy, Paul, Ben, and May Cameron. The two CIA agents, Bill Clinton and Ted Boyles, packed themselves and the people they were sent to protect into the armored suv and Ben's pickup truck. With Ben leading the way, they made their way around Savannah to I95. Then north into South Carolina, at Hardeeville, Ben turned onto hwy US321. Using his cell phone, he informed Bill they would be on this route to the small town of Boone.

Grabbing the encrypted cell phone, Ted pressed the speed dial linking him with his boss in Langley, Virginia.

"Sir, we have left the Cameron house and are on our way to Boone, North Carolina...oh, you've been to the hunting cabin. Yes, sir, we are on US 321 now and should make it tonight sometime, sir...yes, sir, I'll tell him for you." Ted hung up and looked at Bill.

"Um, well, we are going to have company at the cabin. It seems our boss is sending a wet team to help with security. If he and the General can get away, they will be joining us." When Ted finished telling Bill about the plan. Both men looked in the mirror at the two women in the back seat. The agents smiled though neither man felt like smiling. Nobody liked having his or her boss hanging around, especially when the shit could hit the fan.

Zihao smiled when their assassin from America called in and gave him the good news, she killed the traitor Bai Xu. Zihao hung up and turned to another man sitting across the room from him.

"I want you to find that traitor Bai Xu's father and kill him. Let the others know what will happen to their families if they try the same thing." Zihao ordered. Smiling, the man stood and left the room.

This assignment was to be her second. The assassin was told this assignment, if successful, would see her get the first choice from then on. She would be first in line, and the others would have her leftovers. Smiling, the assassin pulled out her PDA and brought up google earth. Typing in the destination of her prey, she zoomed in on the small town of Boone, North Carolina.

Jack watched the sun rise over the mountains separating the two countries of the Democratic Republic of the Congo and Uganda. As Jack turned, he found Joan standing behind him, looking to the east also. Jack knew they now had the men to make their getaway. Jack was getting tired of this shadow group trying to kill him and his friends. Standing in the mountains with the woman he was starting to fall in love with. Jack made up his mind he would have to find the leader of this Group. A man who seemed bent on killing him and Richard and their friends. He would give whoever was the leader of this Group a chance to leave all those he held dear alone. If the bastard was so far gone on this path, then the man would pay the ultimate price.

Chapter. 23

Tran sat looking out at the English channel. He smiled as the memory of him and Jack fishing washed over him. Tran wished he could be with his friend; he even tried to get in touch with Jack and Richard for the last week with no luck. Tran had a bad feeling while he was in the hospital. Jaio and Scott told him not to worry about Jack and the others. He was told to get better, and only then would he be able to help Jack again. Tran followed their orders and meditated every day. He was sent home after his surgery; Tran's doctors told him they had never seen a person recover faster. Now looking out at the deep blue water of the ocean, Tran could only think of his friends. Sitting in lotus position on the front porch of the blue house on the Island of St Martin, Tran sent prayers out for Jack and the others.

Boone, North Carolina, was a small town in the heart of the Carolina mountain range. The hunting was world-famous, along with its southern hospitality. Agent Bill watched the tree line, not feeling too comfortable with how many places he could have hidden. It was a snippers dream area; he worried about the people he and his partner were ordered to protect at all costs. Looking over to his friend and partner, Bill made eye contact, each knowing what the other was thinking. Paul made eye contact with Ted in the rearview mirror and nodded. He also had doubts about being here in the woods of North Carolina.

"Turn at the next laneway." Came the voice of Big Ben Cameron. Looking in the rearview mirror, Ted turned at the next laneway and drove through the forest. Both men wanted to ask Wendy how far down this dark forest lane the cabin was, but they held back, not wanting to seem nervous. Just as they reached the point where both men felt they should ask, Wendy pointed to a log house and smiled.

"There's the cabin." Turning in his seat, Agent Bill looked at her and thought about telling her a house wasn't a cabin. When Big Ben told them about the hunting cabin, both men envisioned a small log cabin with a roof covered in moss. Agent Ted whispered to Bill.

"That ain't a cabin; that would be a house in the woods. I usually get some popcorn and a date to watch a movie that starts like this." Smiling, Bill turned to Ted.

"And just like most of your dates, you ain't going nowhere here either." Bill joked. Wendy sat back and looked at Paul, smiling. She felt safe with him and the two agents, not to mention her father being with her.

The assassin watched as her GPS counted down the miles. Lau didn't know the people she was going to kill, and she could care less about them. For her, killing was something she did; it helped that she enjoyed her job. She was paid well. Also, she lived where she could get anything she wanted was icing on the cake.

The last of the gear was brought into the living. Ben and Paul, along with Agents Ted and Bill, started checking the weapons they had brought with them from Georgia. Once the men were satisfied, all was in working order, and the guns were loaded and ready for action. If it came to that, only then did they go and check out the rest of the house.

"Sir, this is someplace you have here," Paul said as he opened the door to one of the bedrooms on the second floor. Stepping to another room, Ben Cameron smiled.

"Well, Wendy's grandfather built it when I was a cadet at Westpoint. My father never told me he was building this until I graduated. It's been a great place for the family. When I go, it will be Wendy's and yours." Ben told Paul.

"We can wait for a while before we want the keys, sir," Paul said as he looked at the dark wood floors of the house. Ben never thought he would warm up to the man his daughter chose to spend her life with. The more he got to know the young Canadian, the more Ben liked him. Ben had never forgotten the young Canadian marine who saved him from a landmine when he was a young officer in Vietnam.

Ben never forgot the name of the young man or the place where he called home. Years ago, Ben packed the family into an RV and made the trek to Newfoundland, Canada. They spent a week traveling around the wonderful Island Ben, May, and Wendy fell in love with. The people were so friendly and welcoming. They found the views overlooking the ocean breathtaking. The family visited the

Viking settlement in L'anse aux meadows, which enthralled Ben and
Wendy. While May wanted to stay and paint every fishing village,
they came across. Ben drove to the small village of Joe Batt's Arm on
Fogo Island on the north-central coast of the Island.

The young man who saved his life had talked about going out on
his dad's boat fishing. They would return to the place he called home.
Ben remembered some of the other men would tease Bert about his
accent, and the young man would laugh. Standing in the village, Ben
looked out over the bay. At the time, Ben wondered if any of Bert's
family were still here. A young man walked up to him and asked if
he needed any help. When Ben told the young man who he was and
how he knew Bert, the young man smiled and shook Bens's hand.

"So you knew Uncle Bert, eh, well? My old ma will want to meet
you; come with me, skipper ." The young man said as he tugged on
Bens's Arm.

"Best to bring the missus and the lass, too, or I'll be in for it." The
young man said.

Sitting in the small house overlooking the ocean, Ben couldn't
get over how friendly the people were. They wanted to hear about
Bert and if he had many friends. His oldest sister wasn't surprised
when Ben told her the guys would tease Bert, not in a mean way.
He told Bert's sister how the men were deeply saddened when he
was killed. Many of the men thought of Bert as a little brother. Ella
smiled and said that it was Bert; once he smiled, the rest of the room
would smile. Once she learned of her brother, she was happy he
didn't die alone. Ella insisted they have tea and stay for supper. Three
days later, the Camerons pulled out of the Arm, as the locals called it.
Every year they made the trip to the small village in Newfoundland.
Ben and May, with Wendy, grew to think of the people in the small
village as family. Now Ben stood in a house built by his father, hoping
he and his wife would get to see the people of the village one more
time.

Chapter 24

LAU'S GPS SHOWED SHE was entering the town of Boone, North Carolina. All she had to do was go to the cabin and kill the people there. Lau didn't think she had anything to worry about; the reporter's father was old. He retired from the service, and her mother was a housewife. Lau knew the wife would be fat and slow as for the faience. He was a Canadian diplomat, and like all diplomats, he would be a coward. What she had to be concerned about was the two CIA agents protecting the family. As Lau drove, she planned her attack; she would kill the two agents first. This way, she could pick off the family at her leisure. It would be at her leisure; they were stupid enough to come to a back woods town to hide. Lau knew she would be done with these fat, soft people before this night was over.

Agent Bill Clinton was watching the primary approach to the house. He and Ted Boylas had placed wireless cameras around the property after they ensured the house was secured. All the cameras were run through a secure wireless router hooked to three video monitors. Each monitor flipped to a different view every three seconds.

The first feed was from the road approaching the turn-off for the laneway leading to the house. The second was from the front of the house, looking up the laneway towards the road. The third camera was at the back of the house. This camera and the ones on each side of the house were all wide-angle lenses. Each covered an overlapping view into the next camera's view. This way, there were no hidden areas where an attack could come from.

Lau stopped and checked her information before she stepped out of the car. The assassin didn't know Agent Bill Clinton could see her on the monitors. As he watched Lau, Bill spoke softly into a mic embedded in the collar of his shirt. Bill radioed Ted to tell him he was watching an Asian woman who was on the main road.

"What's she doing out in this neck of the woods?" Ted asked. He started to walk around the house; when he reached the corner of the house, he crouched down. Ted waited for his partner to give him more intel on the target's movements.

Lau studied the woods around her. All seemed quiet. A bird chirped in a tree, and a squirrel chattered at her from a branch. Lau was climbing back into her car when she caught movement out of her peripheral vision. Snapping her head around to catch whoever was coming out of the forest. Lau found she was aiming her pistol at a young whitetail deer. The small deer stopped and stared at her with huge brown eyes. She lowered her pistol and smiled as the fawn ran into the trees on the other side of the road.

"Confirm the target is armed, Ted; she is carrying an automatic pistol. I don't know what she has in the car." Bill told his partner.

Lau knew the Cameron reporter had protection. The men sent to keep her and her family alive would be using standard-issue radios for communication. Getting back into her car Lau looked into the backseat. Lifting a blanket, she revealed a frequency jammer. This particular one would jam all radio frequencies; it would also jam cell phones.

This type of tech was highly illegal in the US and most of the Western world. Lau smiled; people here worried about their privacy more than the safety of the country. This worrying about themselves made it so easy to infiltrate their borders. Flipping the two switches and activating the jammer, Lau watched to ensure it was working.

Knowing her targets wouldn't be able to call for help, she opened the trunk of her car. Grabbing the case holding her rifle Lau started into the trees knowing she would be finished with the Camerons soon.

"Hey, Ted...Ted, do you copy...Ted...something is wrong!" Bill said as Ben Cameron walked up behind him. They watched as Ted crouched by the corner of the house. They could see him trying to get his radio to work. Turning around, Ted ran to the back of the house to the door. Walking through the kitchen, he nodded to Wendy and her mom.

"Fine time for the coms to go down," Ted said as he entered the living room.

"Well, with our little stalker out there, I find it a little too convenient. She may have jammed our radios. She didn't get the cameras, though." Bill was saying as Paul came into the living room holding his cell phone.

"Don't try and make any calls. The cells are down too. She must have a multiple signal jammer." Paul said to the men.

"OK, then we use what we know; that's good old fashion hand signals. There are four of us; we can work in teams of two." Ben said. As his wife and daughter walked in the room. Turning, Ben could tell by the look on the faces of his wife and daughter he was going to have a fight on his hands. Before he was going to make it out of this house.

"Now, before you start May, You know I couldn't send these men out to fight for my family without me standing beside them. It's not what I am." Ben was caught off guard when his wife smiled and fixed his collar.

"I know the man I married. I knew if it came to this, you couldn't stay behind. But if you go out there, then you better come back here, clear." When May Cameron finished speaking, it was clear she carried as much authority as Ben did in their marriage.

Paul was checking his Glock pistol when Wendy leaned on his shoulder.

"Be careful out there, OK," Wendy said.

"Careful is my middle name," Paul said and smiled the same big goofy grin Wendy fell in love with when he had flashed it at a dinner full of dignitaries in Washington.

Lau watched the house for any sign; the people inside knew she was there. She knew not to get overconfident. Lau had been taught when people believe themselves better than their adversary, they die.

May and Wendy watched the monitors as the men quietly left through the back door of the house. May put her finger on Lau's image.

"This little bitch should leave us alone. If she hurts any of the boys, I'll kill her." When May finished, Wendy thought about laughing. She didn't think her mother would hurt a bug. When she saw the look on her mother's face, Wendy knew she would kill if pushed to it. Bill went with Paul as they left the house. The two men cut left and disappeared around the corner. Ted looked back to see if Big Ben was behind him. When he made eye contact with Ben, Ted was surprised to see the old marine wink one of his blue eyes at him and nod.

"Don't worry about me, son; I'll be right behind you the whole way." Smiling, Ted turned, then just loud enough for Ben to hear, gave the older man a 'urah,' and then headed to the right of the house.

Lau stopped and listened to the forest; nothing seemed out of place. The birds still chirped, and another squirrel had taken up the warning chattering. Still, Lau waited; she watched; time was on her side. All she had was time with the jammer in place and working. Lau could wait until darkness settled over the house, then use the cover of night to do what she loved.

May watched as the figure of the assassin stopped and crouched behind a large Georgia pine. Looking around, both she and Wendy tried to think of a way to get the attention of the men without warning the killer in the woods. May walked over to the large china cabinet. Opening the cabinet, she grabbed the largest crystal serving platter she had. Then with all her might, May threw her favorite piece against the wall where she knew her husband was. Ben was crouched on the outside of the wall when the crystal platter hit. He could hear May saying something about it being her best piece. He also knew the platter wasn't dropped. Ben knew one of the girls had thrown it. Ben reached forward and grabbed Ted by the shoulder, stopping the man.

"Something's up; there is no way in hell May would drop one of her best crystal pieces; it wasn't dropped; she threw it," Ben whispered to Ted.

"You think she's is trying to warn us about whoever is out there?" Ted asked. Looking back, Ben found Wendy crouched by the corner of the house.

"Mom said to tell you the bitch has stopped; she is crouching by the big pine we used to shoot my old pellet gun at." Ben nodded his head and smiled at Wendy, then pointed to the house. He didn't have to tell her to go back inside. She knew if she stayed, he would worry over her and her mother.

Lau smiled; she promised herself when these people were dead, she would go through the house smashing all the pretty things the woman fawned over. Once she had satisfied her urge to break what the woman loved. Then she would set fire to the house and go back to New York City.

Paul and Bill watched as the small Asian woman hid behind a large pine tree. She seemed to be trying to decide which side of the house to attack first. Paul brought his pistol up, and he took aim at the tree; following Paul's lead, Bill did the same with his pistol. The men crouched beside a woodpile waiting for the killer to expose herself.

Ben knew the tree Lau hid behind was twenty-five yards from the front of the house. Ben crouched behind Ted and looked at another of the large Georgia pines shading the house. Big Ben was just about to make a run for its cover. Before he could move, Ted took off running; it was less than twenty yards from the corner of the house to the tree. Ted covered the ground faster than Lau could react. She caught the movement of the man leaving cover, and he ran to hide behind another large tree. Looking around, she tried to see if she could find a better vantage point. Paul couldn't believe it when he watched the assassin look around and then stand up. Paul didn't think about his shot. When Lau stepped into his sight, Paul squeezed the trigger of his Glock. For a second, Paul thought he fired twice, then he realized Bill had fired a split second after he had shot.

Lau felt the first bullet hit her in the shoulder; her vest took most of the impact though the force of the impact turned her around. The second round hit her in the back between the t10 and t11 vertebrae, breaking her back and severing the spinal cord. The ten-millimeter bullet stopped in her left lung. Staring into the limbs of the pine tree, Lau watched as four men stood over her. The older one crouched down and took her pistol out of her hand. The men looked down at her; each knew she was there alone. They had known she was coming. Lau knew she had failed; Lau lay dying on the ground. She would never see China again.

Ben, Paul, Ted, and Bill watched as the small Asian woman looked at them. She closed her eyes blood ran freely from her mouth. For the men, it was a sign at least one round hit the killer in the lungs. None of them hated this girl. They stood silent and watched Lau draw her last breath, then nothing. Ben shook his head; all he could think of was another wasted life of a young person to satisfy the hatred of old men.

Wendy and May crouched behind the fridge in the kitchen. May pointed to the side of the house where Paul and Bill had been. It seemed like a lifetime before they heard Ben's voice. He called, all clear as he opened the front door. Both women stood and ran to the men checking to see if they were alright. Once May and Wendy knew the men who went out to protect them were unhurt, Ben spoke up.

"OK, now we need to find the car that poor girl out there drove and bring it here. Also, we're going to have to bury her body. So first things first, Bill, Ted, go get the car. Also, see if you can disable the jammer. Paul, you and I can get started on the grave; I know a quiet little clearing not too far from here." Nodding, Paul kissed Wendy, turned, and walked out the front door.

"He's a good man Wendy, when he needed to, he took the shot, he's not happy he did. He took a life in defense of his loved ones. If it could have been different, he would have chosen that path; you've got a good man." Ben hugged his daughter,

"He's a lot like my dad, kind but tough, a quiet man; if you think he's a pushover, well." Wendy winked at her father.

"Go help the boys, Wendy and I will have lunch ready when you get back." Ben kissed his wife and walked out the door. Ben and Paul stood in the yard when they heard the tires of a car crunching on the gravel of the lane. Pulling out his cell phone, Paul was surprised to find service had been restored. Paul and Ben took the time to wrap Lau's body in a heavy tarp. When Bill parked the car, Ted explained they found it with the jammer in the back, and both men helped load Lau into the trunk. The men were quiet as they headed to the clearing Ben told them about.

In the center of the clearing sat an old barn. The old building looked as if it was about to collapse under its own weight. About forty yards to the left of the barn, a stone foundation could still be seen. The house that at one time held the family who farmed this land was long forgotten. As Paul looked over at the old foundation stones, he could see what was left of chared boards. The family who called this place home and worked its fields lost everything to the flames of destruction. Then as in most things, time sought to erase it from memories.

"We'll bury her in the barn; the floor is dirt. We'll drive the car in and park it over the grave. I'll call Wyatt and let him know what we did and where the body is. He'll likely send a team to collapse the barn and hide the whole thing." The men set to work digging a grave for the young woman, who only a short time ago was going to kill them. Working in silence, the men didn't want to disturb the peaceful clearing. Where so many years ago, a family worked, where they laughed and cried. Once Ben decided the grave was deep enough. Paul and Ted placed the body of their would-be assassin into the grave. The men stood around the hole for a minute, looking down at the tarp holding the body of a young woman twisted by the hatred of older men. No words were said; each man held his own communion. The men looked at each other then they placed the dirt over Lau. The car parked over the grave, and as the men left the barn, the sun was setting. Stopping, Ben, Paul, Bill, and Ted turned. They stood; still, and they watched as the sun slowly fell beneath the trees.

When the men returned to the hunting cabin, they found May and Wendy giving four hard-looking men some food and iced tea. The group leader stood and apologized for being late to the party.

"By the time we got kitted up and then found our way here, your wife said it was over; my men and I apologize for being late." Ben smiled and said everything was good. The group sat at the large dining room table eating; none spoke of what had taken place only short hours before. The men sat at the table, each stealing glances at Wendy and Paul as they held each other's hands on the table.

Chapter. 25

Richard thought going down the mountain would be easier than climbing up one. It didn't take long before he realized he was wrong.

"Why in the name of god would anyone want to climb a mountain? It seems to be a foolish waste of time and energy." He complained as he clambered over another bolder blocking his path. Jack smiled as he listened to Richard complain. He looked back to Joan, who was checking to see if Eugene was still making his way with the DeRoux helping him.

"Aw, climbing a mountain ain't too hard, Dick. You could always jump off if you needed down faster." When Richard looked back to Eugene, he found the man grinning at him.

"You know I hate being call Dick," Richard said, then before he could stop himself, he started to laugh. Then Eugene started to laugh, which brought a groan from the wounded man.

"Jesus, don't make me laugh, Dick," Eugene complained. Then before they knew it, both men were off into another laughing fit. Jack looked over to August, who just shrugged his shoulders. Jack told everyone they would take a break until Richard and Eugene regained control.

To this, Richard stuck his tough out at Jack which caused Eugene to start laughing again. DeRoux stood dumbfounded, trying to get the man to stop laughing. Which would cause both Richard and Eugene to laugh harder. With the laughing finally over, the men and the girls had a drink of water. Jack looked to the east into the valley stretching out below them.

"Well, it won't be too long before we're on flat ground." He said as he screwed the cap back on his canteen.

"That's one thing taken care of." Wyatt Whistler said as he hung up the phone.

"Ben just told me your men, and the young man his daughter is going to marry, just killed and buried the body of the Chinese assassin. They need you to send a team to this barn." The General said as he handed a note with coordinates. "And get rid of anything that could prove embarrassing to the Chinese?"

C Steven Wilson looked at his friend and nodded. Picking up the phone on his desk, the Director of the CIA told whoever answered about the barn and what was in it. Steven told the person what he wanted them to do. The man didn't ask questions. He just told the Director it'll be taken care of; turning, he looked at another man in the small office.

"We have a job to do." Nothing else was said; both men just left the office, locking the door behind them. These men were part of the CIA that didn't exist. If you met one and wanted to learn of his past, you would quickly learn they never existed. Once this team found their target, they ensured a body could never be found or identified. Then they would use technology so no one would know the target ever existed. Both these men were very good at what they did. The fact they liked their jobs was a bonus for them.

Jack sat with Joan and August. He knew they had crossed into Uganda. Jack told the others they were one step closer to being out of trouble.

"Here's the thing, I know we can go to Richards family place here. I don't think the men in Beijing will let us go that easily. By now, the men were trying to kill us at the cabin and would have missed a status report. Sure as shit, the one flying the plane who shot yours down would have called in. Or had to call in once he had seen your plane go down. So we can operate under the assumption the group will have men waiting at the ranch." Jack finished. Richard was listening to his friend.

"The people who take care of the place for my sister, their good people Jack. It would kill my sister if anything were to happen to them or their families." When Richard finished, the seals could see the worry on his face. Each of the men gained a great deal of respect for Richard. Though he was from one of the wealthiest and most powerful families in the world. Richard still cared about the people who worked for his sister. Eugene stood beside Richard. He looked at Tish and Tosh; the two girls stood and waited for Jack.

"OK, this is the plan; we get to an airport of some sort, grab a plane, then make our way to safety. Once Richard, Eugene, and the girls are safe, we'll go to the ranch and make sure things are good." When Jack finished, he looked around to see if anybody had any objections, nobody objected.

Richard desperately wanted to go to his sister's ranch to ensure everything and everyone was OK. At the same time, Richard knew he would slow Jack and the Seals down.

"We can get in touch with Washington and see if they can help us in any way," August told Jack as Petty Officer Ricky Topper unpacked the sat phone he had been given before they left the aircraft carrier.

"Call coming in from the seal sat phone, sir." A technician said to General Whistler.

"Put it on the speaker!" Wyatt ordered. All the men in the office looked at the phone, waiting for the call to come through.

"Gentlemen, how is your day going so far?" Came the voice of Richard through the speaker.

"Well, we've been worried about you and the others, Richard; how is Eugene?" Steven Willson asked as he looked at his old friend Wyatt.

"That old war horse is doing fine, though I don't know how. We've made it over the mountain and are now in Uganda. Jack and I are concerned the bastards who are after us won't stop. They might send some people to my sister's place to wait for us to show up." Richard explained what Jack and the seal leader had for a plan. General Whistler turned and looked for someone to take note of the needs of their people.

The survivors of two planes shot down by the group hiked off the mountain range separating the countries of the Democratic Republic of the Congo and Uganda. It took a moment for Jack and the others to realize they were walking on a dirt road. Everyone stopped and looked back the way they came from; Richard breathed a sigh of relief.

"Well, if there ever comes a time where I say I'd like to see over a mountain, lock me in the loony bin." To which Eugene agreed.

The young woman handed the Director of the CIA the list of items Jack and Augusts asked for while Richard was on the phone.

"Well, it seems the first thing we have to do is find a way to get a vehicle to them. Then find an airport so they can either buy or steal a plane." When Steven Willson finished reading the list of transportation needs. He turned and watched as the head of the Joints Chiefs and his oldest friend spoke into another phone.

Chapter 26

THE SKY OVER BEIJING grew dark and sullen as the clouds started to let the rain fall. Zihao Peng stood in front of a window. He watched as raindrops left streaks on the glass. The little water trails slowly distort his view of the city below.

"What the hell has happened? We have been planning this for two years. We had all the right people in the right places." Zihao raged at the window.

"The people in America should have killed the reporter and her family. Now we seemed to have lost our best agents. What is more disturbing than the failure of our people on the ground in America is the loss of the ninth dragon by what seems to have been an American hypersonic drone plane. I want to know how the Americans came by the technology! I know they must have spies here in Beijing. I know it." As Zihao finished, he slapped a porcelain figurine off the table. Just as Zihao finished speaking, the door to the room where the group met burst open. Twenty armed military officers rushed in and surrounded the men seated around the table.

"I know one of you is a traitor; if the traitor tells us who you are, then I will make your death fast. If you do not, I will kill you slowly as your families watch." Zihao Peng said. The others around the table never moved as the armed officers slowly turned their weapons on Zihao. It took a moment for the fact he was the one who was going to be tortured for information, then killed, to sink in.

"I thought this day would arrive. Did you small-minded men actually think I did not foresee this day?" The smiling Zihao asked.

"If I can't bring America and her boot-licking allies to our heel. Then I'll make sure the Americans are ripe for picking. My only regret is I will not see America fall." As Zihao finished his sentence, he pulled out a small automatic pistol and shot himself in the head. The rest of the seated men looked at each other shocked. One of the oldest men in the room cleared his throat, nodded for the armed officers to take the body of Zihao out, and closed the door.

"Gentlemen, I'm afraid the brash Mr. Zihao might have done something foolish. I think we need to check our defensive and offensive missiles to see if they are all accounted for." General Pak Ming assumed command of the group. Unlike Zihao, General Pak wasn't insane; he had grown up in a small village, thanks to a very hard-working father; General Pak received a university education. He had joined the airforce once out of the University of Beijing and risen through the ranks very quickly. His wife of forty years passed away from cancer two years ago. Now he spent his time in this room or with his grandson. While he wished for his homeland to be a world leader, General Pak wasn't about to kill millions to get his point across. As for the UN, hell, he could care less what a bunch of politicians thought.

Chapter. 27

The sliver plane looked like an angel to the battered and worn friends. They thanked the elderly man for the ride in the back of his delivery truck. The group of friends stood at the end of the dirt runway in the town of Kasese. Steve Duncan looked at the DeHavilland dhc6 twin otter as if it was sent from heaven.

"I haven't flown one of these in years. My grandfather had one outfitted with pontoons for landing on the lake where his fly-in fishing and hunting lodge was in Alaska." The two airforce pilots walked around the twin-engine Dehavilland plane, checking the wings and the struts connecting the aircraft's body to the overhead wing. Once they were happy that the plane was in good flying condition, Alex checked the fuel to make sure the tanks were full, and water hadn't contaminated the fuel.

"OK, everybody, get in, and let's get the hell out of here." Came the order from Jack once he had received the nod from Alex. Steve was behind one set of controls and was already priming the engines. Alex joined him and finished a significantly shortened take-off checklist. There was a loud pop, which caused the seals and Jack to draw their weapons. Each man looked out the windows for any armed men who might be shooting at them. Turning around in his seat Steven smiled and gave everybody a thumbs up. Alex started to push the throttles forward, causing the plane to roll as the propellers clawed at the air.

The lone air traffic controller sat in his uncomfortable chair, watching the plane start to roll onto the only taxiway. The frightened man knew this plane didn't have a flight plan. He also knew it was being stolen. The man behind him with the mask and the large automatic weapon told him he would sit and watch this happen. It wasn't his plane; he didn't know who owned it. Right now, the lone controller could care less. He just wanted to live to see his wife and son at dinner tonight.

"V1," Alex shouted over the sound of the roaring engines of the twin otter as it powered its way down the runway.

"Check," Steve replied; he knew they were past the point of no return. He listened as his copilot and best friend told him they had reached one hundred and fifty knots. Both men knew they could have taken off at that speed. They also knew the climb would be slow. Knowing this, Steve and Alex held the shuttering plane on the runway, gaining more momentum.

"Two twenty, let's do this," Steve shouted as he and Alex started to pull the nose of the twin otter into the Ugandan sky. Once the plane reached thirty feet, both men knew they had cleared the aircraft's tail. Steve pulled the nose into a hard climb, the engines screaming as Alex poured on the power, at the same time as they climbed into the blue sky of Africa. Steve looked out his window and then banked the Otter hard over to the north. The maneuver brought screams from Tish and Tosh. Jack looked over to Eugene and Richard. Both men had their eyes closed; Joan was looking at him and smiled. One of the seals was laughing; he shouted this was better than the rollercoaster at Disney World. Once Steven finished his maneuver, he pulled the plane out of the bank. Then leveled his rate of climb to something that didn't have the people in the back crushed into their seats.

"OK, we know where we need to be; we can't go with the injury Eugene has. We need to get Richard and the girls to safety. So we will have to come up with a safe area to set our friends off at. Then we go to the ranch and get those people out of there." Jack told the others. The seals gathered towards the cockpit as they came up with a plan.

The air traffic controller jumped when the masked man with the big automatic pistol patted him on the shoulder, then dropped an envelope into his lap.

"That's for your trouble. I'll drop another one off at your house in a month if you keep your mouth shut. If you talk about what happened here today, well, you think about it." The masked man said as he squeezed the controller's shoulder. Once the controller heard the door to the tower close, the man looked in the envelope. What he found made him laugh, American one hundred dollar bills. He tried to count them, but he was so excited he would lose count. Good to his word, the controller never spoke of the plane or the group of people he watching stealing the plane. Thirty days later, a man caught him tending his little garden and gave him another envelope. Inside this envelope was the same fifty thousand American dollars. There was something else he and his wife had almost given up on.

Immigration papers granting them and their son landed immigrant status to the Atlantic province of Nova Scotia in Canada. The man stood stunned as he looked at the envelope when he turned to thank the man. The controller found his wife looking worriedly at him. He never told her where the money had come from; he just pulled out the papers they had been praying to receive for the past two years.

Chapter. 28

The strike team watched the Windsor coffee ranch on the Victoria Nile north of the Ugandan town of Paraa. The last order the strike force commander received from the group's leader Zihao. Told him he and his men were to watch for the escapee and the rest of their targets. Once his targets arrived, his force was to kill everybody at the ranch and spare nothing. Nobody was to be left alive; even the children were to be killed.

Richard and the girls watched as the runway of the Entebbe international airport came into view. Tish and Tosh held hands as the plane carrying them to safety gently landed. Steve and Alex landed the ancient Otter so smoothly that the seals sleeping in the back of the plane never stirred. It was smooth until Steven used the brakes, causing one of the seals to fall forward into the back of the seat in front of him.

"Are we there yet, Dad?" Petty Rick Topper asked as he rubbed the sleep from his eyes. From the back of the plane, the voice of medic Angle DeRoux was heard telling Rick he had pissed the bed and it was a bad dream. This brought laughter to the exhausted people on the plane. Alex taxied the plane into an open hanger; four men stood inside the shadows out of the African sun. He and the others had been ordered to help the injured off the plane. Then get them onto the awaiting aircraft as fast as humanly possible. Once Alex brought the plane to a stop inside the hangar, things happened quickly when he shut the engines down. Jack opened the door of the twin otter, and one of the unknown men pushed a set of stairs to the plane. Jack looked at him, and the man stood looking up into the eyes of a man he knew would kill him before he made a move, If he didn't get things just right.

"Mister, you better know the key phrase, or we are going to have a problem," Jack said to the man, looking up at him. For the first time, the man really didn't want to have a problem, not with this man.

"Hi, I'm Nurse Betty." The CIA medic gave the key phrase, to which Jack smiled.

"OK, you're the real deal; how in the hell did Steven and Wyatt come up with that for a lock phrase?" Jack asked, then told everybody it was OK; they were safe. The first ones off the plane were Jack and the seals. They went to the large hangar doors. Jack wanted to make sure their landing and taxi to the hangar hadn't caught the attention of any curious souls. Once the seals and Jack were satisfied it was safe, Joan and the girls were next off their plane. As each one stepped off the plane, she was hurried to another and was ushered inside by an armed steward. Richard hadn't wanted to tell anyone. For the last hour, he wasn't able to move his legs, let alone stand. He wasn't in any distress; his legs just refused to carry him out of his seat. Jack was surprised to see Richard still sitting in his seat. It terrified Jack; he could see Richard was trying to stand for whatever reason his friend and leader just couldn't.

"OK, what's up, old boy?" Jack asked as he climbed back into the Otter.

"Well, it would seem my lower half doesn't want to listen to my upper half. I can't seem to get my damn legs to work." Richard informed his friend.

"Are you in pain, anywhere, in your neck or back? Are you numb anywhere?" Jack asked as he reached Richard. He felt the plane move and knew August had stepped into the cabin.

"Can you get DeRoux over here?" Jack asked the seal leader to get his medic. Once Angle DeRoux checked Richard out, he couldn't find the cause of his paralysis. The seal medic turned and shook his head. Jack looked at August, and without a word, the men manhandled Richard out of his seat. Jack wrapped his arms around Richards's chest under his arms while August grabbed Richard by his ankles and walked out of the plane.

Richard could see Joan and the girls were concerned when he needed to be carried out of the plane. He could also see Joan wanted to run to him to help. Richard smiled at Joan and waved her back inside the waiting plane. Two of the CIAs medics ran to Richard and took him from Jack and August. They carried the portly Richard into the leer jet and started a complete examination. Jack smiled. He knew his friend would be fine when he could hear Richards complain about having some privacy, that he wasn't a slab of beef to be manhandled. Jack looked at the team of seals; the men had been going hard for over twenty-four hours. He knew these men were exhausted, and Jack also knew they would fight until they had nothing left.

August, the team leader, was looking his men over. The big Texan knew his team was ready for a fight; they had run long enough. Now it was time to take the fight to the bastards. Jack was about to tell the men it was time to kick some ass. Before he could get started, Angle, the team's medic, nodded behind him. Jack turned to find Joan walking towards him. He was surprised to see her pointing at him and then out into the bright African day.

"You go and save those people at the ranch; you better come back," Joan told the much larger Jack; behind him, he could hear one of the seals chuckle.

"That sounds like an order." Jack quipped, smiling.

"It god damn well is an order, mister," Joan said. Then she grabbed Jack behind his head and drew him down into a long hard kiss. One of the seals whistled another chuckled. When Joan released him, Jack turned to see who had whistled. He found a team of seals looking out of the hangar doors into the heat of Ugandan day beyond. Turning back to Joan, he smiled down into her green eyes, and she looked into his.

"You come back, there will be more of that, but you must come back. Do you understand me, Jack? Come back to me." Joan told Jack as she placed her hand over the heavy scar on his face.

"Nothing will keep me away from you, nothing," Jack promised the beautiful Irish Chief Warrant. Nodding, Joan turned and walked back to the waiting leer jet. Just as Jack started to look away, he saw Richard and the girls looking out one of the plane's windows. Tish and Tosh ducked back, trying to hide. Richard just lay there smiling at him. Jack smiled and shook his fist at his friend, who laughed and turned away from the window.

Jack and August stood in the hangar watching as the leer jet lifted into the faded blue sky of the Ugandan afternoon. Jack knew it would carry his friends and the woman he loved to safety. Turning, Jack looked at the men he knew would fight and die with him if that's what it would take. For the first time in his life, he felt as if he was part of a team.

"This is going to stop with us. This group runs around the world, killing whoever they think is a threat. This group's only reason for being is their quest to bring China into control of the world." Jack told the seals.

"We know this isn't what the government of China wants. So through diplomatic channels, Richard has received the green light to take out the group's strike team. We know they are watching Richard's sister's ranch once this team is dealt with. Then we go on the hunt for the bastards who started this. Gentlemen, this is what I was built for; you don't know my past. I have been trained for war, built for a fight from the age of four years old, by the people who grabbed me when I was young. They weren't looking to train a warrior to bring the fight to people like themselves. However, that is exactly what they did.

They built me to hunt and destroy the groups of the world who want to throw it into chaos. I have worked with one of the finest men you will have the opportunity to know. When this is over, and we have achieved our goal, your government will offer you the chance to come work for Richard and the unit. This is strictly voluntary; it is your choice. You can not be ordered to come with us; this choice has to be yours and yours alone." When Jack finished, he looked each of the seals in the eyes and knew he now had a winning team to take on the group. Steven and Alex were watching the twin otter being refueled. They turned and watched as Jack talked to the seal team.

"Do you think he's giving them the same speech Richard gave us?" Alex asked as he watched the big scared Jack finish and look at each of the seals.

"I think we are going to make a real difference here in the unit," Steven answered. With the Otter refueled and idling on the taxiway, Jack reached up and patted Steven and Alex on the shoulders.

"It's good to have you two on the team and in the unit now; let's go do some good." When Jack finished. The big twin otter started rolling onto the runway. Without hesitation, Alex shoved both throttles to their maximum and smiled as they raced down the runway and into the sky.

Chapter. 29

The leader of the strike team held his binoculars to his face. They hadn't seen any movement for the last three hours. Turning, he looked back at the men Zihao sent with him. He was to kill the family of the man who was the head of the unit. He didn't want to kill unarmed women and children like himself. Most of the men he led had children and wives. If he gave the order, he knew they would do what was ordered. Captain Seun Lee wanted to walk away from this mission. He just wanted to go home and kiss his wife and play video games with his son. The Captain knew most of the men behind him wanted the same, or at least he hoped so. For the last two days, Captain Lee wondered if he had told his men of his feelings. He wondered if they would say they, too, had wanted to go home. Or if they would tell his Colonel and have him shot for being a traitor.

Jack watched the Ugandan bush as the twin otter carried him and the team of seals toward a fight with the group's strike team. A team that, at this moment, watched the main house of the ranch. Looking over to August, he nodded; leaning over, he tapped Steven on the shoulder. August knew by the smile on Jack's face he had something brewing for the Chinese.

"Can you land this thing on the driveway of the main house, you know, come in fast and land on a short runway?" Jack asked, smiling. When he looked at August, Jack could see the team leader knew where he was going with his plan already.

"Um, it should be possible with this plane; what do you think, Alex?" Steven asked, his copilot smiling.

"Hell, let's do it!" Alex said that was the answer Jack wanted to hear. Looking back at the rest of the seals, Jack could see most used the time of the flight to grab some much-needed sleep, and August leaned over.

"We need to work out what we are going to do once we reach the ranch; you want to land in front of the main house. Bold, once we are out of the plane, then what?" Jack looked out at the bright blue sky and smiled.

"That's the fun part. Once Steven and Alex get us on the ground and close to the house, we run and gain cover inside. Now the plane is going to be no good after the Chinese pound lead through it. That's fine; we're going to be in the house. Richard told me the house has a stone cellar, and there's a tunnel it will take us to the back of the house. The main house sits on this hill overlooking the river valley. His sister keeps a power boat docked for day trips. We are going to get the family out of there and get them to safety, then we are going start to tear the group in China apart." Once Jack finished, August smiled and nodded.

Richard could feel heat spreading from his lower back to his legs. He began to worry when the heat started to burn. The pain was starting to become unbearable. It involved his whole lower back now and was beginning to slide down his legs. Leaning over, Richard looked at Joan; she leaned into him, thinking he was going to tell her not to worry about Jack.

"I don't want to alarm you, Joan, but there is something very wrong with my back; the pain is unbearable." Joan stood up and waved to one of the CIA medics. The medic rushed to Richard's side. He looked at Richard's back to ensure there wasn't a wound they had missed. No injury was found. The first medic turned and waved to his partner. The other medic came down the isle way of the leer jet with a backboard and a large bag with a bright red cross on it.

"What we think is you have a preexisting medical condition, with being forced to hike through the mountains has probably forced it to present. Now, this is a good and bad thing... it's a good thing because once we get to one of our medical units, our doctors will be able to diagnose the problem and take care of it." The second medic told Richard and Joan.

"What is the bad thing?" Richard asked through clenched teeth.

"It's going hurt like a bastard until we get there. I don't want to give you anything but acetylsalicylic acid for the pain." The young medic answered. Richard hissed with the pain as the medics laid him on the backboard. He didn't want to complain, knowing Eugene's injury was much worse than his back ache. Richard was placed with his friend in the back of the plane and given two small white pills for the pain. Looking over at Eugene, Richard smiled and, with his best American accent, asked.

"So how ya do'in pard." With a smile, Eugene nodded to the two male medics.

"Be better if the nurses were better looking and less hairy." Both men started to chuckle and then groaned from the pain. Both medics turned and scowled at Richard and Eugene, then went back to what they were doing.

Chapter. 30

Alex looked at Jack and the seals he pointed down, indicating he wanted Jack to see something on the ground. Looking out his window, Jack could see a large house surrounded by smaller outbuildings. Nodding to August, Jack shouted over the sound of the twin engines noise.

"That's the place; some of those buildings will give us cover when we land." When Jack finished, he could see August nodding.

"Well, this ain't going to be so bad." One of the seals said. Then before anyone could say anything more, Steve made a tight hard bank and shoved the nose of the plane toward earth.

"Oh fuck!" One of the seals cried out as the unit's newest pilots pushed the Otter into a dive for the ground. The sound of the plane flying overhead changed, catching the leader of the Chinese team off guard. Turning, the leader tried to locate the plane. When he finally located the plane. He realized the twin-engine aircraft was lining its nose up to land on the ranch's driveway.

"You ever hear the term don't drive angry? Well, don't fly angry, Dodo." John Bowen yelled from the back of the plane. Jack sat looking out the window. He could make out the men on the ground looking up at the plane. Then he could see a mist trailing out the back of the wings.

"What is the vapor I see behind us," August asked.

"It's fuel, we don't want to have a bullet find the tanks, so we are dumping it before they start to shoot," Alex answered. To August, it seemed out of place as they watched mother earth rush up at the nose of their plane. Shouting over his shoulder, Alex tried to be heard over the screaming of the engines.

"If you know the crash position, this would be the time to use it!" Alex yelled. From the back of the plane, someone could be heard saying the in-flight service sucked.

"Hey, at least we have our luggage." Someone answered then; all at once, the noise stopped. All the man in the plane could hear was the sound of the air rushing around the plane. The men in the back of the aircraft could hear Alex shouting their altitude out. Then they heard Steve yell flair, and the nose of the plane shot up. Seconds later, the landing gear of the plane slammed onto the dirt driveway of the ranch. The men and plane were still moving at better than sixty mph; when they landed and were racing down the drive heading towards the main house, the Chinese started to open fire at it.

The seals could hear the bullets thumping into and through the aluminum body of the plane. The men grabbed extra combat vests with armor and held them by their sides for protection. It seemed to take forever for the plane to reach the house; in reality, it was a few seconds. Steve and Alex aimed the plane for a large bay window and drove the nose of the plane through it into the living room.

The leader of the kill squad couldn't believe his eyes. He stood shocked as the plane raced along the driveway and crashed into the house. For a second, he thought the aircraft suffered a loss of power and crashed for real. Then he could see men jumping from the plane with packs and rifles. In earnest, his men opened fire, pounding the back and the sides of the plane with bullets. Captain Lee could see holes appear in the plane as he shouted for his men to cease fire.

All the others had made it out of the plane and were taking cover in the house as bullets started to rip and tear their way through the aircraft. Steve was climbing through the front windshield of the battered Otter when he heard Alex curse behind him. Looking back, Steve could tell the dash of the plane had pinned Alex's legs. His friend couldn't get out from under it without help. Steve was trying to climb back into the plane when August grabbed him by the collar, drug him out of the way, and climbed in to help Alex.

"This is not the time for a sit-in 'A train,'" August said as he looked under the dash trying to see if there was a way to free his new comrade.

"Well, I was going to use this time to bring the plight of myself and my fellow farmhands to the forefront," Alex said as he moved his legs to show August, they weren't broken.

"What's the hold-up?" Jack asked, looking into the cockpit.

"Alex here has some issues getting out of the plane, the main one being the dash has his legs pinned," August said.

"What do we need to get out and mobile?" Jack asked.

"Leverage, get me something I can use to pry this off his legs, and we're out of here." Just as August finished telling Jack and the others what he would need to get Alex out, another round of automatic fire thundered into the plane.

Alex and August ducked, trying to make themselves as small as possible. A heavy six-by-six-inch timber was slid in through the front windshield.

"I think this will do fine," August said as he placed the timber under the dash and started to lift. Alex could feel the weight ease off his legs, and all at once, Alex slid out of his seat. Once both men were out of the plane and in the house. DeRoue took a second to check Alex's legs. The men all looked around the living room. Jack pointed to a hallway heading to the back of the house.

"Off that would be the kitchen; in the middle of the hallway, there should be a door. This door should lead to the basement." Jack told the others. Unknown to Jack or the seals, Richard's sister was in the house.

Richard's sister Victoria stood holding an African woman and two children behind her. She stood holding a Berretta over-under double-barrel shotgun. She loaded both barrels with buckshot and had twenty more shells. She made herself a promise no harm would come to this family she loved. Jack pointed to a door halfway down the hall; turning, he whispered.

"I'm betting the family has taken shelter in the basement." The rest of the men looked at the closed door and nodded. Jack and the seals knew the people they wanted to save from the group were in this house; they hoped they were downstairs.

Victoria listened as the floor creaked; she knew someone was in the house. They all heard the crash and then the sounds of men jumping in the living room. She was standing in the basement, trying to hold two small boys behind her. Their mother was trying to keep their sister from crying and giving away their hiding place. They all listened as the sounds of boots started down the hallway. The small group held a collective gasp as the sounds stopped by the door. Looking back at Kissa, Victoria turned and raised the shotgun. She had never wanted to kill anyone or anything before. She also knew she would kill to defend these children she loved and her friend.

Jack could feel August's hand on his shoulder. He knew each man would be covering a different sector of the house. The only part of the house they didn't have covered was the basement. Jack looked over his shoulder at the men behind him. Then with a simple nod of his head, the men knew Jack was about to open the door.

Victoria listened as the footsteps stopped at the door leading to the basement. Straining to hear anything other than the pounding of her heart and the frightened breathing of the boys. Victoria raised the shotgun to her shoulder and started to squeeze the trigger.

Chapter 31

JACK HAD JUST STARTED to turn the doorknob when the blast from the double barrel shotgun tore through the wooden door spraying splinters across Jack's face and rattling off the wall opposite the now crouching men.

Pulling Jack out of the way, August kicked the door and then spun out of the way. He was about to throw a stun grenade when Jack grabbed his hand.

"No, wait, I think the family trying to protect themselves," Jack told August.

Looking at the ruined door and the stairs leading down, August nodded.

"We are here to help; we have been sent by the brother of the woman who owns this ranch. Please don't shoot anymore. Just hold your fire." August shouted down the stairs. The men were shocked when a strong woman's voice came back to them from the dark recess of the basement.

"If her brother sent you, then you know her name," Victoria asked.

"Victoria, her name is Victoria, and from the English inflection in that voice, I would place money. I'm talking to her right now, and it's you holding that shotgun." August said. He turned and looked at his men and Jack, who was still on his feet even though his face looked like a pin cushion. He could tell Jack was shocked, along with his men, that Richard's sister was at the ranch. The last intel they had on her said she was back on the family's estate in England.

"I'm going to come down. I am coming unarmed; please don't shoot me with that cannon, OK?" August told Victoria. He looked back to Jack and started taking off his weapons. The stairs only counted sixteen; for some reason, they seemed to go on and on. August spoke softly to Victoria as he stepped down each of the steps. Stopping at the last stair, August cleared his throat.

"I'm at the bottom, just around the corner, don't shoot, OK?" August stood and waited for a response. Nobody said anything. August knew people were there. His years of training told him he wasn't alone; he could also hear their breathing. Using all his courage and some faith, he peeked around the corner.

"Hello, how are you all doing?" Was the only thing August could think to say. To his surprise, he was looking at a tall, pretty, light-haired lady who, at the time, was holding a very ugly double-barrel shotgun.

"Oh, I suppose it could be worse as days go, so one must be positive," Victoria stated as she lowered the gun. She watched as August stepped fully around the corner and looked down at the boys hiding behind her skirt. August looked at the children and smiled; one of the boys smiled and waved shyly at him. Turning and looking back up the stairs, he called quietly; it was clear. Then he walked over to Victoria and gently took the shotgun out of her hands. Victoria watched as August's big hard hands gently took her father's shotgun. She liked the feeling when August held her hand for a moment, his thumb stroking the back of her right hand, his brown eyes smiling down at her.

The sounds of boots on the wooden stairs brought Victoria out of her moment and back to the present. The first one behind August was DeRoue he was followed by Jack. The rest of the team filtered down with Ricky Topper, who stayed at the top of the stairs as a lookout.

"You need to sit down so I can get those splinters out of your face before they get infected. Or I'll have to explain to your lady how it is I didn't do my job while she's kicking my ass." DeRoux said as he pointed to a chair. Jack was going to argue when he looked at the others in the basement. He knew he was outnumbered. Besides that, the splinters hurt like hell. Sitting on the offered chair, Jack looked around the basement and couldn't see the tunnel Richard spoke of.

"Oh my god, did I do that? I never wanted to hurt anyone; I just wanted to scare them away." Victoria said as she walked over to Jack. To his credit, Jack looked up at her and tried to smile before DeRoux turned and looked at him.

"For god sake, man, don't smile. Your cheek is a pin cushion. Now I'm going to rub this on the area it's supposed to numb it; I've never seen it work." DeRoux said. Setting to work DeRoux applied the cream and waited. The seal medic started to tease splinters out of Jack's skin. The people in the basement tried to look elsewhere as the medic worked. Jack wanted to laugh when, unlike the others in the basement, the two young boys found it completely fascinating. The two boys would dodge out of their mother's grasp to keep watching. Once DeRoux said he had gotten the last one out, Jack stood and thanked him.

"So you would be Richard's sister Victoria; you are supposed to be at your family's estate in England, not here," Jack said as he tried to touch his cheek, and DeRoux gave him an angry look.

"Well, as it would happen, I was at my family's estate, then I received a call from my brother asking if he could stop by the ranch, and of course, I said yes. I miss Dicky. I wanted to be here to see him, so here we are." Victoria stated as she took a step forward. August liked this lady. Jack is a very intimidating-looking man at the best of times; now, with his face bleeding and unshaven, he looks like he would kill at the drop of a hat. This proper English lady was standing almost toe to toe with him. The whole basement was stone silent when Jack started to smile, and then he chuckled.

"Dicky, you call Richard, Dicky?" Jack asked.

"Yes, he hates it; I've called Richard Dicky since we were children. What do you call him besides Richard?"

"Mushtasheio, he tried growing one once, but it didn't turn out, so I give him a bit of a time about it once in a while," Jack told her.

"Your Jack, Dicky told me about you. He also told me you are fiercely protective when it comes to what you consider family, and you think of him and your friend Tran as family."

"They are my family, just as these men are; I will storm the gates of hell with a glass of water to protect them, as well as you and these kids. Make no mistake, I'm not a nice man when it comes to those who mean to do my family harm." Jack told her.

"Well, I love big families. Growing up, it was only Dicky and I. Then our father sent him to Eaton. I went to school, so I'm ready for a big family." Jack looked at August. He wasn't sure, but Jack could have sworn Victoria's last statement was aimed at the big Native America.

"Follow me, gentlemen; the tunnel we need to open is over here. We tried to get the door open. It had been sealed for too long and might have a little more muscle than we have." Victoria told them. She led them to the darkened side of the basement.

Chapter 32

THE LEADER OF THE CHINESE strike force knew the women in the house now had help. He just wanted to get the hell out of the sun and the heat of Africa. Turning, he looked at his second in command and ordered the man to set the house ablaze. At this point, the Captain wanted to go home. He wanted to see his son, sit at their small dining table with his wife and listen to how her day went. He watched as two men ran toward the crashed plane with cans of gas. As the men reached the plane, they each threw their can and ran back to cover. Two other men ran for the plane with flares. These men threw their flares into the aircraft, and the two men turned to run for cover as the fuel caught fire. The sound was muffled; each man outside the house knew those inside would soon burn to death. The leader of the strike team knew his job here was done, The Captain didn't like it, and he gave the order to pull back. If he had to kill these people, he wished he could have done it quickly, not by fire. The Captain couldn't think of a death crueler than burning.

Jack and August looked at each other as the gas cans thumped into the plane; they could guess what was coming next. When the whump of the gas was lit by the flares, their worst fears were realized.

"We have to go right now." Jack was saying as the rest of the seals listened to the boots of Ricky Topper thunder down the stairs.

"We are out of time, boys and girls. They lit the plane, and it's burning like a Roman candle." Ricky said as he slid to a stop in front of August. The others looked at the barred door as John Bowen set his pack on the ground and started to whistle a tune. Jack turned to look at the seal; he realized the others had taken the boys and then started back to the other side of the basement. Jack watched as John began to unravel some kind of detonation cord. Then he could hear someone trying to get his attention. Turning, Jack found the rest of the seals waving him over to their area of the basement. It was then Jack noticed John stopped whistling. Jack found the man standing beside him, holding a short length of explosive cord, smiling.

"Like they say, a little will go a long way," John said as Jack started to run to the other side of the basement.

Tran watched the dock where the powerboat was tied, waiting to be of use. The four men who were supposed to be watching for Jack and the others were lying dead at his feet. He could see the smoke rising over the trees of the ranch. Tran knew Jack and the others would be fine. The person he was most worried about was Richard's sister. She was of a class that never did for themselves; they had servants. She wouldn't be used to the hardships about to befall her. Richard was beside himself with worry.

The leader of the strike heard a small explosion from somewhere in the house. Captain Lee was convinced it was a small gas bottle or something along those lines. Tran also heard the small explosion and smiled. He knew it would be Jack or one of the seals with him forcing the old door to the tunnel.

The two little boys clung to Victoria as the dust settled. Everyone in the basement was amazed that the baby girl wasn't crying. Jack took the lead and started down the dark tunnel as the smoke from the fire began to drift into the basement. August took the last position in the group, with Victoria just ahead of him, holding the two boys at her side. The flashlight beams lit their path ahead. The shafts of light also showed how fast the tunnel was filling with smoke. Not wanting to break out into a full jog, Jack did his best to hurry through the darkness without seeming to.

The men in the strike team just wanted to be gone. The leader knew his men didn't want to stay and watch as the house with the women and children burned. Turning, the Captain gave the command to leave the area, and he told his second-in command-to to go get the men at the dock.

The beam of the flashlight caught the wood of the door blocking the end of the tunnel. This door was easier to open. Something told Jack to stop and check out the area before he opened it. August moved to the front and watched as Jack studied the door. August knew what Jack was doing. August knew Jack was looking for a trap of some kind. At the same time, the smoke was becoming thicker. It was starting to burn his lungs and eyes, and the two boys with Victoria had begun to cough. With a smile on his face, Jack stepped back and, without warning, kicked open the door.

Chapter 33

TRAN KNEW HIS FRIEND, and he smiled when Jack did what he had expected. Jack stood and inspected the door until he found a symbol. It let Jack know all was well on the other side. Then he unleashed a brutal kick tearing the door from the frame and allowing the sun of the African afternoon to blast into the dark tunnel. Jack couldn't believe his eyes, was it real, the mark he knew and it was fresh. It was a stick figure with a halo. Tran drew this; it was a joke between them. Now it was on a door in Africa. The name of his friend bounced around his head. Before Jack could stop himself, he kicked the door open and ran outside to look for Tran. The others followed, trying to shield their eyes. The sun was blinding as Jack ran through the door. He found the four men Tran killed. The others were standing behind Jack as someone cleared their throat; they all turned, the seals bringing their weapons to fire positions. Jack stepped in front of them and started to laugh as he went to the smaller Asian man, who bowed and shook Jack's hand. The others knew the man Jack ran with was Tibetan. They knew he had just survived a brain tumor.

"Are you ok to be here?" Jack asked.

"I am ok to be anywhere. Here is just where I need to be, little brother." Tran answered as he smiled up at his big scared friend.

"But your head, is everything? Do you still have pain?" Jack asked.

"No pain, it is, as the children say, all better. Now let us get our new friends out of here. Richard is just about to lose his mind with worry, and I worry if I have to answer this phone again, I might get another tumor." Tran stated, holding up a satellite phone.

The seals already had the mother and the two boys, along with Victoria, on the boat. Jack and Tran climbed into the boat, then with a roar of the boats mighty V-8 engine, they raced down the river heading towards Lake Victoria.

With the sound of the house burning, and men moving off through the bush, the Chinese never heard the sound of the power boat.

"Has transport been arranged to get these people and us out of the country?" Jack asked Tran.

"Yes, it's all waiting at the airport in Entebbe; we have a boat waiting in Bukakata. We must use this boat to get to our larger boat, which will drop us off at the end of the airport runway. We cut the fence, and our plane will be waiting for us." When Tran finished, Jack and the seals were quiet; they didn't want to get their hopes up.

"We can't take Kissa with us; she has a family, her husband, and her children." Victoria was saying as they looked at the woman holding the baby and the two boys.

"Yes, your brother has reached her family, and they are going to meet us at the airport. They will be safe and be able to get away." Tran told her. Once the boys knew they were going to see their dad and grandparents, they became excited again. The rest of the trip to Bukakata was quiet. The men who staged the rescue looked over their equipment and slept, thankful for the safety the boat gave them. Jack listened to the growl of the powerful engine as it pushed them closer to safety; for the first time in months, he felt whole again. Tran was by his side. Other than the lack of hair and a scar, Tran was himself before the tumor.

Richard watched out the window of the jet as the rolling waves of the English channel crashed into the white chalk cliffs of Dover. Unlike other times when he would come home, his heart didn't flutter at the sight of the cliffs. Richard knew this time was different; his little sister was running for her life with Jack. Richard knew Jack would give his life to save Victoria. He also knew if Jack was to die, it would crush Joan. The Irish redhead tried to hide her tears when they had taken off from Africa. He had seen the streaks as they ran down her face.

"You know he's going to be alright," Richard said to Joan; Eugene looked over and nodded his head, then closed his eyes; the two girls never left his side.

"I know Jack and Tran have the skills along with the seals. Richard, we have added an unknown into the mix, your sister, along with the others. I also know those men will give their lives to save them." Joan said as she turned from the window.

Jack and the others sat in the idling boat. The men watched the edge of the airport where the runway met the waters of Lake Victoria. The men listened as another boat approached theirs, and the seals took up firing positions on top of the wheelhouse. While Jack and Tran waited at the handrail. The other boat slowed and seemed to come to idle before its engine was shut off. Out of the darkness, a small power boat drifted.

"Can we help you?" Jack asked as he lifted his Heckler and Koch MP5 to show starting something wasn't going to end well.

"Yes, sir, I have come to take my wife and children home." A man said.

When the boys heard their father's deep baritone voice, they broke free of their mother and almost leaped from the boat into their father's arms. Jack and the others smiled as the father scooped the boys into his arms and covered their faces with kisses. Then he walked to his wife and softly kissed her forehead and lips. This loving father then gently took his daughter and did the same. The men who saved his family knew this was a man who loved all in his life; he was a good man.

"I can never repay what you men have given me. If I lived for a thousand years, I could not. All I can do is thank you." Before Jack knew what was happening, he was wrapped in a hug from this stranger. Each man in the group received a hug, and a thank you. When the thankful man was done, he scooped his daughter from his wife, then helped the others into the small power boat. Jack, Tran, and the seals watched as the two small boys waved until the night claimed them.

"Well, that's the easy part over with, now to wait for our ride the hell out of here," Jack said. Minutes later, they watched as a plane started down the taxiway. The men who crashed into a house hours ago to rescue a family they didn't know now sat at the edge of an airport. Jack turned and looked each seal in the eye; he thanked the man for being there. Then he turned to his friend and brother; Jack couldn't believe Tran was here with him.

"Yes, little brother, it's me, and I'm not going anywhere," Tran told him.

"This will be our ride, gentlemen; let's hit the shore and be ready when it stops," Tran said as the engine of their boat came to life, pushing them towards the rocks making up the shore. The boat came to rest at the edge of the runway with a heavy thump. The team seemed to be over the railing of the boat and on the rocks in one fluid movement. August cut the fence, and his seals silently crept through, laying in the grass when Jack and Tran crouched beside them. They all willed the plane to stop so they could just stand and run in the door. To their surprise, the aircraft did just that; it came to a stop. The door with the stairs built in was being lowered, and the men started to file in with Victoria caught in the middle.

Richard looked at his phone. He was trying to decide whether to call Tran one more time just to hear his voice.

"You know if you call him again, he's apt to throw the phone in the lake," Eugene said, looking at his friend.

"I know, for some reason, I feel better when I hear his voice. It's as if I can hear Victoria simultaneously; it's stupid, I know." Richard said as he placed the phone back on the bedside table.

"It's not stupid; it's a sign you care for both of them. One is your family, and the other you've come to think of as family." Eugene said as he watched the two girls he called his daughters walk past the window.

"Look at those two; they aren't my daughters. I love them like they are. I would die for either one of them. I never met the right woman for me; I have long ago cut ties with my sister and the rest of the people who call themselves family for reasons I won't bother you with. Those two girls are my family, and that is that you feel the same way about Jack and Tran." As Eugene looked away from the window, he saw Richard nodding his head.

As Jack entered the plane, the man who had lowered the stairs turned and knocked on the cockpit door. The engines spooling up was the response. Before Jack took his seat and his belt fastened, the private jet was screaming down the runway, its gleaming white nose being lifted into the air.

"We will be back in England before you know it, gentlemen. Once I get the ok from the pilot, you can stow your gear; I'll have some food ready." Jack and the others listened as the Steward listed the emergency exits and where the washroom was; before he finished, some of the seals had fallen asleep. Jack was watching out his window when a 'ding' was heard, and the Steward started back through the plane. He was informing the men they could place their gear in the back two rows of seating if they wished.

Jack and August watched as the young man went from seal to seal, asking if they wanted a drink and something to eat. He never offered to help with the gear, and the Steward never came close to any of it.

"That young man is experienced with how we work," August stated, to which Jack nodded. The young Steward had all the drinks out and was starting through the cabin with the food before all the gear was moved. Victoria sat and sipped her tea, then, to her shame, began to cry. She was shocked at her loss of control, and her embarrassment deepened when August sat beside her. He never put his arm around her or said anything. He just sat there and let her have her time. She knew then, and there this man was the one she had been waiting for. She just leaned into his shoulder and fell asleep.

Chapter 34

THE WARBLING OF THE sat phone woke Jack from a light sleep. Looking at his watch, he realized he had slept through his call in time.

"Sorry, Richard, I fell asleep and missed our check-in," Jack said as he answered the phone.

"So all is well, I take it?" Richard asked, knowing the answer already. He had been talking to the pilot one minute past the check-in time; he just wanted to hear Jack's voice.

"Everything is fine; also, I think we may have a budding romance on our hands; I'll tell you all about it when we get home," Jack said.

"Ok, get back quickly; Joan is just about ready to fly out and meet you halfway," Richard told Jack.

The vice president gave Wyatt and Steven the lowdown on the conversation he and the president had with the leaders of China. The vice president told the head of the Joint Chiefs and the director of the C.I.A.

"The men who formed the group were at fault for the attempts on the lives of Richard and others in the Unit. They are going to be dealt with." The V.P. told them.

"Well, sir, do you believe him? Or should we let the others know we don't know where or when the next attack will happen?" Wyatt asked the vice president.

"Christ, he sounded as if he was sincere; then again, it was a conversation over a secure phone line with China, so take it for what it's worth." The vice president said before he ended the call.

"This is something else; we have got to inform Richard," Steven said as he watched his old friend nod his head.

The leer jet carrying Jack and the rest of the team landed at the small Cotswold airport. From there, a small convoy of armored land rovers rushed everyone to Richards and Victoria's family estate. Everybody decided with not too much coxing from Richard and Victoria, they would all stay at their family estate. The house had forty rooms, more than enough for everyone. Angle DeRoux was able to keep an eye on Eugene and Richard. The others sat around and relaxed most of the day. For Eugene, his days were filled with healing. For Richard, it was spent trying to get back on his feet for more than ten minutes at a time. When they did an M.R.I. on Richard, the doctors found a pinched nerve in his lower back. They were hoping that weight loss and physiotherapy surgery could be avoided.

Jack and Richard would nod and point conspiratorially when they would see August and Victoria standing next to each other or holding hands. Whenever Joan would catch them at it, she would tell them it was time for the kids to go out and play. Or she would drag Jack away on some made-up chore. Tran was teaching the girls meditation. He was happy with his new students as they were eager learners. He was looking more and more like his old self as the days passed. As Richard, Jack, and the rest of the team relaxed at his home in the English countryside. General Pak Ming and his team sat in a Hong Kong highrise, planning how they would kill Richard and Jack.

"We know to go after this Unit's leader and its chief assassin is not going to work. I have, over the years, placed more than one operative in crucial positions in the U.S. government. We also have people in the British and Canadian governments. We will try to get one of these people into the Unit, then wait for the right time to strike. The other men in the room nodded; they thought the same as the General. If you wanted to kill people like Richard and Jack, you had to go about it quietly.

"Call coming in, Richard. It's from Steven and Wyatt." Joan called out as she entered the dining room. Richard thanked her as he headed for his office.

"Richard, we are not sure, but we think we have the chairman in China. The man is telling us about the group that has been trying to kill you and Jack. Exposing the Unit to the general assembly has been taken care of. We don't know whether to believe him or not." Steven Willson said. Richard knew by the silence hanging over the line there was another reason for the call.

"I can tell by your silence you have another reason for this call, so let's have it," Richard said as he looked into the monitor. Both Steven and Wyatt smiled at their friend.

"There's no fooling you, is there. Well, here it is; we think it's time the Unit left the U.N. The heat is getting a little too much, and sooner rather than later, we are going to be found out." Wyatt said as he watched for a reaction from Richard.

"You know the funny thing is, gentlemen, I was thinking the very same thing for the last month. As long as the founding countries say it's so, then we will break ties with the U.N. It saddens me to say this, the general assembly has become a non-starter these days. With all the politicians out for their own gain and fame. Rather than helping people as the U.N. was meant to do." Richard told the men.

"Good; what do you say to a meeting at your estate in a week with the others? There, we can hash out any details," Steven asked, and Wyatt nodded.

"That sounds great; till then, be safe, gentlemen," Richard said and ended the call. He watched as Jack and Joan walked through the garden hand in hand. He wondered what it would mean for them. Would Joan stay with the Unit, or would she choose to return to the regular British army? Richard wondered how many of his people would decide to return to their home countries. Richard knew those who would stay. He silently hoped there would be more staying than leaving. First, Richard was going to have to explain to the others what was going on, he decided to do it tonight during dinner. Until then, he needs to work on the separation of the Unit.

Chapter 35

THEY ALL SAT AROUND the dining room table. The meal was one of the best Richard and Victoria could remember with all their friends around them. Once the meal was over, deserts were served; Richard stood leaning against the table and cleared his throat.

"I have some news that will affect us all and the unit as a whole." Richard started, and the others stopped and looked at him.

"I wanted you all to hear it from me before the rest of the crowd gets here; we are going to hash out what is going to become of our unit." Richard stared.

"What the hell are you talking about, Richard?" Jack asked.

"Well, Wyatt, Steven, along with a few of the founding countries, feel it's time the Unit breaks all ties with the U.N. We would be following our own path. With the sanction of our founders, of course." Richard answered.

"Ok, will the people sitting here at this table still be needed in the Unit? Will we still be able to act to help others?" Joan asked. Hoping she would not be told she would have to return to her old Unit.

"No, everyone here today is still with the Unit. That will not change unless you wish to return to your country's military." Richard explained. Eugene looked at his girls and smiled.

"Well, I can tell you I ain't planning on leaving; however, I'm requesting a raise, old chum." Everyone chuckled at Eugene's statement.

"We'll have to talk about that after the meetings this week. Please take your time and talk it over with the others. Once everyone is on the same page, we'll meet again." Richard excused himself and started back to his office. He knew Jack and Tran had left the dining room behind him and were following him to the office.

"Ok, Mushtasheio, you know Tran and I are going to stay. So what the hell happened to bring this monumental change on?" Jack asked.

"It was the last couple of weeks, with the group in Beijing, almost losing Victoria. Well, and me goddamn, it's me, Jack. I'm so useless in the field. Eugene, with a busted shoulder, could outpace me. So I've made up my mind when this is over, and the change is finished... I'm going to step aside as the head of the Unit." For the first time, Jack and Tran could see how discouraged Richard had become.

"O.H. fucking no, your not old, boy. If you think that you had a bit of a hard time getting over a hill in Africa is a reason to quit. Well, my friend, hang the hell on because Tran and I are starting you on a diet and exercise. It's not going to be easy; I promise you will start to feel better mentally and physically." Jack said as he put his hand on Richards's shoulder.

"I know what you are trying to do, Jack; let's be honest; losing a few pounds won't make up for the fact I'm completely inefficient at all forms of combat." Before Richard could finish, he was cut off by Tran.

"That is where I come in. I will teach you some basic fighting techniques so you can defend yourself and those you love with. Along with that, you will be on the range with Jack and me every afternoon, no excuse, ok." Tran told Richard. He sat and looked at his two friends and wondered how or why he had ever been blessed with these men.

"Now that desert you enjoyed, well, it's your last for some time, pal. We start at 0500 hours, so get some rest." Jack said as he and Tran left the office.

True to his word, Jack was standing on the back veranda of the main house at 0500 hrs. He turned to find Richard in a set of sweats and running shoes. Tran was standing at their friend's side, waiting for Richard to step through the door.

"To start, and seeing it is your first day, Tran and I are going to limber you up a bit with some stretching. Then we thought a nice easy run around the perimeter of the estate." Jack said, smiling. He watched the look on Richards's face change to horror.

"This estate has a perimeter of ten miles," Richard said, as the thought of running for ten miles scared him.

"Well, it's a good place to start. We'll see how far you get before you can't go on." Jack told him. Richard liked the stretching part of the program; he felt his hips and legs loosen. Then Jack and Tran said it was time for the run. The two men set the pace, Richard knew either one of the men could have been gone like a shot, but they wanted to stay with him. Jack said he wanted to run on the estate's groomed lawns to save Richard the hard impacts of running on the road. Also, if he tripped when he got tired, grass hurt a lot less than pavement.

"I don't think I can go any further. I'm just about done in chaps." Richard panted beside Tran.

"Ok, stop, don't turn around. Tell me in your best guess how far do you think we came?" Jack asked as he looked at Richard.

"Oh, I'm hoping for one mile; I know it's more like a quarter mile if I'm lucky."

"Turn around, and you tell me," Jack said. Both he and Tran knew Richard had run a full mile.

"My god, I can't believe I made it this far. Chaps, I won't let you down if you stick with me. I'll be around this estate before you know it." Richard said as he looked at the house.

"Here's the best part, old chum, we get to walk and jog all the way back," Tran said, smiling. Richard groaned. Joan watched with Victoria as Jack and Tran coaxed Richard until he was a mile into his run.

"He did pretty well for his first run," Victoria said. Watching the three men in the distance.

"He did very well; it will be tougher tomorrow. He'll be sore; we better run him a very hot bath with some Epsom salts." Joan offered, and Victoria nodded.

"You know August is a good man. You couldn't find a better one." Joan said. As the two of them watched, the men started back.

"I know, and I want him to stay. I can't tell him how I feel, though; I don't want him to stay with Richard because of me. I want him to stay because it's what's right for him." Victoria told Joan.

"Well, I know Jack is staying, and so am I. I would have either way, but this made it easier." Joan said. The seals were sitting around the kitchen table having a light breakfast of fruit. It was Angel who brought the discussion to what they were going to do.

"Guys, I've made up my mind. I decided to stay with Richard, as long as it's ok with the Whisper." Angel DeRoux told the others. He watched as the others stopped eating and looked at him.

"Well, shit, I thought I was going to be the only one who decided to stay. It ain't that I want to quit the teams. It's just I feel I can do more good with these folks, boss." Ricky Topper said as he looked at August.

"Ok, it's ok. Who else has made up their mind to stay?" August asked his men. He watched as the remaining, and John put his hand up and smiled.

"So that's all of us then; good, I didn't want to be the only one." The big seal and Native America told his men. They all walked out to the veranda and watched as Jack and Tran encouraged Richard to finish the last one hundred meters of his first run. Without knowing who started it, the seals began to shout encouragement to their new boss.

Looking up, Richard could see the seals standing on the veranda, and he could hear them shouting for him to make it. Each of the seals told Richard he could do it. Richard could hear Tran speaking to him; Richard told himself he wasn't going to quit; no way was he going to stop. Richard thought, just put your head down and, like the bull, push through, and that is what he did. Then all at once, he felt Jack grab him. Looking up, he realized he was at the first step of the veranda.

"That, my friend, is two miles, one out and one back. Now before we are done, we are going to stretch again, then you are going to take a very hot bath, ok." Jack told him.

"As long as I don't have to run to the bath, you are on," Richard said.

After his bath, the seals gathered in Richards's office to tell him they all decided to stay with the Unit. As long as the Joint Chiefs gave their ok.

"I'm so very pleased, gentlemen, so very pleased. Have you informed Jack and the others yet?" Richard asked.

"No, we wanted to tell you first," August said as the rest of his team filed out of the office.

"Will you do me a favor before you tell Jack and the others? Will you go to Victoria and tell her first. I know she is very taken with you. From what I can see, it would mean so very much to hear it from you first." Richard watched as August smiled.

"She was my next stop; I was going to be all proper and ask you if it's ok if I start seeing your sister, formerly Richard?" August asked.

"Not that I could stop you both. I couldn't see a better man for my sister than you. If it is my blessing your looking for, you most certainly have it by god; man, you saved her." Richard smiled; he knew he would never have children. Maybe he would have nieces and nephews to spoil. August stopped at the top of the main staircase. He knew where to find Victoria at this time of day. She would be sitting in her favorite spot with her feet tucked under her reading a book. August couldn't help himself; he just wanted to stop and look at her for a while. August couldn't believe he had found someone like her. The English sun fell through Victoria's golden hair and splashed across her shoulders.

"What are you looking at, mister?" Victoria asked as she blushed a little.

"You, only you." Augusts said as he knelt down beside her.

"I want to tell you something that is going to affect the two of us." He could tell she was nervous.

"I've spoken to your brother, and my team and I are staying with the unit, staying here with you." Augusts was surprised when Victoria hopped out of her chair and landed on him, kissing his face. Laying on the floor, he looked into Victoria's green eyes.

"So I take it you approved of this outcome," August asked.

"I most certainly do, mister," Victoria told him.

"Well, being the old fashion man that I am. I also asked your brother if I could start to court you; he also approved of that young lady." August told her.

"Oh, so my brother handed me over as if I were a slab of beef. Something to trade off, well see here, good sir, you are going to have a job ahead of you." Victoria smiled and kissed August again. This time he rolled her onto her back, finished the kiss, and helped her off the floor and into his arms.

Chapter 36

STANDING ON THE STONE veranda, Jack and Joan held hands, looking over the manicured lawns of the estate. If they could have seen through the groomed forest surrounding the estate. They would have seen the Asian man setting up a small camper so he could watch the manor house from the woods surrounding the property. He had placed all of his cameras where he thought they would get the best angle. From his little caravan, he would sit and watch the people come and go. This poor man didn't want to spy on the people in the house. He wanted to be with his wife and little girl. Earlier, when Jack and Tran were running with Richard, he had placed cameras in the trees across from the front of the manner house. Now he waited for the lights to go out in the house so he could place other cameras in the estate's trees. One very special camera needed a clear line of sight to the office window so he could record what was being said in the room. The spy was surprised when the last light went out in the house at eleven pm. Three hours later, he was back in his caravan in time to answer a call.

"Yes, sir, I have placed all the cameras around the property and have set myself up in a small clearing in the forest." The Asian man said, then listened for a moment and nodded.

"Yes sir, it seems they are taking some time off as they say here. No, they will not see me, sir. Are they safe, sir?" With a disappointed look, the lone man hung up the phone. His job was surveillance only, the General barked. He was to record the people who came and went from the estate. He was to do this for one month, then he could return to his job in London and his family. The man sat in the caravan and feared for his wife and daughter in London. He knew the kind of men he was dealing with in Beijing. They liked to think of themselves as enlightened men. In reality, the men in Beijing were nothing more than killers. The lone watcher watched the monitor, its camera set to record the back of the manner house. This had been a week ago. The solitary watcher sat in his caravan, wondering and worrying about his wife and daughter. Nobody came or went from the estate; most evenings, the house went dark around eleven pm. Around this time, the watcher would yawn and drift off to sleep.

This one morning, the watcher woke to see the Tibetan man standing next to the assassin and the red-haired woman on the back veranda. Unlike the big assassin and the woman, the Tibetan watched the forest where he was hidden. As he watched Tran stare into the forest from the house, an uneasy feeling crept into the watcher's mind.

Jack went inside to see Richard, and she turned to follow Jack. Joan caught Tran standing on the back veranda, looking at the forest behind the property.

"What has you so enthralled with the forest Tran." She asked as she stood beside him.

"I can not say. I have an uneasy feeling. It is as if something there watches us; I have felt this before; it was when I was in the army. Then we knew it was cameras." Tran told Joan. Before Tran could stop her or step back, Joan wrapped her arms around him and kissed his cheek. When she felt Tran stiffen up with the contact, Joan smiled at him.

"I'm not letting you go until I get a hug," Joan said, holding Tran until he relented, then hugged her back. She knew with his training,

Tran could have gotten away from her. Joan also knew he would never hurt her, so he hugged her back.

"I'm going to stay with the unit and you guys, so I expect a hug every day," Joan told him.

"Ok, one a day. Now if you let me go, I'm going to prepare Richard's breakfast, crazy lady." Tran joked. He stepped back from Joan and then kissed her hand. She knew he was lonely, and she also knew he wouldn't tell any of them he wished for someone to fall in love with. Tran finished Richard's meal and brought it to his office. Jack was there; he and Richard were talking about the house on the island of St Martin that he and Tran shared.

"I want to buy another house on the island. The older lady who lives in the next house wants to move in with her daughter in London." Jack was telling Richard.

"I want Tran to have our house, he loves that house, and the woman at the end of the lane is kind of taken with him." Tran smiled as he walked into the office. He noticed both his friends became quiet about the subject.

"I brought your breakfast, Richard; you two don't have to stop your conversation because I'm here. I know Jack is talking about buying the house next to ours; I think it is a great idea." Tran told them.

"How the hell could you have known about that?" Jack asked.

"Well, first off, I went and helped her with her tomato plants; we would talk. When you approached Margaret about buying her house, she thought you and I were breaking up. I quickly informed her we were not a couple, and after that, she spent her time trying to set me up with her daughter. The one in London, oh, and she thinks we are war correspondence." Tran told Richard and Jack.

"She thought we were a couple, us!" Jack blurted out.

"I know; I always thought I could do better," Tran said as he and Richard laughed. Jack looked at his two friends, shaking his head. Richard started to eat his avocado toast with soft poached eggs.

"Another reason I came besides bringing you breakfast, Richard, I have a feeling we are being watched. It is when I'm in the back of the house." He told Jack and Richard.

"I wasn't going to say anything. When we reached the point where we turned around, I had the same feeling. I didn't want to say anything. I thought I was being paranoid." Jack told the others.

"Well, tonight, why don't we do a little recon of our own around the estate. Just to make sure we are indeed alone out here." Richard suggested.

"We'll let August and the guys in on the night's activity over dinner," Jack said as the three friends joked about Tran and him being a couple.

Sitting in his little caravan, the lone Asian man found it hard to keep his eyes open. He never understood why the men in Beijing never sent another so they could work in shifts. The lone watcher knew this job would mean his death when it was over. He had known too many other surveillance men who were sent on assignments before, only to never be seen again. As he sat in the wood outside the estate, he desperately tried to think of how to save his wife and daughter. The men who gave him his orders were, in fact, the ones who created the group.

The General had only been with their creation because the one they put in charge was straying from what they wished. Zihao Peng brought the existence of the group out of the shadows and into the light. If Zihao hadn't killed himself, the General was going to do it that very day. The men who gave the watcher his orders didn't know he had surveillance on all of them. The general and the others didn't know this was what he had been doing for years. The watcher worked for many aspects of the People's Party of China.

Chapter 37

EUGENE WANTED TO GO and have some fun; as he put it, Angle DeRoux wouldn't let him saying he was still healing. Eugene looked at the medic and snorted, then waved off the seal medic. He turned to the girls for help, and they wrapped their arms around the older marine who gave in, saying, 'It ain't fair.' Richard stood at the grand window looking out over the back of the estate. Eugene stood beside him, and each man tried to see if they could pick out their friend's movement in the dark.

"I've got to give them credit; those boys can move. Have you picked them out yet?" Eugene asked Richard.

"No, I haven't," Richard answered, trying to pick out anything he thought might be one of his friends.

"Neither have I. I thought I saw a bush move a bit ago. It turned out to be a magpie." Eugene said.

Tran was the first to see a camera; he watched until he was sure it was fixed and not rotating. Turning, Tran watched for his team; when he picked out Jack, Tran pointed up into the tree and mouthed the word' camera.' Jack looked to where his friend was pointing. He could make out a knot; it didn't seem to belong. Now they knew what to look for, Tran and Jack retreated to August and the others.

"Ok, Tran found a camera; how he spotted it, I don't know, magic, I think." Jack joked, to which Tran waved his hands in the air.

"They are meant to look like a cut-off branch. When we find one, mark its location on your G.P.S." When Tran finished, the seals and Jack slipped into the night. The men were in the kitchen when the sun started to rise; they were talking about the cameras and their location.

"Guys, I found something I think is important. I found three cameras pointed directly at Richard's office. They seem to be the only ones where whoever placed them was forced to alter the trees, so the cameras would have a line of sight. He cut branches out of the line of these cameras, is what I'm saying." Ricky Topper looked at the others as he told them about the cameras.

"You think these cameras have some kind of eves dropping device?" Jack asked.

"I do. It's most likely a laser acoustic device. If it can touch a pane of glass, it can hear what's being said. Also, it can be used over a distance; no need to be close." Ricky told them.

"So they could be listening to us right now?" John Bowen asked as he looked out the window.

"No, those cameras would have to be pointed at the window. The cameras are only pointed at Richard's office. Well, to be exact, at the two windows in his office. So after I found these two cameras, I started to search using the cameras as the center, knowing the house was behind me. I went south first, then west, and about half a mile into the forest, I found a small travel trailer." Ricky told the others, who stopped sipping their coffee.

"I crept in. I saw no movement, and I looked it over, being careful not to touch anything. Inside I found one Chinese male and a shit load of electronic equipment. All of it for some heavy-duty intel gathering." Ricky finished.

"Well, we have to assume it's the group we've been dealing with," Richard said, looking out of the dining room window.

"You have the meetings this week. We can't have that guy reporting back who was here. Sure as hell, we can't let him send any recordings back." Joan said as she sat down at the table.

"No, your right there. At the same time, we can't just grab him. That would send a message to this new group, forcing them to go under. Doing so would make it much harder to find them again." Richard said as he looked at the others.

"So how do you plan to do that, Richard? It's not like we can move house out of the way," Jack said.

"No, however, we can move the rooms around. You said the cameras with the listening capabilities are pointed at my office. So we hold the meeting where there are no windows. I think the cellar would be a good spot." Richard smiled as he thought about the stone cellar. He remembered all the times his mother would go down and pick out a wine list for a party he and Victoria's parents were hosting.

"It would; we can bring the large table in father had. I do believe it's in the carriage house." Victoria added.

The watcher wanted to go to the house just to see what the people inside were up to. This morning he watched as the big man and the Tibetan ran with the fat one away from the house, then back. They spoke for a bit when they stopped, then the three of them jogged back to the house.

The four females, with the other five men, went to a smaller building. He watched as they brought out a large wooden table. The watcher used a parabolic dish to listen to what was being said. He listened as the men grunted and complained about how heavy the table was. The younger girls talked about a party and how having all their friends at the house would be nice. The watcher thought it was a strange time to be throwing a party, then what did he know of the wealthy.

"Have you called about the tent and awing?" Richard asked Victoria.

"Yes, I have; it will be here as requested," Victoria answered

"Also, I took the liberty of bringing in Joan's family. She doesn't know; I wanted it to be a surprise. I tried to find Jack's family, but the girls were telling me he has none." Victoria said.

"Oh god, don't bring that subject up to Jack. His family was murdered in front of him when he was a child." Richard told Victoria, who stood shocked; Richard hugged his sister.

"I'll tell you about it later," Richard told Victoria.

"Oh, I'm glad I came to you first. The girls told me they don't have anything to do with their families. They said Eugene long ago cut any ties with his?" Victoria added.

"Yes, the girls came from very abusive homes. Terrible spots for girls, and to tell you the truth, I never asked why Eugene never goes home to visit his sister. I know the girls spoke to her and asked for some of his mother's recipes; I don't know if the woman sent them or not." Richard told his sister.

"Well, I've invited some people I know, and with Joan's family, I'm sure we have enough to pull off what seems to be a nice party."

"If we turn on the big lights in front of the house, then turn them so they shine down the drive. They would cause a glare on his infrared night cameras, rendering them almost useless. Our little spy would see cars coming and going. He couldn't see the people before we brought them into the tent." Joan told Richard as Jack and the others came down the stairs into the cellar.

"God, I remember Mother coming down here to pick out the wine when my mother and father threw parties. I would follow her down and pretend we had a dungeon." Victoria told Joan and the girls.

"This place is cool; I can see some dude hanging by his wrists chained to the wall over there," Tish said, pointing to the wall at the end of the cellar. Tosh looked around, then walked to the shelves and started to feel under each one. Joan and Victoria watched the girl as she looked under and behind each shelf.

"If you are looking for a secret lever to open a passage in the walls. You're wasting your time; Richard and I searched the whole house over the years and have never found one." Victoria told the girls.

"Well, that sucks," Tosh stated, though she kept looking, joined by Tish. The girls stood off to one side in whispered conversation. Joan and Victoria smiled at each other. Joan couldn't get over how the girls could come from homes where abuse was heaped on them. Still, the girls held onto their child like innocents and curiosity.

Chapter 38

THE DAYS PASSED AS the lone man watched the estate and the people who called it home. Delivery vans came and went, more tables were brought in, and a large tent was set up in front of the house's main entrance. The two men still ran the fat one every morning; they were getting further and further from the house on their runs. The weird girls with their piercings would stand and cheer the men on as they made their way back. Then when this was done, the Tibetan would come out and sit with the weird girls and meditate. As he watched the weeks pass, then came the day of the party. He knew whoever went to this party would be of interest to the bastards in Beijing.

The first ones to arrive at the estate were Joan's family. Richard met the cars at the front of the house. He told Joan's mother they were keeping their coming a secret from her daughter. The watcher sat looking at the monitors for the front of the house. He wondered why the big lights on the front of the house were turned on and facing out along the driveway? He was by himself; this is why he should've had someone to help with this surveillance. The watcher made up his mind he was just going to have to move the front cameras. He stood and grabbed his pack when the first of the cars started to arrive. Sitting back down, the lone Asian man watched as the first car pulled into the big tent. He watched as people began to get out of the vehicle. With the glare of the lights, the cameras were useless. He wished the lights were off so the cameras could make out the faces of the people. The general told him to capture the faces of people going to the party, so the group could use them to see what countries supported the Unit.

As the afternoon turned into evening, he watched as limousine after limousine pulled into the tent. He watched as the fat man and his sister met whoever stepped from the car. Once the greetings and hands shakes were exchanged. People would walk to the front of the house through an awning set up with the tent. It was time for him to send his daily email packet to his leaders. Once the video of the previous afternoon and this morning was sent, the man leaned back. If these spoiled rich people wished to throw a party, he didn't care. He only cared about his family.

Joan couldn't believe it when she saw her mother and father standing at the entrance of the manor house. Jack was walking behind her, eating a cookie he had stolen off the tray. He almost walked into her when Joan stopped.

"Ma, Dad, how?" Joan said as she hugged her mother and father; then she saw her sister with Lilly.

"Richard and Victoria thought it would be nice for you to have your family around for the weekend. Also, your dad wanted to meet this Jack lad to make sure he is a good man." When Joan's mother finished speaking, Richard smiled and turned to introduce Jack.

"Well, Jack is right here...." Richard and Joan turned to find Jack had disappeared.

"If you're talking about the big fella, he turned and walked through that doorway." Joan's sister said as she nodded to the back of the house.

Joan took her family to their rooms, and along the way, she found Tran leaving his room.

"Tran, I would like you to meet my mother and father." As Joan made introductions, Tran bowed deeply and shook hands.

"It was you who escaped from Tibet with Joans Jack." Joan's sister stated to Tran as she returned the bow.

"Yes, along with our four friends, we made our run for freedom," Tran told a shorter version of Joan. Lilly Joan's niece looked around her mother and smiled at Tran.

"Hello, little one," Tran said to the small red-haired girl. He was delighted to see her smile, and in one of the most innocent voices he had ever heard, Lilly returned Trans hello.

"Once you're freshened up, I'll come and get you for dinner." Joan hugged her mother and father again, then started down the hall to find Jack.

The general sat in his office and looked at the video packet surveillance sent in this morning. On the audio portion of the email, they could hear the bastards planning a party for the weekend. Then the lights at the front of the house came on; at that point, the cameras were rendered useless. They could see cars arriving at the house and people getting out. The problem was with the lights on; they couldn't make out their faces. Once in the house, the people who came to the party were out of sight. The General and the others in the office with him knew Richard and the others were up to something. They just needed to find out what.

Richard greeted Steven Willson and Wyatt Whistler, then led them into the house. Introductions were made all around. Richard led the men down into the cellar.

"We'll have the meetings down here; we know the chap in the caravan has placed cameras all around the property. The ones our spy place to watch my office have laser audio surveillance. For this reason, we thought this would be a better place." When Richard finished, both the C.I.A. director and the head of the Joint Chiefs nodded.

"This place is great; how thick are the foundation stones in this house Richard?" Steven asked, running one of his hands over one of the granite slabs that held the manor house up.

"Well, if I remember correctly, the stone used to build this house over three hundred years ago are three feet thick by three feet long and two feet high. The whole house is built of the same stone, all quarried and brought from Scotland. Here is a bit of trivia for you, the stone used for this house is from the same quarry as curling stones come from." Richard told Steven. Richard and Wyatt watched as Steven walked around the cellar running his hand along the walls. Both men knew Steven loved architecture. He had a particular affinity for English manner houses of the sixteenth century. Victoria entered the basement and informed the men more of their counterparts were arriving. The three men followed Victoria back upstairs. Car after the car arrived, their counterparts from Canada and the British governments were greeted by Joan. It was then the Canadian informed the others that France once again refused to participate in this meeting. Once the men returned to the cellar, the Canadian spoke to the others.

"The French did inform the British, whatever the outcome of this weekend is. They would not be interacting with the Unit. Essentially the French have cut all ties with the Unit." The Canadian diplomat informed them.

"It's not as if we'll miss them. They haven't been helping out for years." Wyatt said and watched as the rest nodded.

"So, gentlemen, I suppose we could get this meeting started if there are no objections. I have informed Steven and Wyatt about our unique situation. We have a Chinese male hiding just off the property; he has placed cameras all around the house. The ones facing my office upstairs have audio surveillance; this is the reason for the cellar." Richard explained once again. He turned as Victoria, Tish, and Tosh brought trays of food, pitchers of water, and some scotch for the meeting. The girls walked over to Wyatt and smiled at him.

"Hello, girls; how's Eugene doing?" The big gruff General asked as he hugged each of them.

"He's getting better. He wants to have a drink once you're all done here." Tosh answered. Wyatt nodded.

"That will be great; you tell him we all need to have one after this," Steven added as Tish and Tosh hugged him. The men sat down and started talking about the future of the Unit. Each man knew there was a future. This entity was needed in so many places. Disbanding it was out of the question. This weekend was going to be the beginning, a new start for the Unit. Each man at the table knew innocents around the world needed the Unit and the men and women in it. It saddened them that they were forced to take the Unit started by good men decades before and remove it from the united nations. A place where governments from around the world came together for world peace. Now that once fine body of peace is a stepping stone for globalists seeking power.

Joan found Jack sitting in the kitchen; she watched him twisting his hands together, his knuckles cracking.

"Why are you in here?" She asked as she stood beside him.

"I don't know. When your mother came in the house, I just turned and walked away." Jack answered. Joan looked down at the man she had fallen in love with. For the first time, she saw how vulnerable he was.

"I'm worried your family, well, that your family will see this scared-up thing. They will think I'm only good for fighting." Jack said, looking at the wooden floor between his feet. Joan ran her fingers through Jack's short hair as she thought of what to say to this man. A man who has fought and survived things that would have killed any number of men. A man Joan knows who can kill and chooses to save a life whenever he can. As Joan looked at the bowed head of the man, she fell in love with. She knew Jack was so afraid of his own hands he refused to hold a baby out of fear he'd hurt it.

"Jack, I'm going to ask you a question. It's an important question," Joan said as she knelt before him.

"Ok," Jack said as his heart seemed to want to stop.

"Do you think we have a future together? I do, but I need to know if you do?" Joan asked.

"I do. I want to have you with me." Jack answered.

"You have been learning about your mother and father. Do you think they would approve of me?" Joan asked.

"God, yes, from what I have learned, they would have loved you," Jack answered.

"Well, I know my family is going to love you like I do." When Joan finished, she stood up and held Jack's hand, gently coaxing him out of his chair. Looking up at her, Jack knew Joan said she loved him, and he knew he loved her.

"You know I love you too, Joan; I don't know what I ever did to deserve you in my life," Jack told her.

"I don't know either, but it must have been monumental because I'm a catch," Joan said as Jack stood laughing.

"Yes, you are," Jack said. Holding his hand, Joan led him out of the kitchen. She could feel Jack wanting to pull back; she loved him more with every step he took.

Richard was pleased with how well the meeting was going. The men sitting around the table in the cellar of his family home. Agreed from the start, the Unit must keep doing its work around the globe.

"So we all agree, we have to keep the Unit going. However, it can no longer be part of the united nations." Richard said to the others.

"As for the budget, that shouldn't be an issue; for the most part, the Unit was self-sustaining. When we did need a boost, you have all come to help." Richard said as he nodded to the others.

"However, with the investments, we have made with the money recovered when we nabbed Chow Yang. I can happily say we should remain self-sufficient. The only thing the Unit would need from the founding countries would be weapons and some logistical help." Richard knew this was where the actual negotiation would start.

"The U.S. is prepared to outfit the unit with weapons, along with any logistical ground support such as mobile bases of operation," Wyatt said as he checked some papers, then handed them over to Richard.

"And we'll help with any personnel transportation, along with the new cells being built in the north." The Canadian minister added as he handed Richard another file.

"As always, Britain will do all she can for the Unit and her friends. Australia said the same when we spoke this morning. He added his apologies for his absents." The man from Downing Street finished.

"I think the Unit will be stronger and better able to do the tasks the founders intended now. We will still have to be kept in the shadows. The sitting body in New York can never know about us. However, we have made it this far. Let us together make the world a safer place for everyone." Richard finished as he raised his glass for a toast. The others in the room raised their glasses and toasted to a better future.

Jack walked behind Joan; he couldn't believe he was so nervous about meeting her family. Joan turned and looked at him, and he tried to force a smile, then silently scolded himself not to smile.

"Mom, Dad, I want you to meet Jack," Joan said. Jack realized he was standing in front of her mother; all he could think about was how short this woman was.

"Ma'am." Jack heard himself say as he held out his hand.

"Oh lad, in this family, we hug, so bend down and give me a hug." Joan's mother said as she pulled Jack down for a hug.

"A handshake will do me, lad." Joan's father said when he stood up. Joan's sister Katherine hugged Jack, then he saw a little girl trying to hide in a corner. Joan stopped her sister when she tried to get the girl to come forward. She knew how intimidating-looking Jack could be, and to her tiny shy niece, he would be terrifying. She watched as Jack got down on one knee and held out just the index finger of his right hand. They all watched as shy Lilly looked at Jack, then to the end of his finger and back to his face. At first, Joan thought the girl would run and hide. Everyone in the room was shocked as they watched Lilly step out and move toward Jack's outstretched finger. Jack watched as this small girl walked to him. Then with her index finger of her right hand, she touched his finger, then looked at his face. Jack was stunned to see Lilly had the same jade-green eyes as Joan.

"They hurt you," Lilly said as she ran her hand over Jack's scared arm.

"Yes, they did." Was all Jack could think to say.

"What they did was bad. They shouldn't have hurt you." Lilly said as she cupped Jack's face in her little hands.

"It's ok. I'm here now, and I have met you." Jack returned; he watched as the girl nodded and hugged him. Jack didn't dare hug Lilly; his fear of hurting a child rushed back to him. Joan and her family could see Jack start to shake as Lilly hugged him. Joan knew Jack's greatest fear was hurting a child, but she never knew how bad that fear was until now. Joan wanted to step in and free Jack from it, then Lilly let go of Jack and smiled at him.

Chapter 39

SITTING IN THE SMALL caravan, the watcher wondered what was happening at the house. Everything had gone quiet; his audio equipment hadn't picked up anything in the office. He didn't think this was strange; after all, it was a party. No one should be in the office while the party was going on. He didn't understand, some cars had left, and the lights in front of the house were now off. He could see clearly now through the cameras; some people must have stayed behind, but why. Sitting in his little caravan for weeks now, the lone Chinese spy jumped when his satellite phone chirped. He looked at the thing for a second then it chirped again. Knowing it would be Beijing on the other end of the call, he picked it up.

"Yes?" The watcher answered.

"In your last information packet, it showed the highest ranks of the Unit, and our targets were at the house. We think the Americans were at the party. Though we are not sure, has anything changed in the last twenty-four hours?" General Pak Ming asked.

"They had a party with many guests; they have all left, and the house is now quiet." He answered.

"Good, we are thinking we should attack while they think all is safe," Ming said as he watched the others nodding their heads.

"What do you need of me, sir." The spy asked.

"Keep up your good work; the very moment something changes, call me, and start sending your packets every twelve hours." Ming ended his call. The man sat in the small travel trailer, looking at his satellite phone, then sat it on the counter. He wondered if the men in Beijing had lost their minds. He wouldn't be calling them for any reason. He was planning on leaving and trying to rescue his family.

"How is our friend in the trailer doing?" August asked John as he walked into the kitchen.

"Well, he got a phone call, and you ain't going to like what it was about. We need to get Richard and the others in on this." John told his friend and boss.

August watched as Jack and Richard, along with Victoria, talked with Joan's family. The last thing he wanted to do was break up the gathering. At the same time, August knew Richard would want this information right away. Jack watched as Augusts waved him and Richard over to the doorway.

"We need to talk now," Augusts told them and turned, heading back towards the kitchen. Richard and Jack both knew it was serious and followed August.

"What's going on?" Jack asked as they entered the kitchen and found John Bowen standing at the sink.

"Well, yesterday Ricky and I went for a walk, you know, down the road. When we were having a close look at the bushes, we saw that Chinese fella leaving in his car. So Ricky and I snuck into his trailer, and we placed some of our own bugs. I thought what's good for the goose is good for the gander, you know. Anyway, there was a satellite phone there, so we also slipped a bug into it. Our friend just received a call from General Pak Ming." John told them. Richard's jaw hung open at the name.

"Your sure it was General Ming?" Richard asked.

"Yes, we're sure, and the old shit said they were thinking about attacking us here at the house," August told Richard and Jack.

"We have got to get Joan's family the hell out of here then," Jack said.

"Well, here's the shit on that part. August and I think the fuck might have his team here already, just sitting waiting for the word." John said.

"Then we have to let the others know; we have to get set up," Jack said as he worried about Joan's family.

"Gather everyone in the parlor; we have got to warn them, my god," Richard said as he turned and left.

"John, I want you, Rickey, and Angel to go over the weapons we have in the house. Also, do a count of all the ammo, please." Jack asked as he and August left.

"We'll have to let the girls know what we think is about to happen." Jack was saying to August when Tish and Tosh ran up to him.

"You two need to find Eugene," Jack said as the two girls stopped in front of him.

"We will, but first, you need to see this; where's Richard and the others?" Tish asked.

Jack was about to scold the girls, but he stopped. Jack could see they had something important to tell everyone.

"I think I saw Richard heading down to his office. I'll get him, and you guys get everyone else and meet us in the dining room." Jack said as the girls turned and ran to get Eugene, who was doing physical therapy with Angel.

"We have something to tell everybody." As they practically dragged Eugene and Angel to the dining room. Everyone stood wondering why the girls wanted them here; Richard spoke first.

"What's going on, ladies?" He asked the girls knowing they were excited.

"Do you remember when Tosh and I were saying how cool it would be if this place had secret passages in the walls?" Tish began

"Yes, what of it?" Richard looked at the girls wondering if they had found something.

"We measured the outside of the house and the inside, accounting for the building material and the era for the house; it doesn't add up," Tosh said, looking at Richard.

"Ok, how far apart are the numbers?" Richard asked, knowing they needed to be preparing for the Chinese.

"Well, if our numbers are correct, this wall should have a three-foot wide passage in it, and we think it links with others throughout the house both up and downstairs," Tish said as she placed her hand on the east wall.

"Ok, so how do we get into the secret passage?" Victoria asked.

"Well, we've been looking, and as far as we can see when the house was renovated. Whoever did the work covered the openings with wallpaper and wainscoting." Tosh told the others.

"However, we found one place no one has ever changed because it was perfect, and we found a long-forgotten entrance," Tish said as she looked around the room.

"Oh, for gosh sake, girls, tell us before we burst," Eugene told the girls.

"It's in the wine cellar, one of the shelves rotates away from the wall, and there it is. Dusty and filled with cobwebs, it's an honest to god secret passage." The girls said as they started out of the room with the others following. As he followed the girls, Richard looked back at his sister. He knew Victoria was wondering how they could not have known about the entrance. After all, he and Victoria had searched the house repeatedly when they were kids looking for an entrance. When the girls walked past the table brought in for the meeting of the Unit. Richard thought they said the wine cellar and the girls turned a corner of the cellar.

"I forgot this was even down here, Richard," Victoria said as they stood at a long-forgotten part of the wine cellar. There it was, a secret passage; Richard and Victoria stood and watched as the two girls shifted a shelf. Then everyone heard a loud click, then the whole wine rack was pulled away from the wall revealing the passage.

"I knew it. Didn't I say our house must have one when we were kids?" Richard exclaimed, looking at his sister.

"Didn't I say it?" Richard asked again.

"Yes, you did. This would have been great to have back then." Victoria answered.

"Where does it go?" Jack asked.

"Well, that's the thing if we're right. This should branch out and go all over the house." Tish said she and Jack looked into the darkness. Jack grabbed a flashlight, then looked at Tish and nodded; he smiled when the girl nodded back.

"You're not going without me," Richard said as he asked Victoria to hand him a torch.

"Knock on the walls so we know where you are, and we can map out these passages," Joan told them as she watched the bobbing light fade. They followed the passage to the first branch, where Tish knocked on the wall. The three explorers smiled when they received an answering knock from the other side. The three walled explorers stood undecided on which way to go; all three looked down a different passage.

"If I remember correctly, this should lead to the underground garage; its entrance is on the north side of the house," Richard told Jack and Tish.

"There's an underground garage?" Jack asked.

"Of course there is. We are standing in a secret passage in a three-hundred-year-old house. Hell, we might find a dungeon, unused, of course." Tish finished looking at Richard. Smiling, Richard winked at the girl and shrugged his shoulders.

"Well, let's see this underground garage," Jack said as Richard led the way. They stopped knocking on the walls as the wood gave way to the heavy granite on the house's outer walls. Standing at the end of the passage, Tish took one of the torches and started to search the walls for a latch hoping to find one to unlock a doorway. Smiling, the girl turned and pushed a brick into the wall, a click was heard, and the door popped open. The three friends stood in a large underground garage. The beams of their flashlights shone off four cars sitting covered in dust.

To Jack, it looked as if they had been abandoned in the dark for twenty years. All at once the lights came on, causing the two men to whirl around to find Tish standing by a fuse box.

"Good job Tish, Richard; what the hell are these doing here, my god man?" Jack asked as he looked into the first car.

"Well, to tell the truth, I had forgotten my father even had these. Both my father and mother loved to go for drives when they came here from London. I think my father lost his love for the country drives after his mother passed away. He told me he had put them away, and over the years, I must have forgotten."

"This looks like a 1938 Rolls Royce Wraith. My god, man, that's a 1924 Sliver Ghost; it is one of the most sought-after cars in the world." Jack told Richard as he brushed twenty years of dust from the car's glass.

"That was my fathers; he restored it himself. It took him years to find all the original parts." Richard said as he walked over to a lock box mounted on the wall.

"The other two he bought for my mother."

Jack turned and found two more Rolls Royce cars sitting, both models from the fifties and sixties. The first was a 1959 silver wraith, and the second a 1965 silver cloud.

"When was the last time these ran?" Jack asked Richard as he looked under the cars.

"Oh, it has to be at least twenty-five years; they would need to be worked on," Richard told Jack as he held up four sets of keys.

"We can fix these when we get through this," Tish said as she walked up to the men.

"Yes, we will," Richard stated as he put the keys back in the box. Richard took one last look at the four cars before Jack shut the door. The rest of the day was spent mapping the passages running throughout the house.

"It's freaking amazing down there. The first place we found was this old underground garage." Tish was telling Tosh. Victoria turned and looked at Richard.

"Are they still there?" Victoria asked; Richard smiled.

"Yes, all four of them are there, though father and mother would be terribly upset at the state of them." Richard watched as Victoria smiled and then walked over to him.

"That's the best part; I can remember how Father would let you drive around the property. He would smile and pat you on the back, telling you what a good driver you were. He couldn't say he loved you, but Father had his way of showing you. When you fix his cars, it will be like part of him is still here." Victoria said.

"He was a man's man. A true British officer and member of the royal family, an Eaton man, I still can smell his pipe." Richard said as he nodded in his remembrance.

Chapter 40

RICKY AND JOHN WATCHED as the lone Chinese surveillance man drove his car out of the woods and turned to the north, heading into the next village. It took over an hour to find and disarm the i.e.d the man had left to guard his operation. Once they were sure it was cleared, the two men searched the small trailer. Turning up nothing, the men checked and placed more listening devices of their own. Then plugged a flash drive into the lone computer sitting on the table. They watched as a download bar told them of the progress of a virus Tosh gave them as it loaded. When the bar reached one hundred percent, John unplugged the flash drive, and the men left the trailer. They made sure everything was back as it was found, even the i.e.d was rearmed.

"Ok, we can now listen, and that virus thing you gave us loaded like you said," John told Tosh as she started to type into her laptop. Within minutes her screen began to fill with encrypted emails, both sent and received.

"This is what he has sent to China about us, and this is the reply he's received. The encryption is good; it might take some time to crack it; Tish and I should be able to." The two girls sat down and started to work on the encryption. They were engrossed in their work when Lilly walked into the room. The little girl watched as Tish and Tosh typed on their computers.

"Look at the faces," Lilly said, pointing. Tosh turned and looked at Lilly.

"What faces? Where do you see the faces, sweetie?" Tosh asked as everyone stopped and watched the little girl.

"Here and here, see this man is looking at this man," Lilly said as she climbed onto Tosh's lap and pointed at the screen.

"Your so smart," Tish said as she leaned close to her screen, then kissed Lilly on the cheek.

"What's up?" Joan asked, looking at the two young ladies and her niece.

"What's up is? The great and all-knowing Lilly can see the encryption. To her, they look like faces because that's what it is." Tosh answered.

"Ok, um, I see what looks like random letters and numbers; where are the faces?" Eugene asked, trying to lean in to get a better look.

"One face is here, and another is here." Lilly pointed to the screen.

"The important bit is because of Lilly, we can now work on the part of the encryption that counts. Other than the faces, the rest of it is just fodder." Tosh told the others.

"How is it Lilly can see this and we can't?" Victoria asked.

"Well, there has been a debate about how young children have what some call an artists eye. These children can see this type of encryption. These kids are so rare and special; if you meet one, you meet one in about one hundred million." Tish said, holding Lilly on her lap.

"Come on, sweetie, let's go find Mommy?" Victoria said as she picked up the girl.

"Mommy's taking a nap. I was supposed to, but naps are boring, so I came to find Aunty Joan; she's not so boring." Lilly told Victoria, to which Jack laughed.

"Not so boring, just a bit boring, is she Lilly?" Jack asked.

"Most grown-ups are. Does that happen when you get old? Why do grown up stop playing?"

"Well, I'll tell you a story; it's about playing." Victoria offered as she and Lilly left the room. The two hacker girls were busy working on their computers; they seemed lost in what they were doing, so Richard, Jack, Joan Eugene, and August decided to quietly step out.

"So what is it we know about this General Pak Ming?" Jack asked.

"Well, to start with, I thought he retired; I haven't heard his name in years. When he was an up-and-comer in China's military, he had a reputation for being tough. When there was any kind of uprising or talk of unrest, the central command sent in Ming, and within twenty-four hours, all would be quiet. Of course, the people who wanted more freedom and democratic reforms were never seen again. In most cases, their families would soon disappear, also. It was this man who trained Trans Colonel. He was to take over for the General until the night Trans sister ended his raping days." Richard told the others.

"Then he is as much to blame for the suffering of Tibet as that monster was," Tran said from the doorway.

"I was starting to wonder where you had gotten to," Jack said as he nodded to his friend.

"I wondered if the man who was sent to watch and report on us knew about Jack and me, so went to talk to him," Tran told the others to their shocked expressions. Tran smiled and finished his story about his meeting with the Chinese surveillance.

"As it turns out, this man knows who it is he is watching. He told me the only reason he is here is that the General knows he has a wife and young daughter. He's afraid they will be hurt or killed if he fails." Tran told his friends.

"Got it!" The girls exclaimed from in the other room. The friends all turned and started to walk back into the room.

"What have you found?" Richard asked.

"Nothing good. The encrypted file wasn't a watch order; it was a kill order. You better sit and read it." Tosh told Richard. She stood and gave Richard her chair. The others gave Tish and Tosh a questioning look. They all wondered what the file had in it. It took less time than Jack thought for Richard to turn and look at him and the others.

"My god, the man is insane," Richard said as he looked at his friends.

"Ok, that sounds bad," Jack said as he looked at his friend.

"It is bad, Joan, don't panic. Is there a place where your mother and father could stay with your sister and Lilly for a short time?" The leader of the Unit asked as he stood from the chair.

"Yes, I suppose so. Why, what is in that file.?" Joan asked, knowing the answer to her question.

"You already know this file has a kill order for your family and mine. We can get your family anywhere you feel they would be the safest." Richard told her as Jack put his arm around her shoulder.

"Mom has a twin sister who lives in Nova Scotia. They haven't seen each other for fifteen years," Joan told Richard in shock; some faceless bastard wanted to kill her family to get to Richard and Jack.

"Go tell your mother and father you're sending them to Nova Scotia for a holiday. Since my only family in the world is standing right here, we know someone will be coming for us." Richard told the others as he held Victoria's hand.

"John, would you and Ricky go to the garage in the back and check the white land rover out, make sure it's good for a road trip?" Richard asked the two seals.

"I have got to inform the others about this development. August, please don't let her out of your sight." Richard as he looked at his sister.

"Best job ever." The big native Texan said as he stood behind Victoria with his hands on her shoulders.

Jack and Joan walked down the hallway heading towards her mother and father's room.

"What are we going to tell them?" Jack asked as he neared the room.

"The truth is my mother has a better nose for bullshit than any polygraph machine ever built," Joan answered as she stopped in front of the door. Once Joan had explained to her mother what was going on. That they had a threat to her family's lives, the older woman stood and took her daughter's hands.

"You see these two hands; I still can remember the day you were born. You never cried. You were too strong for that. You've never run from anything in your life; how do you expect me to do the same?" Joan's mother asked as she held her hands.

"Because if you're around, Jack and I can't do what might need to be done," Joan said, pleading with her mother.

"Ah, daughter, when was the last time your mother did something she didn't think was right?" Joan's father asked as he placed his hands on his wife's shoulders. All Joan could do was smile and shake her head. She looked at the two people who raised and loved her and her sister.

"Ok, if you won't go, then you're going to follow some fundamental rules, the first being if we say run, you have to run," Jack said, looking at Joan.

"Also, Lilly can't stay. This is not going to be a discussion. She must go; they must be safe." Jack finished.

"Yes, Katherine and Lilly. They can go to Nova Scotia for a vacation; I'll not be leaving my home." Joan's mother stated.

"Mom, what about the rest of the family? You need to think about everyone. We know you would never run from your home Dad built. We all need to go until Joan can take care of this matter." Katherine told her mother.

Chapter 41

JOAN WATCHED AS HER mother, for the first time, didn't know what to do, then Jack held out his big scared hand.

"You see this hand, this is the hand of the man who has fallen in love with your daughter. This hand is the hand of a killer; I'm not proud of what I am. I am proud of what I do with my ability. Your daughter is my anchorage in the rage that storms within me every minute of every day. Nothing happens to my family. I will wipe the earth of whoever is behind this." When Jack finished, Joan watched her mother place her small hand over Jack's. Then she reached up and put her hand on the left side of his face.

"Son, I see in you so much pain it hurts my heart. I also see the best kind of man for my Joan, you go, and you take care of this for your family." She said Joan's father looked at his daughter, then he looked at Jack.

"Young man, you watch yourself. We will have a talk when this is over." Joan was astounded by her father. Usually, her father was so quiet and unassuming that he would inform Jack of an upcoming talk completely shocked her.

"Yes, sir, I will, sir. I look forward to our talk," Jack said. Then he looked at Joan and nodded, then left the room so she could talk to her parents. Joan's sister followed Jack and caught him in the hallway.

"You say you love my sister, and so do I, Jack; my father is a proud man. He has worked the whole of his life to provide for his family and never has the man once complained. When he says he wants a chat, you had better be ready for a chat and a good one. Now as for my sister, she is the fiercest of us. Also, the kindest and the one with the biggest heart, so don't you break it, mister. Or you'll be dealing with me." Katherine said as she stood with her hands on her hips.

Jack looked at Joan's red hair sister, and for a brief second, he was going to turn and walk away; then, for a reason he didn't know, he stepped toward her. Jack wrapped his big arms around Joan's sister and kissed the top of her head.

"It's going to be fine; Joan is going to be fine. I won't let anything happen to any of you. I will rip those responsible from this world to protect you all." Jack let her go, then turned and walked down the stairs. Katherine watched Jack's back as he walked down the stairs. Walking back into her mother's room, Joan looked at Katherine.

"What happened?" Joan asked when her sister walked back into the room.

"Well, I went out there trying to be tougher than I am; I told Jack if he hurt you, he'd have me to deal with," Katherine told Joan, who laughed.

"Oh, how did that go over?" Joan asked, smiling.

"Well, he is a strong man and tall," Katherine said, smiling.

"Oh god, what happened? What did he do?" Joan was starting to regret what she had asked.

"Well, there I stood, hands on hip, my best 'I'm not afraid of you' face on, and your boyfriend reached out, wrapped his arms around me, and kissed the top of my head. Then tells me in his deep voice, 'He won't let anything happen to you or any of us.' Joan, what happened to him? I know from the scares he's been in battles. There's something else he is very intense; what happened to him?" Katherine asked her sister.

"I can't tell you right now, just know Jack, well, Jack has been doing this the whole of his life. A very sad and painful life; the things that happened to Jack would have killed anyone. I'm going to be fine; I need you to start getting Mom and Dad ready, please." Joan pleaded with her sister.

Joan stood on the steps of the manner house, tears rolling down her cheeks as the black armored land rover sped out of the driveway heading for the closest airport. That night a private jet left a small airport, and a flight plan registered to show the flight was landing a Boston's Logan Airport. It refueled and then took off its new flight plan showing a destination of Toronto, Ontario, Canada. It never made it; the flight plan was removed from all the N.T.S.B. and Transport Canada computers, as well as ever being in Boston. An hour later, the plane landed at Halifax Stanfield international airport. Joan's family were happy to be on firm ground again. Two large suv's waited to take the family to their assigned hotel.

Chapter 42

WAITING THERE WAS STEVEN Willson and another man from the Canadian secret service.

"Joan told us to make sure you, Mrs. O'Driscoll, do not find a way to get back home until this is over," Steven told Joan's mother, who smiled.

"My Joan thinks me a super spy?" The older woman said with a smile.

"No, Mother, she knows how stubborn you can be," Katherine answered as she hugged her mother with Lilly.

"Sir, I know you don't have to tell me a thing. We need to know the very second this is over that our Joan is alright." Mr. O'Driscoll said to Steven.

"You will; I give you my word as an officer, sir," Wyatt promised the family as he shook Mr. O'Driscoll's hand.

"I know you might have heard this before, with Jack beside her. Nothing, and I mean nothing, is going to happen to your daughter." Steven added.

"You both talk about Jack as if he is some kind of superhero," Katherine said as she finished tucking Lilly into bed.

"Well, ma'am, in a way, he is too many of us. Jack's story starts at a very young age; he's Canadian. His mother was a lawyer, and his father was a journalist. If the family had been left alone, Jack would have gone on to be a fine young man, one who would have done any number of things with his life." Wyatt started to say when he paused, Steven took over.

"Years ago, my predecessor was a spoiled man whose family was very wealthy and held a lot of power in our government. Jack's father somehow found out about a program this man was operating. My predecessor tried to scare Jack's father off, then Jack's mother became involved." Steven told the now-sitting family looking at Joan's family.

"This is all of the highest confidentiality; none of you can ever repeat what I'm about to tell you, agreed?" Steven asked. Joan's mother, father, and sister agreed to keep what they were about to learn to themselves.

"The man who ran the C.I.A. before I was brought in thought he was above reproach. So when he thought someone was going against him, and what he thought was best, he would have them killed." Steven started, then Wyatt took over.

"In Jack's case, the man had Jack's mother and father killed in front of him. Then he placed Jack in a program called 'the cradle operation.' This program was thought up by some sick bastards. Jack was placed in this program when he was only four years old. They tortured him for god knows how long until they broke his young mind." Wyatt told Joan's family. Steven watched Mr. and Mrs. O'Driscoll sitting, shocked at what they were hearing. Joan's mother sat silent, her face paled. Katherine wiped tears away before they fell. Joan's father's face was red with a barely contained rage when Steven took the story.

"Jack was tortured with everything they could use once his mind turned in on itself. They started to build another in its place; once this was done, they called Jack John Smyth. This program was thought up by the top men and women in the field of child psychology. They knew what to do to get the best results.

As they built this, John was placed in a school run by this program. His education was academic in the mornings. Then in the afternoon, he was taught how to hunt men and kill. Before he was allowed to go on his first mission, his instructors at this school were all afraid of Jack. He was so fast and strong that he started to hurt most of the male instructors. So at the age of eighteen, Jack was used to hunt and kill a terrorist leader in Iraq. Over the next few years, Jack was the most successful operative ever. The terrorists started to refer to a mysterious killer as the angle of death." When Steven stopped to take a drink of water, Wyatt took over.

"Well, the man who thought up this program was in Hong Kong. He was working for a station chief who had started to take over all the drugs and weapons coming out of Asia. This sick bastard brought Jack to help eliminate any competition. This man and the Hong Kong station chief would tell Jack his target had plans to attack an American or an allied country or installation. Then Jack would do his duty until the day he was to kill a man in Hong Kong. Jack could have killed the man any number of times. Instead, he watched his target as the man had lunch with his wife and young son. It was then Jack knew something was wrong. So he started to research his previous targets and found they were all heads of drug and weapons syndicates. So he ran, trying to get away until the bastards sold him to a corrupt Chinese general. This general placed Jack in a secret prison deep in China by the Tibetan border." Wyatt and Steven watched as Joan's father raised his head. They both saw the man knew who Jack was. Steven raised his hand to stop him from asking any questions.

"In this prison, Jack was tortured again; god almighty, we don't know how he survived. The General and his Assistant tore at Jack every day for hours, and he was kept on a starvation diet for months. When the guards thought Jack was too weak to do anything, he escaped killing any guard in his way. Jack walked naked and with broken feet into the mountains of Tibet, where he was found and taken to some monks who hide in the mountains. There he was helped and brought back from death's door." Steven told the now stunned family.

"Well, this is the part of the story where we two become involved. When Jack was better, the monks said goodbye to him. They even gave him a backpack and some supplies for his hike down the mountain. On his way down, Jack met another man. Tran had just found out his family and village were. Well, everyone and everything in the village was killed one night. Killed by a colonel who had tried to rape Tran's sister. She slashed the man with his own knife ending his raping days." Wyatt told the family as he handed Mr. O'Driscoll a glass of bourbon.

"The two men had a meal together and talked until the stars came out. As Tran said, it seemed to be fate. Tran told us he knew he was going to die avenging his family and village until he met Jack. It was then he thought there might be hope. The two men found the man who killed Tran's family and the General who had held and tortured Jack. Jack and Tran freed the B.B.C. men, and with the journalists, Jack and Tran ran and fought their way out of Asia. Bringing back the story of how there are dark forces at work in China. Once out, Jack used what he had found out during his run to hide all the money his former boss had made from the drug and weapons sales. Jack then turned it over to Richard so the money could help the Unit save people around the world." Steven finished, and by this time, he was sitting and holding his own glass of bourbon. Wyatt and Steven watched as Joan's mother gently took her husband's glass of bourbon. Nobody said anything as the matriarch of the O'Driscolls took a sip from the glass and cleared her throat.

"So this innocent child saw his mother and father butchered by a monster. Then they tortured him so they could turn him into a killer?" She asked.

"Yes, ma'am, the man responsible for it was hunting Jack down in Tibet when Jack found him first," Steven said.

"Well, where is the bastard at?" Mrs. O'Driscoll asked.

"Jack got all the information he wanted out of him, and well, the man is no longer with us," Wyatt told her.

"Well, may the bastard rot in hell; now, why have you told us all of this?" Mrs. O'Driscoll asked as another man walked through the door.

"Hello, my name is Phillip Peters; I work with Jack. I've been trying to help him remember his childhood up to the point they grabbed him."

"Why, why in gods name would you want him to remember what the bastards did to him?" Katherine asked.

"Well, for him to start to heal, you see, Jack was raised to the point when his mother and father were killed. They were very good and loving parents, so his sense of right and wrong was instilled in him early. Now for years, he knew what he was doing was right. Even if he knew the men he was working with were less than desirable. However, it's the way they tore down Jack's young mind, then rebuilt it by installing their programming. It's this programming I want Jack to come to terms with."

"Will he be alright if you can do this? Will he be able to live and be happy with Joan or..." Mr. O'Driscoll never finished his question. He just looked at Phillip with a concerned look.

"Will he be able to lead a normal life?" Phillip asked the question everyone was thinking.

"Absolutely, yes, you see, Jack is about the strongest person I have ever met. His physical stamina is off the chart. However, it's his emotions, his mind. Once he found out what his mother and father called him as a child, his friends started to use his real name. His mind started to find ways around the blocks the others installed in him as a child. We are telling you this because I feel when Jack starts to have a real family again, these blocks, well, these blocks will start to fall like dominos, and I'll need to be there." As Phillip spoke, he watched Mrs. and Mr. O'Driscoll for any sign they were afraid; he never saw any.

"Well, if our Joan has chosen Jack to spend her life with, then he is family." Mr. O'Driscoll stated as he held his wife's hand.

Chapter 43

"WHEN DO YOU THINK THEY will make their move Jack?" Richard asked as he looked out the window into the English night.

"Well, if it were me, I would make my move the next time you stick your head through the curtains," Jack answered as Tran eased Richard back from the window and closed the curtains again.

"I don't think they will come tonight. I believe they will wait until the whole family is together. Then they will attack, hoping to kill everyone." Tran said as he answered Richard's question.

"Well, if it were me, I would have done it the way they are. This has a lot of thought behind it." Joan stated as the others turned and looked at her.

"Let's think about it; we found their man and the encrypted message, and a young child was able to see the picture. From that, we now know their intent, so we sent my family away. So it's just us here in this house, in the middle of a large estate. With suppressed weapons, they can unload, and no one would know." When Joan finished, Richard, Jack, and the others looked at each other and knew Joan was right. It had all been to get these people alone.

"Well, there you have it, boys and girls; we have played right into the hands of the people who want to kill us the most. So instead of sitting around waiting for them to have it all their way, I say we take it to them." August said as he held Victoria's hand.

"Hell, you know we are with ya, you name the time and place, and we'll tear it up." Rick Topper said as the other seals nodded in agreement.

"Ok, well, let's set up and see if we can catch these people before they catch us," Richard said as a plan started to form in his head.

The landing plane had all the proper paperwork, and it was even on time. The lone air traffic controller sitting behind his radar screen at the small airport in Greare, France, listened as the pilot informed him of their impending arrival. The man thought to himself, of course, you are arriving; the flight plan and my radar tells me so. He watched as the private jet settled to the tarmac, slowed, then taxied to a hangar where it was met by French customs and emigration. The ten Chinese men were cleared by customs, and four S.U.V.s sat waiting for the men. An hour later, they were inspecting weapons smuggled into France aboard a fishing trawler owned by an Albanian organized crime family centered in Calais, France.

Once the weapons passed the inspection of the Chinese team, the money was handed over, and the family turned to leave. The four Albanian men never heard the shots as the bullets plowed into their bodies. The last sight the older man saw of his three sons was their bullet-riddled bodies as they bled out on the dock. After the money was recovered from the father. The Chinese leader ordered the others to load everything into the S.U.V.s. He then turned and shot each of the brothers and their father in the head to ensure they were dead.

Standing in the shadow of the forest, the youngest of the Albania family watched her brothers and father being gunned down. The young daughter desperately wanted to rundown and save her brothers. The teenage girl also knew if she was killed on the dock, her mother would be left, never knowing what happened. The daughter sat and watched as the Chinese loaded everything into black S.U.V.s. The leader walked over to her father and brothers, looking down on her family. She watched as he shot each one in the head like they were no more than dogs. The fucker even smiled before he walked back to his men. She could feel the scream of rage and anguish climbing inside her. Looking away, the last child of the family started to run. The daughter never realized she had run home until her mother was helping her through the door. Through her tears, the girl who spent so much time in this home being bounced on her father's knee. Told her mother how her husband and sons had been murdered. To her surprise, her mother stood up and picked up the phone. The girl sat in stunned silence as she listened to her mother tell someone to go and retrieve her fallen husband and sons.

"Mama, what are we going to do?" Alexandria asked.

"We are going to get our men back, then we will hunt these Chinese bastards down and skin them alive." Her mother answered. That night Alexandria helped her mother as she washed the blood from the bodies of her brothers and father. Then all four men were cremated, and their ashes spread over the waters they smuggled in.

"Now we hunt the animals who did this to our family." Her mother stated as the sun started to rise over the trees. Twenty men stood around the fire pit in the backyard, and each one took an oath to avenge the family.

Chapter 44

GETTING THE WEAPONS into England was easier than even the leader of the Chinese squad could have hoped for. After taking the Euro tunnel, they checked in with English customs and then were let go on their way with nothing more than a paperwork check. Smiling at the lack of security, the leader thought. Killing the people on his list would be easy, then he and his men would be back in China in time for his brother's wedding.

Richard's phone rang; Jack and Joan watched as their friend and boss answered, then nodded his head. Smiling, Richard thanked whoever was on the other end of the line and then pressed the end call button.

"Well, a group of ten Chinese men just crossed in from France through the tunnel. If they are our killers, they should be here in about 6 hours if they drive straight through." Richard told the others. Jack nodded and looked at Joan.

"Well, what do you think? Will they come straight here and try to do the deed?" Jack watched as Joan thought it over.

"No, if they stick to s.o.p, they will start by doing fresh intel work. Then report any deviations from the intel they have been receiving from their man on site. If all is the same, then they will proceed." Joan informed the others.

"And if something changes or is different than the intel?" Ricky asked.

"Well, it goes one of two ways. The first way will be they kill their man and return to China. Then they wait until they get another chance. Number two is they kill their man and then firebomb this place. Then go back to China and wait for word on whether we survived. If we survived, then they wait until they get another chance." Joan answered Rick's question.

"Either way, we have to get these guys before they get us," Richard said as the others agreed.

John watched their Chinese surveillance as he started to pack what little personal belongings he had brought with him.

"Hey, in the house," John called over his radio.

"Yeah, what's up, John?" August asked.

"Well, our would-be get-smart is looking as if he's going to bug out. I mean, the dude is packing personal shit and acting real sketchy." John answered, still watching the lone Chinese man.

"Tell John to grab that man before he gets away," Richard ordered. Jack looked at his friend and then smiled. Turning, he and Tran ran out of the room and then out the back door. Both men sprinted across the backyard heading to where they knew John would be.

"Don't let our peeping Tom leave. Jack and Tran are on the way to you now." August told John.

"Roger that." Was the only answer John gave before he started to move. He began to move, knowing he couldn't wait until Jack and Tran arrived. Their Chinese surveillance would be gone by then.

The house had gone quiet days ago, and now he couldn't hear anything. All the cameras around the estate were still working. It was the people in the house; they stopped going into the fat one's office. Now they stayed in the rooms at the front of the house. The cameras covering that part of the house could see clearly now that the large tent and awning had been removed. He could make out the people moving around. He watched as the curtains were pulled shut for the night. This was his time to send the last intel report then he could leave before the team arrived. He knew they would kill everybody here, even him, if they were ordered to, and he didn't trust Beijing. Looking around, the lone Chinese surveillance man pressed send on his last encrypted email to Beijing. Turning, he started to back out of the trailer. He stepped right into a sleeper hold by John Bowen.

John was so much taller than his target. The watcher was lifted off his feet, dangling in John's arms, causing more pressure on his carotid arteries. It only took a few seconds for the man to lose consciousness. Tran and Jack found John walking back through the woods with the Chinese man draped over his shoulder.

"Dead?" Tran asked, hoping John hadn't been forced to kill their target in self-defense.

"Sleeping," John answered with a smile.

"He's gonna have one hell of a headache when he wakes up," John added, patting the unconscious man on the leg.

Sitting in the kitchen, Jack and Tran, along with Richard and August, watched as the spy started to show signs of recovering. They watched as their watcher slowly came to, only to realize he had been captured. It was then he realized he had failed his wife and daughter.

"You have to let me go. He will kill them if he finds out you have me." The panicked Asian man stated to Richard.

"Who will kill whom?" Richard asked, seeing the genuine concern on the man's face.

"My wife and daughter, the general will order them killed," Quan answered.

"Where are they right now," Richard asked as he held a cellar phone.

"At our small apartment in Oxbridge, men are watching them encase I fail; they are to be killed." Quan didn't know why he was telling these people what he was. Quan was just hoping someone would save his family.

"I'll call Scott at MI6; he'll get them out and would be happy to get his hands on their team for questioning," Richard said as he left the room. Tran helped Quan sit up straighter and gave him some herbal tea to help with the headache he knew the man had.

"You are lucky to have been sent to watch us. These men will help your family; they don't expect anything in return." Tran told the scared surveillance man.

"I do have some information for them; when they have my family safe, I'll tell them what targets the teams are going after and the timelines," Quan told Tran, who nodded.

Quan watched Jack whenever he entered the room. He had been told Jack was an assassin. He was also told if he was caught, Jack would kill him. Then his family would be killed for his failure.

"Why do you fear my friend so much that you shake when he comes nearby?" Tran asked.

"I was told he would kill me if I was caught. They said he is an assassin, a killer without any compassion." Quan told Tran, who smiled at the scared man.

"Well, I can tell you that is not true. That man there hates himself when he has to take another life. Even if that other is the worst kind of person. He has saved more people than any other person I know of. He will not hurt you or your family." When Tran finished, he stood and then left Quan alone with Jack.

"Would you like something to drink?" Jack asked the frightened man. Quan looked at Jack and shook his head. Quan thought he might have insulted Jack and quickly changed his mind and started to nod. To Jack, it looked as if Quan had a mild palsy attack.

"Are you alright, pal? It's only water," Jack said as he offered a bottle of water.

"Yes, I'm sorry; I didn't want to spy on you or your friends. It is just that my background in surveillance and my work at the offices of the Ministry of Defence forced me to do this. They said if I didn't, they would kill my wife and daughter in front of me." Quan explained.

"I know, and we don't blame you for any of this. We know how the men who are forcing you to do this work. We also know they wouldn't think twice about killing your family." Jack told Quan. Jack knew he couldn't offer comfort to a father waiting to hear if his daughter and wife were safe. All he could do was be here for the man. An hour later, Richard walked back into the room.

"We have them. Your lovely wife and daughter are safe. They are at MI6 headquarters having dinner and waiting for you. Your wife is an ingenious lady. She figured it all out about a week after you left. She has been taking pictures of the team watching her and your daughter. She also gave the men at MI6 their schedule. Their surveillance team was picked up as their order of pizzas arrived." When Richard finished, he opened a laptop, and on the screen were Quan's wife and daughter smiling at him. The man left the room so he could speak with his wife and daughter. A few minutes later, the door opened, and Quan looked at the men who had helped rescue the loves of his life.

"They have sent ten men to England and five to Ireland." Quan started as he opened his laptop.

"The men going to Ireland are to kill the family of the head of your security. The men coming here have two jobs; the first is to kill all of you. Then to invade and expose something in Scotland. This house is the first stop for them. They are to start the attack after they kill me, and the team in London was to kill my family." Quan told Richard and the others.

"So now we have the London team, and we need to stop the other team here," Richard said as he looked at his watch.

"So if they haven't run into any delays, we should have about four hours left before they arrive to find Quan no longer at his post. Then they will call the London team and find the line is no longer in service. So we either take them at the caravan, or we wait until they start to pull out, and we take them then." Jack said as he looked at the seals.

The team leader watched as the English night passed by his window. The second and third SUVs followed close behind his. Bau knew in four hours, he would be standing over the dead bodies of men who obstructed his leaders. Bau knew his leaders, the men he pledged his life to, and their plan to gain supremacy over China and North Korea. All the men in the suv with Bau knew they were on a path to make China the only superpower in the world. Once these people were dead, his leaders were going to assassinate the leaders in China, along with the whining shit Kim Jong-Un. Once these assassinations were completed, a new country would be formed with North Korea. The new China would force North and South Korea to become one under a new flag at last. The Americans will be powerless to do anything about it.

"These men who are coming here to kill all of us are not Chinese," Quan told Richard and the others.

"They aren't, then what are they?" Richard asked.

"They are North Korean; this is what the world doesn't know. What the world would never suspect, Pyongyang has been seeding the highest levels of China's military and government for the last fifty years. The general, Pak Ming, is really North Korean. He was sent to live with the Mings when he was a boy. His mother and father were assured Pak was from a family with a son. The Mings couldn't have children, so when presented with a baby. They raised him as their own; when Pak was in university, he learned about his real origins." As Quan told Richard and the others about the twisted plans of the group's leaders, they all stood stunned.

"He and the team hold no loyalty to either government, only to this Ming and the three others who make up the group, the real group." When Quan told Jack and Richard, along with the others, about the killers and who they really were. Richard and Jack turned and looked at the others in the room. Everybody stood silent, looking at Quan.

"How did you ever find this out?" Joan asked him.

"Well, that's the easy part, I'm North Korean by birth, and I was part of this group. I planted many listening devices in offices all over Beijing. I always listened to the recordings, and one of the offices I had a device in was the General's hotel suit." Quan answered.

"My god, man, do you still have this recording?" Richard asked, hoping beyond hope Quan hadn't destroyed it.

"Yes, it is on my laptop, hidden in a game called the end of Times." When Quan told Richard the name of the game, he called Tosh and explained to her what he wanted. A few moments later, the two hacker girls walked into the room carrying their laptops and showed Richard the files.

"These will help shut down the group; the only drawback is it will save that spoiled man-child sitting in Pyongyang," Richard told Quan.

"I have a question. How in the hell did they find out about Scotland?" Jack asked Richard. Turning, Richard looked at Quan and was about to ask if he knew when the man nodded his head.

"They don't exactly know what is up there." Quan started.

"The group knows something exists. A few years ago, one of our trawlers was off the north coast of Scotland. A helicopter was seen flying with no lights on. The crew of this trawler watched as this helicopter landed on a barren island. This happened after you escaped through Tibet and India." Quan said, nodding to Jack and Tran.

"So they saw a chopper land; what of it?" August asked.

"Once the trawler reported this chopper, it was ordered to stand offshore and watch the island. Not long after, more choppers were seen, always at night and in bad weather." As Quan told Richard and the others how the island was discovered.

"The choppers seem to be ferrying people back and forth. The leaders of the group think you have a secret lab or base. General Pak Ming believes you have created a super soldier because of him and how he escaped after Trang interrogated you." Quan motioned to Jack when he mentioned the dead General.

"Also, he was seen on one of the choppers," Quan told them.

"I have to get these to Wyatt and Steven. They will know how to get the leader of China to listen to these." As Richard said, leaving the room with Tish and Tosh behind him, Tran smiled at Quan.

"You will be with your family soon," Joan said.

"I can not repay any of you for my family's life," Quan said to the men, along with Joan and Victoria. As they stood in the grand foyer of the house, Quan watched a car pull up in front of the house. Richard and the others watched the man run to the car. It was a run to his family more than it was away from them.

"How in the hell did you get these, wait, don't answer that; I don't want to know," Wyatt said as he watched Steven call the White House emergency line. Wyatt could hear Steven explaining why he was calling. They needed to wake the president and have him meet Wyatt and himself in the situation room. Thirty minutes later, the president of the united states was sitting in his customary chair at the head of the table, his hair still tussled by his pillow.

"I don't want to know how you guys came to get these. I just want to wait until they are confirmed authentic." The president said.

Chapter 45

THEY ALL WATCHED A man working on a computer. They watched the technician as he looked up from his laptop with a shocked look on his face.

"They are as real as it gets; the voice is an exact match along with speech patterning. The men speaking on these recordings are General Pak Ming, internal security minister Ping Wong, Admiral Wo Dong, and multi Billionaire Sing Woo." The specialist told them he turned his computer around so everyone could see how the men's voices matched other known recordings made during public speeches.

"Well, I've got a call to place." The president said. The man packed his computer up, nodded to the others in the room, and left. It was the strangest call the president had ever made, and the leader of China was more than a little skeptical. When he asked how the president came to have this information, the storyline of a hacker trying to break into the Pentagon was given.

"During the raid on this person's house, the computers were taken, and our people found these. We have been having good relations for some time, and I wanted you to have these. I know you'll want to take care of this. My people are sending them to your people now so you can verify them for yourself. I hope the next time we speak, it will be about fishing. I know a beautiful river where we can fly fish for trout." The president said.

"That I will look forward to; good night, Mr president." President Chang said, then ended the call.

"Tell me it is a lie; tell me this is something cooked up by the Americans," Chang ordered. A man looked up from his computer and shook his head.

"Sir, I'm sorry, the Americans have it right; it is indeed the General and the Minister along with the Admiral and Mr. Woo; it is a 100% match, there can be no doubt." The technician told his leader. Chang looked out at the courtyard and wondered how far this cancer had spread through his government. Turning, he looked at the man still sitting behind his computer and ordered him to send his personal guard. A moment later, Chang's personal guard stood waiting for his orders.

"We have a problem," Chang said to his guard and friend.

"Ok, who is the problem?" The guard asked back.

"Spies, North Korean spies, you will not believe who they are." The Chairman said.

"It doesn't matter who they are; spies do not survive in China." The guard stated.

"Right now, they are meeting across the courtyard in that building. General Pak Ming, Admiral Wo Dong, internal security minister Ping Wong, and Mr. Woo. They are conspiring to take over this government." Chang knew a friend and guard had left his office. The man didn't say or ask anything. One moment he was standing by the sofa. The next moment the door softly closed behind him. Chang never saw his guard walk across the courtyard of the central government offices. Chang's guard walked through the basement, down a long, darkened corridor leading to another building, then into a stairwell of another.

The guard knew which room the traitors were in, thanks to a vast security system monitoring every hallway. As he moved through the building, cameras would fail. When he would leave that building, the cameras would work fine. Chang watched the building across from his office. He knew no camera would pick up his guard as the man saved China. The four men never heard the door open in the next room. The leaders of the group had no idea they had been found out. Each man thought they were safe from discovery until the first bullet from Chang's guard blew apart the skull of the billionaire Mr. Woo.

The others scrambled to get out of the way when the guard stepped into the room. The minister was the second man to fall to the guard's gun. The minister was reaching for his cell phone to call for help when the second bullet fired by the guard blew most of the left side of his head into an ice bucket, holding a half-empty bottle of wine.

The Admiral dove over a chair and was crawling, trying to get out of the room, when the guard fired a third time. This bullet found the Admiral crushing his brainstem, plowing its way through the soft tissue. Then it hit the hard bone of the spine being diverted up into the brain like the others death was instant.

The General tried to leap behind a sofa when the fourth bullet fired by the guard hit Ming in the chest. The force of the impact turned the man slamming him to the floor. General Ming could feel himself dying. He could see the guard standing over him, smiling.

"You have failed. If I could, I would go to your family and wipe them from the earth. Know this. You and this other filth will be buried in a landfill someplace." The General watched as the guard raised his weapon for the last time and shot him in the face.

The guard slipped quietly back into his leader's office. When Chang turned from the window, he found his friend and guard standing at his usual post beside the sofa.

"It is done; a team will have to be sent to the minister's office suit there is a bit of a mess; I do apologize for that." His guard stated.

"You have saved China from a terrible crime; there is no mess big enough you need to apologize for." Chairman Chang told his friend.

Chapter 46

THE SARGENT MAJOR WATCHED through his starlight scope as five Asian men filtered down the street. He and his team watched as the men moved from building to building, slowly making their way to the O'Driscoll house. From the way the men advanced, he could tell they were well-trained. The Sargent Major smiled; he knew his men were better than the men they waited for. He loved the little town of Baltimore in the county of Cork; he could smell the ocean. This Sargent Major knew Joan; he was Joan's trainer when she joined the special armed services. For these men to go after her innocent family like this was, in his and his team's eyes, the most cowardly thing he could think of.

"Alright, men, when the fuckers get to the line, kill them." The Sargent Major ordered. The line the Sargent Major spoke of was the cloths line Joan's mother still used to dry her linens on during the warm days of summer. As the last would-be killer of Joan's family crossed under the line, the men opened fire from the upstairs windows. It was so fast and brutal that the Asian team never had a chance to return fire before they lay dead in the back garden. Once, the Irish team made sure the killers were well and truly dead. A call was made moments later a van pulled up.

Men helped with the bodies, and the house was put back as it was before the night's activity had taken place. Once the team left, another van pulled up to the house. A cleaning crew went over to the house to remove the smell of burnt gunpowder from the automatic weapons, and any stray brass missed by the team was picked up.

"Your mother and father's house is safe, Joan," Richard said as he thanked whoever he was talking to on his cell phone. Joan hugged Richard and kissed his cheek.

"Now we have to get our team, and then we can go on the hunt for this group." Richard was saying when another phone warbled to life on the table. Everyone in the room knew this phone was encrypted, and only a handful of people had the number. Walking over to the telephone, Richard looked at Jack and mouthed Wyatt's name.

"How are you tonight, Wyatt?" Richard asked as he answered the phone.

"Well, I'm getting better, Richard, and so is Steven. A word from Beijing is that three very high-ranking officials and one very rich and powerful businessman died tonight. It seems their plane crashed in the Makan desert no survivors were found. The bodies have been recovered; however, due to the severity of the crash only way to make a positive identity check is through DNA." Wyatt told Richard.

"That is a shame; well, send my condolences," Richard said, then hung up the phone. Turning, Richard looked at his phone and called the car carrying Quan to his family in London.

"The four men who had your family held and forced you to spy on us here are dead. They were killed by the Chinese government after it had been found out that they were trying to overthrow it. So because you helped us and others tonight, our government is offering you asylum." The others felt good when they heard how grateful Quan was for the chance to stay here and for his daughter to be truly free.

"Can we do something about Quan's trailer? Can we rig another explosive? It would take out most of the team coming here?" Richard asked.

"You bet we can. I can pack ball bearings around it so those not caught in the blast will be caught by the shrapnel." John Bowen offered.

"It's not nice. It will have to be done to end this quickly." Jack said as he and August agreed.

Bau knew he and his men were close to their targets when the roads turned from four-lane highways to the two-lane country road they now traveled on. He watched the GPS locator leading his team to the small trailer of the man his leader has watching the unit leaders. Bau's orders are to kill this man and then call a team in London; they would kill the surveillance man's family. Then he and his team were to bomb the house and kill any who tried to escape; they were not to get into a firefight with these people. Once they were done here, he and his men were to go to a small island in Scotland to see if they could breach an installation there.

"It's done," John said as he entered the house.

"How many did you get made and planted?" Jack asked as John took a bottle of water.

"Five made, four planted around the trailer, one in the trees of the laneway. All are rigged to impact tremblers. A step near any one of the devices will set it off. The blast wave from the first one will trigger the others." John reported. Jack and August nodded, knowing John had covered all the bases.

"Ok, when things go boom, we wait; then, when MI6 gets here, we head in to see what's what," August said as the team rechecked their weapons.

Bau looked at the GPS as it beeped to indicate a right turn into the lane. This lane would take him and his men to the trailer, where the man who had been watching the people was. The leader of the hit team wondered why the group leaders wanted this surveillance man dead. Bau told his driver to stop the suv next to the man's car. The second suv stopped ten meters behind. He could see a light from the trailer, and he decided his men would just shred the tin trailer with automatic fire, killing the man without having to hear him beg for his life.

Chapter 47

IT HAPPENED FASTER than Jack or the others thought it would. The first explosion caused Richard and his sister Victoria to jump up from their chairs. Victoria whirled around, looking for the cause, when August grabbed her hand and smiled at her.

"That was a lot faster than I thought it would be. They must have been closer than we allowed for." Richard commented.

Bau and his men line up five meters from the side of the trailer. When he snapped his fingers, the eight men opened fire. They were engulfed in flames and flying debris the eight men died instantly. The second suv was hit by another explosion on its left side. The ball bearings blowing through the driver's side of the suv tore metal and flesh to shreds. The steel projectiles smashed bones to power before tearing off into the forest to imbed themselves into trees. Lying beside his suv, the Bau could see his men were all dead. He hated the surveillance man now. Bau knew Quan told his targets they were on the way; it had to be him. Bau's last thought wasn't of his family. It was of the surveillance man's family. He hoped they would suffer, especially the daughter. She should be made to suffer for this.

Jack, Tran, August, and the Seals readied themselves when they heard the helicopter over the house. They watched it land on the front lawn, and four men climbed out, each wearing a suit and carrying a briefcase.

"Sir, we are from the home office. The prime minister sends his regards." The older of the four said, shaking Richards's hand.

"Well, thank him for me when you see him next, please; come in, gentlemen." Each man gave a slight bow to Richard and a deeper bow to Victoria as they entered. At the same time, Jack and August, with John, Ricky, and Angel, slipped out the back door and made their way to Quan's trailer.

The devastation was more than any of the men expected, except for John. Whole trees were blown apart from the ball bearings John used. As the men entered the small clearing, they found what was left of the ten men sent to kill them. Most of what could be identified as human were severed arms or the lower part of a torso. The trailer was gone; it had been vaporized when the propane tanks were ruptured by the ball bearings as they ripped through the trailer; it all added to the carnage. The first suv sat on four flat tires, the passenger side door open, and a mostly intact body lay outside it. The left arm was missing, and what was left of the lower abdomen spilled its contents onto the ground.

The second suv was parked right next to the fifth device John planted and took the full force of the blast and the flying ball bearings. When Angel knelt down to see if there were any who survived. He quickly surmised surviving while having your head removed by the flying bearings was impossible. The men stood in the center of the carnage and looked at one another, then turned and quietly left the clearing heading back to the house.

"Well, that's that," Jack reported when Richard came out on the veranda.

"Bad?" Richard asked.

"For them, it was fast; they never knew what hit them," August told the others.

"I'll call Wyatt and Steven and let them know it's safe for your mother and father to come home," Richard told Joan.

"If it's alright, I would like to be there when they get home?" Joan asked.

"I think that's a grand idea. Both you and Jack should be waiting for them." Richard returned.

"I am going to see Jiao and my godson," Tran announced.

"Is everything ok?" Jack asked Tran.

"Yes, everything is fine. I just wish to hold my godson, to be around his innocent smile. Jiao was telling me of a group of Tibetan ex-pats who met by her place, and she wanted me to go. I think she is trying to set me up." Tran smiled as he thought about meeting people who could speak his native language.

"So it's official, we are all on vacation until further notice," Richard told everybody. He watched as Victoria and August stood off in the corner and discussed how they would break up their time. Victoria wanted to introduce him to the rest of her family and friends. August agreed as long as they had time to fly back to Texas and for her to meet his family.

"Well, what are you going to do, Richard?" Jack asked.

"Oh, I have too much to do to take any time off. I have to plan for our futures together," Richard said as his sister turned to him.

"Damn it Dickie, you have never taken a vacation, not from the time Father sent you to Eaton. You know he never thought you were lazy, and even Father took time off." Victoria told Richard. Richard smiled and reached out to take Victoria's hands in his.

"I know, however, I do have mountains of paperwork to get through. We are on our own now; I have to prepare all new forms so when we need something from the four countries who support us if we need it. Also, I have to bring in our ships and whatever other assets we have in the field." Richard told his sister.

"Well, I'm staying to help him out," Eugene said as he entered the room.

"And we don't have any other family except for Eugene and you guys, so we're going to stay also." The two girls said as they walked in behind Eugene.

"And besides, when Tran is done with his visit with Jiao, we want to keep studying with him. It's fun and relaxing, and we can run with Richard every day." Tish offered.

"Well, Joan is going to make sure her family gets settled back into their home, so I'll be here to help keep you from straying, old boy," Jack said, then caught an elbow from Joan.

"Ah, excuse me here, mister Jack; you will be in Ireland with me getting things ship shape for Mom and Dad to come home to," Joan told Jack.

"As it turns out, I have a previous engagement I let slip my mind," Jack answered in his best Irish accent to everybody chuckling. The rest of the night was spent dealing with the aftermath of the explosions at the trailer in the small clearing and the cleanup of the area. The sun started to rise over the trees to the east of the house when Jack and Joan left, heading for her parent's house in county Cork. Victoria and August headed back to London to visit with family and friends for a few days before flying to Texas. They told Richard they would be back in ten days. Rick and John left with Victoria and August; they were flying back to the States for a vacation with family. Angel was an orphan. He had no one to go home to, so he decided to stay and keep up Eugene's physical therapy.

Chapter 48

SITTING IN THE DARK of a house in the south of Ireland wasn't his idea of retirement. He told the General twice he wasn't interested in one last job. The old fucker told him he would let the authorities in on his new identity. Also, the four million euros the General placed in his secret account helped change his mind, so here he was, waiting to kill some man with a scar on the left side of his face. When he first arrived at the house, he could still smell the blood at the back of the house. He watched as a man stopped a truck with a tank on it and sprayed the lawn and flowers. Now the coppery scent of the blood was gone, clean up complete.

"So everything is fine, you and Dad can come home, yes Mom, we will be there, yes I said we, as in Jack too. Mom, you don't have to cook a big dinner. No, I'm not telling you what to do in your house. I'm just saying we are going to be happy to see you, Dad, Katherine, and Lilly, that's all. You don't have to go through the trouble. Ok, I'll ask him." Joan said, exasperated, holding the phone away from her ear; she turned and asked Jack.

"Would you rather have a turkey or roast beef for your first meal? I'll do you in if you say something else." She warned him.

"Turkey is grand," Jack answered with a Scottish accent this time, to which Joan glared.

"Yes, fine, Mom, I'll get them; no, I won't forget; I love you to tell Dad I love him, and we'll see you soon." Joan smiled at Jack, then walked past him slapping his butt.

"You know you were no help, Mister." She said, laughing.

"I know, but it was fun." He answered.

"So you are going to be alright, Richard; no joking, you will call if anything feels the least little bit off," Jack said as he looked at Richard and Eugene.

"Yes, if Angel or Eugene have the littlest inkling something isn't right, we will leave right away and call you; I give you my word," Richard promised.

The assassin knew the team in London had failed to kill the woman and the girl. He watched as the team from MI6 grabbed them for the team going to the house outside Gwynfe in the Brecon Beacons national park. The assassin never heard if that team were successful or had met the same fate as the London team. He wasn't told about the team sent here; he knew what must have happened to them.

Jack and Joan took Tran to the train station. It was only a three-hour ride to Jiao and Scott's place. For Jack, he felt like he was abandoning his friend. When he told Tran how he thought he wanted to drive him to see the baby, Tran laughed.

"You could never abandon me, little brother; you don't have it in you. Now I want you to go and have a good time with Joan. I will have my phone so we can talk anytime; remember, we are brothers, family." Tran shook Jack's hand, then turned and walked into the train station. The drive to Liverpool was fun for Jack. He watched the road and held Joan's hand as the English countryside sped past outside the car. Jack stood holding Joan on the pier, waiting for the ferry to take them to her parent's house. He was amazed when they boarded. Sharing a sleeper birth shocked Jack, and he laughed when Joan showed him their room. In his mind, Jack thought it would be like a cruise ship with one queen size bed. On this ferry, their birth had two small cots attached to each wall.

"It's going to be hard to get romantic on these beds." Jack laughed.

"Oh, I'm sure you'll figure it out," Joan answered as she turned on the shower.

Tran sat and watched the English countryside fly past the window of his train car. He was excited to see Jiao and Scott though he was more excited to see the baby. People around him read or played games on their cell phones. This was something Tran could never do; it seemed such a waste of time when one could be meditating. The train started to slow as the station came into view; soon, people were standing to get their bags from overhead. Tran could see Jiao and Scott standing with his godson Scott Jr. They called the baby by his middle name Tran, and he would smile. He loved the boy and had come to think of him as his grandson. As the train stopped and the other passengers stood with their belongings.

Tran noticed one man seemed overly interested in him and the people he was there to meet. Tran didn't know why; for some reason, this rough-looking Spanish man appeared out of place on the train. As Tran gathered his things, he watched as the Spaniard kept watching him. Just when Tran was about to ask if he could help the man with something, the Spaniard pulled a knife and tried to stab Tran in the chest.

The attack was sloppy, and Tran had easily stepped back from the thrust. Others near the attacker screamed and started to rush for the exit. Tran sidestepped another attack from the Spaniard and turned slightly to ensure he wasn't being driven into another attacker to his rear. When Tran was sure this man was working alone, he turned and faced the would-be killer, then waited for his opening.

Jiao watched as the man attacked Tran. She looked around to see if Scott and her baby were being stocked by another attacker. Jiao wanted desperately to run onto the train and help Tran. Jiao knew she would be in the way and could get Tran killed.

The killer wasn't very skilled in his method of attacking when the stab and thrust hadn't worked for him. The attacker turned to the slash, hoping to cut his prey. Tran waited, then with a final slash, he drove the stiffened fingers of his left hand into the right eye socket of his attacker. Tran felt the resistance of the man's eyeball as he drove his fingers in deeper. Tran felt the eyeball relent and pop under the force. The man screamed, dropping his knife. The attacker grabbed his face, exposing his throat. Tran saw this and drove his right hand into the bobbing Adam's apple of the killer crushing the man's windpipe. Tran watched as the Spaniard sank to his knees, then onto this side dying. He never looked back. Tran just wanted to get to Jiao and the baby. As he walked down the aisle, he saw the reflection of the Spaniard. Tran hated someone who forced him to kill when he was so close to others and children. Taking out his cell phone, he called Richard and explained what had happened. Tran knew he would have to explain to authorities how the man ended up dead.

"Of course, go with the police. I'll have someone waiting for you when you get to the station." Richard told Tran. Richard started to pick up another cell phone. Tran waited for the police to arrive, and he explained what had happened. Two other officers went and checked if the attacker was armed and beyond medical help, as Tran said. Once the officers came back and confirmed the other man was indeed dead. Tran was escorted to one of the idling police cars and placed in the back seat while officers interviewed the other passengers. Jiao and Scott sat in the train station and talked to a detective about what they saw. The other officers and the detective stood in a circle and reviewed the interviews.

"Come out, sir. The other officers and I talked to the passengers. They all say the same thing, the man attacked you for no reason, and you only defended yourself, in doing so, were forced to kill him." The detective told Tran.

"I believe them and you. Also, the cameras in the train car tell the same story. Do you have any idea why this man wanted to hurt you?" The detective asked.

"No sir, I don't. Until a few weeks ago, I was under a doctor's care for post-surgery of a brain tumor; I've just come to visit my godson and family." Tran said as he stood next to the detective.

"Well, sir, I have all your information, and if I need you to answer any more questions, I'll be in contact." The detective told Tran as he shook his hand. Jiao ran to hug Tran as Scott pushed Jr in the stroller.

"I have to call Richard; we need to warn Jack," Tran told Jiao as he hugged her.

"Richard, the detective didn't arrest me. The people stayed to tell the police what had happened. He said he may want to talk to me again, though. Have you called Jack to warn him to be careful?"

"Yes, all I keep getting is his infuriating voicemail with that idiotic English accent he puts on," Richard told Tran.

Tran smiled; he remembered the day Jack recorded it, telling him he had hoped Richard called so he could hear it first.

"Don't give up, Richard. I have a bad feeling," Tran said as he ended the call and tried to call Jack himself.

Chapter 49

AUGUST WATCHED VICTORIA as she picked out a suit and tie for him. He thought she was going to pick out a nice dark blue or black suit. He was surprised when she came back with a tan suit, a light cotton shirt, and a darker tie with oxfords.

"I would have thought a proper English lady would have preferred a dark blue or black suit." He teased.

"With that beautiful native skin color, never," Victoria said as she stood on her tiptoes and kissed him. Victoria noticed August turned her so he could see out the front window.

"What's wrong? What are you looking for?" She asked, trying to get a look at the street.

"Do you trust me?" August asked.

"From the very first moment, I saw you in that basement standing there with your hands up," Victoria told him.

"Then trust me when I say I'll be right back," August told her and turned and slipped out the back of the tailors. He held the back door from slamming and giving away his presents. August watched as the man who'd been watching Victoria and him shop all afternoon stood at the corner of the clothier. The small pile of cigarette butts spoke of his need for nicotine rather than how long they had been in the shop. August was about to grab the stalker from behind when a shadow passed over the wall next to him. Turning, August found he was in the presents of five spec opp soldiers; the leader smiled and winked at him. August answered the wink with a sweeping gesture of his arm and a salute.

The man never knew what had happened. One second he was waiting for a member of the royal family. This member of the royal family was the sister of the fat man who headed up some unit. The next, he had a bag pulled over his head, and he was on the ground being zipped, tied, and carried off to god knows where. In less than a minute, August walked in the shop's front door to a thankful Victoria.

"So what was it?" She asked.

"Well, it's hard to say; I think we owe your brother a thank you," August told her as he gathered their packages and thanked the shopkeeper.

The recorded voice woke Joan; she didn't hear what was being said. She knew they were docking. She looked at Jack as he was lying on his cot, staring at her.

"Is everything alright?" She asked, looking around.

"Everything couldn't be better." He answered as he leaned over to kiss her. As he was about to kiss her again, his cell phone chirped several times, telling him he had more than one voicemail.

"Something's up." He said as Joan started to get dressed. Turning, Joan looked at him as Jack listened to the first message.

"What is it?" She asked.

"Richard said someone is still targeting us. Tran was attacked on the train. He's fine; he was forced to kill his attacker. Also, Victoria and August were being followed. Richard had a team from MI6 grab the guy; they have him now." Jack reported.

"Do you think someone will be after us?" Joan asked, knowing the answer to her question.

"I going to operate under the assumption we are targets. I'll lay money; whoever it is will be at or near your parent's place right now." Jack told her as he picked up their bags.

"What are we going to do?" Joan asked.

"First thing is somehow to get a hold of your parents and have them diverted to someplace else. There we can have a security detail waiting for them. Second, I'm going to their house and find whoever is waiting, and either they will listen to reason, or I'm going to kill them." Jack said. Joan knew trying to stop him was out of the question.

"Let's get going; we can talk about your plan on the way," Joan said as Jack held the door for her. To Jack, it seemed to take forever to get off the ferry and on the road. Then he was forced to deal with the traffic caused by the ferry landing. To Jack, every mile seemed to take longer and longer until they were out of town and in the open country heading south.

Chapter 50

THE SUN HAD RISEN OVER the water hours ago; his contact on the ferry had called him. The daughter was coming home, so he thought her family would be along anytime. He was about to unwrap a sandwich he had made the night before when he heard the voices of two women walking down the path leading to the back door.

"Well, I know she said she was going to the bingo. I think her sister in Canada took ill, so we'll just crack a couple of windows to keep the place fresh until she comes home." The killer heard one of the old ladies say as she looked under a potted plant for a hidden key. Sitting upstairs, he thought about killing these two; he wasn't getting paid for them. So if they didn't find him or posed a threat to him, he would let them be on their way. If they got nosey well, then he would have no choice.

Joan pointed to the roundabout for the R595 road. It would take them to Baltimore; it ran through the Skibbereen golf course. Then through the village of Lockahane, Joan knew when they reached the town where she grew up, Jack would have to turn at the castle. Then her mother and father's house was the third on the seaward side of Castle end road.

The two women opened a window on either side of the house so a breeze could flow through the rooms. They never ventured upstairs, they came to do a small kindness, and he let them live. The assassin watched as the two old ladies left, placing the hidden key back where they had found it.

Joan was about to tell Jack to slow down when they hit the roundabout. Instead of going around the way the traffic control was meant to be used, Jack cut the circle in half. When Jack entered R595, Joan glanced over at the speedometer. They were entering a secondary road at ninety-two miles per hour.

"We are going to get there long before Mom and Dad know anything was ever wrong; you can slow down a bit," Joan said as Jack passed a slower car.

"I have a bad feeling; I can't explain; it's bad," Jack said, not taking his eyes off the road. The golf club flew past the windows as Jack managed to get the car past the one hundred miles per hour mark on the speedometer, then the signs for Lockahane came into view.

"Jack, you have got to slow down; this is a small village. Children cross the roads on their bikes and old ladies." Joan warned, then gave a sigh of relief as she felt Jack slowing down. She watched as their speed dropped to fifty miles per hour, then to the posted thirty miles per hour.

Once they left, the village of Lockahane Jack sped back up to sixty miles per hour. For some reason, he didn't feel the need to go any faster. Jack knew the killer would be there. He wouldn't have to worry about this killer popping up in a month or a year. No, Jack knew the killer would be waiting for him and Joan.

"I don't know why or how, but I know the person they sent to kill your family is a professional. He has never been caught because most people would never think twice about him." Jack told Joan.

"Ok, so how are we to know him if he has been at this for years and the best law enforcement officers couldn't catch him. How the hell are we going to?" Joan asked, knowing they were heading into a trap.

"That's easy; the bastards who set this up know me. They know my weakness and my strength. They came after my only weaknesses. My friends and my family they've been studying for me. This is going to sound crazy. I would bet they somehow got their hands on my personal files." Jack said as they passed the first sign for Baltimore.

"I'll call Richard to see if he has any luck diverting the plane," Joan told Jack.

"I have talked to the pilot. He has diverted to the Cork Airport. It was the best he could do on such short notice. We are on our way right now on the other plane and will be landing in moments." Richard told Joan.

Jack could see the castle which gave the town of Baltimore its name. He switched off the car's headlights and coasted to a stop in the parking lot.

"It's going to be on foot from here, and it will take time; I'll need you to be our eyes behind us," Jack said to Joan; they left the car and cut through backyards. No one saw Jack and Joan as they hopped over fences separating the backyards of the people in this quiet little town in the south of Ireland.

The assassin had no fear of the man he was here to kill. The general told him this man was a traitor. He escaped justice by running to the British, so he was doing the world a favor.

"That's it, the house with the yellow trim and the flower garden is the house I grew up in." Joan pointed out to Jack.

"Ok, I need you to stay here; stop anybody from investigating what's about to happen," Jack told Joan, then leaned in and kissed her.

Chapter 51

HE COULD STILL HEAR the seagulls flying over the harbor, crying for their share of the catch. The sound of a car's tires humming on the pavement caught his ears. Sitting in the dark of the house, he could let his senses reach out. The killer could hear everything except Jack, who was at that very moment standing under the open window of a room where Joan spent her childhood. Where she had faced her demons and won. Standing under the open window, Jack could smell the killer's soap. His shampoo, even the sandwich he'd eaten earlier.

The killer knew what the general wanted; the sick old bastard wanted the people of this house to die except for the sister. The assassin's orders were to use a hatchet on Mom and Dad. The general wanted it messy. When he was alone with the sister named Katherine, he was to call the daughter, the one who headed security for the unit. He was to give her the message as he gutted her sister. It wasn't really his style, he usually garrotted his victims, but this is how the old man wanted it done.

Jack looked around for something to use as a distraction; he smiled when he looked down at the garden gnome. The cement creation seemed to be smiling back up at Jack as if saying a good idea. Without a second thought or hesitation, Jack reached down and picked up the concrete gnome. He headed around to the front of the house. Finding an open window, Jack smiled at his good fortune, and before he knew it, he was standing in the living room, the concrete gnome sitting on the window sill.

He heard something, a creak of a floorboard? He trusted his instincts. He held his breath, straining to hear anything. The killer remembered hearing older houses settled, that they would creak in the middle of the night. Nothing, it was nothing it had been about five minutes since he had heard the creak, then nothing.

Jack stood still; the board under the window creaked when he placed his foot down. He knew the killer in the house would be listening for another sound giving his presents away. Jack counted to sixty-five times, then one more for good measure. The house was strong as he moved; Jack was careful testing each step before he committed his full weight to the step. Now he was at the foot of the staircase looking up to where he knew the killer was. The thought to rush up and confront the man came to him, then Jack dismissed it as fast as it came. He had another idea; a smile played on his lips, turning Jack saw the television remote. Still smiling, Jack picked up the remote.

He sat up so fast his sandwich wrapper fell to the floor, the television was on downstairs. He knew no one was in the house beside him. He would have known if someone had tried to gain entry. All the doors were locked. Then he remembered the windows the two old betties had come and opened earlier. Someone broke in using one of those windows. Now he had an intruder to deal with before the family came home.

Jack sat in the armchair facing the staircase. He knew the killer would have to come downstairs to deal with the intruder eventually. Jack heard the man stand up in Joan's bedroom and walk across the floor. The shit didn't even try to conceal his movements; he was trying to frighten what he thought was a kid who broke in; Jack smiled.

Standing at the top of the stairs, the assassin waited for whoever broke in to start running; when he walked across the floor, all remained quiet. Well, the killer thought it was your funeral kid and started down the stairs into what he thought would be an easy kill.

Jack listened to the killer as he took his time, coming down one step at a time. This man made his living by killing people who never had a chance to fight back. Now the killer was trying to intimidate him. Jack smiled as the killer's shadow started to crawl across the floor at the foot of the stairs.

"You might as well come the rest of the way down. This way, we can talk before you decide whether you're going to live or I'm going to kill you." Jack said.

Fuck, the killer had almost blurted out the word when the man in the living room spoke. He'd been killing for years. This was the first time someone had ever gotten to him. Something told the assassin whoever was in this house with him was a predator. The assassin knew what he was, a killer he would kill only for money, and if he knew, it posed no risk to his life. The other here in the house was a predator. This man would stand face to face and always be alive at the end.

"You might as well step into the light; I know you don't have a gun, or you've used it by now. Come on, let's chat, then you can be on your way." Jack enticed the would-be killer.

"How do I know you don't have a pistol?" The killer asked.

"Because if I did, I would have put one between your eyes while you were sitting in that bedroom up there," Jack responded. Then watched as a slight man wearing a dark suit looked around the corner into the living room. Jack held up his hands, showing the man he was armed only with his K-bar knife. The killer pointed his blade at Jack and then pointed to the corner of the room.

"Throw your knife over there." The killer ordered.

"Yeah, how about fuck you instead? You're in the house of the parents of the woman I love. That makes them family, so you tell me why I shouldn't just kill you now and cut you up for fish bait?" Jack said.

"You can dig yourself out of this if you wish. The general and the rest of the group are dead. So you could walk away from this with whatever they paid you, just go on your merry way...or we can see what option two holds." As Jack finished still holding the K-Bar. The killer knew he would never beat this man in a fair fight. The killer knew he was looking at a true predator. Looking at this man sitting in the armchair as if he didn't have a care in the world, the killer knew he was going to take the out.

"Well, if there is no client, then there is no contract." The killer stated and started to turn away.

"Know this, friend, I know what you look like. If I ever see you again, I'll kill you; no second chances...father...no second chances, fair." Jack told the assassin.

"Fair enough, and you will never see me again. I think it's time I bring the word of god to others in a dark part of the world." The priest said as he walked out the door of the O'Driscolls house in Baltimore, Ireland.

Chapter 52

JOAN TURNED THE CORNER in time to see a slight man walking towards her. It wasn't until the light hit him that she saw the priest's collar; she smiled at the man of god. Her smile turned to shock as the priest pulled a knife. He was about to stab her when Jack grabbed him from behind and drove his K-bar under his left arm into the priest's heart, turning the older man so he looked up into Jack's scared face.

"Fair enough, son." The dying man whispered with his final breath. The older man managed to take two last steps and then crumpled into a bush beside the road.

"He was a priest. A priest was the hitman?" Joan stammered.

"Yeah, I don't know why; somehow, I remembered Mike and Chow used a guy on more than one occasion. This assassin was a real priest once. He would always use some form of a garrotte. I talked to a man once who said he heard the sick fucker praying as he killed a kid." Jack told her.

"Is that it? Do we have to worry about others out there?" Joan asked, looking up at Jack.

"No, not for a bit; Richard will have more information in the morning." Both Jack and Joan turned at the sound of a racing engine and tortured tires as the suv Richard, and the others were in came screaming around the corner. Jack started to pull Joan behind him when he recognized Richard on the passenger side.

"Everything ok?" Richard asked, looking at his friends.

"No, there's a dead priest in the bushes," Joan said, then started walking to her childhood home.

"A priest?" Richard asked, looking at Jack.

"Yeah, Chow and Mike Styles used this guy to kill others. He would always get away with his dirty deed; who would think a priest would be the killer. I remembered him, and well, the rest is not important." Richard nodded, then turned and asked the driver if he would take care of the cleaning up and then come back to the house. The driver nodded and started to work moving the body. There wasn't much to do at her parent's house. The former priest was a neat man. He kept his movements to the upstairs mostly. The only time he ventured downstairs was to get a glass of water. Even then, he had rinsed the glass and placed it on the drying rack beside the sink. The only evidence he had been in the house was the wrapper he dropped when Jack turned on the television.

Richard knocked before he entered the house and was greeted by Jack.

"The body has been taken care of; Joan's parents and her sister are on their way now. I'm going back to the airport; if you need anything, just call." Richard told Jack.

"I will; you be safe. I'll let you know how long we are going to be." Jack said as he shook his friend's hand and watched as Richards's car pulled up to the drive. They heard Joan coming down the stairs; she was almost running, trying to dust the house.

"You are not going anywhere, Richard, not until Mom and Dad get here to thank you for your help. Once we have tea, you can excuse yourself; until then, you will come in and have a seat." When Joan finished, she turned and rushed into the kitchen to get everything ready.

"Well, you had better let your driver know you are going to be a while. He had better come in also, or there'll be hell to pay." Jack told Richard.

"Yes, I had better. Does she know I'm still the boss?" Richard asked Jokingly.

"Not tonight, you're not," Joan said from the kitchen. Jack and Richard, along with Richard's driver, stood waiting for their orders from a frantic Joan. Who raced around getting her mother's house into what she called an expectable state. Jack was relieved when she stopped and looked around,

"Now, Mom and Dad can come home," Joan said to them. Fifteen minutes later, they watched as a suv pulled up outside the house. Joan ran out of the house when the car carrying her family pulled into the driveway. Richard and Jack walked out into the night and watched as she gathered her family into her arms. Jack knew they would be fine. Jack was content, he knew he had the best kind of friends, and now he had a family.

Jack smiled as he patted Richard on the shoulder, then went to Joan and her family. He was surprised when Joan's mother turned and looked up at him. Then ever so gently, she placed her hand over the scarred left side of his face as a tear fell from her cheek.

"Give me a hug Jack." The matriarch of the O'Driscoll family told him, and Jack happily hugged the older lady. When Jack stood up, he reached out to shake Joan's father's hand, and the smaller man took his hand.

"Come, son, let's go for a walk and have that chat." Mr. O'Driscoll said as he shook Jack's hand. Joan was about to protest when her father raised his hand and stopped her. Before she knew what was happening, her mother had ushered her and Richard into the house for a cup of tea.

Chapter 53

JACK FELL IN STEP WITH Joan's father as he chose the direction of their walk.

"We met some of your friends. They told us a story of a young lad. This lad had the most terrible time of it; his parents were murdered, and he was forced to become something he was never meant to be." As Joan's father spoke, Jack desperately wanted to stop him. What Jack feared was happening. He just couldn't get the words out. Jack just kept pace with the older man. Before Jack knew why they stopped, when Jack looked around, he found they were standing on the docks. The rigging on the fishing boats clinked. The ropes holding the boats in place creaked and groaned under the strain of the waves.

"Wyatt and Steven told us some of what happened to you as a child, then later when the Chinese had you. It's enough to make anyone go mad; you didn't. Jack, you took it all, and now you help people around the world. Son, as a father, I can tell you your father would be so proud of you, of what you do; I'm so proud of you. Mother and I are more than pleased you and our Joan have gotten together, but I need something from you." Joan's father said as he looked up at Jack.

"If I can, sir, I'll give you anything," Jack said, relieved Joan's father wasn't about to tell him not to see his daughter anymore.

"I need you to talk to us, to me, if you are having a bad day or feel overwhelmed. You just need to tell me, and I'll make sure you get some breathing space." When Joan's father finished, he looked at Jack. He knew what had happened to this man his daughter loved. Men who have worn uniforms all their lives told his wife and him Jack was one of the kindest men they knew. He was also one of the deadliest on earth.

"Yes, sir, I can do that," Jack answered as the two men stood watching as another boat was tied up. The men started walking towards them on the dock. Jack was surprised when each man tipped his hat towards Mr. O'Driscoll. The last man off the boat was the captain, and he walked up to Joan's father.

"Evening, skipper; everything alright?" The burly fisherman asked as he looked at Jack.

"Oh, everything is grand." Joan's father answered.

"Jack, this here gentleman is Joan's cousin Corey; Corey, this is Jack, Joan's lad." Jack stuck his hand out, and Corey smiled and shook.

"My god, you have got be a hell of a lad for Joan; good on ya." Joan's father and her cousin laughed as he turned and walked towards the pub.

"Well, we had better go for a pint. The lads will want to have a look and meet you, then Mother will want you home for the night." Mr. O'Driscoll told him as they followed Corey to the door of the pub.

"You mean Joan will want me home?" Jack asked Joan's father, who laughed.

"No, son, mother, the boss, she told me not to keep you too long. I was to have the talk and a pint, then straight home so she could get you squared away." Jack stood holding the door open. For a second, Jack wasn't sure he had heard right.

"You're in the family now, so when Mother says she wants you home, you go home." Joan's father finished as he ordered two pints.

"Dickie, give my lads a round and put it on my tab, please." When Jack heard Joan's father order a round for his lads, he turned to see who the lads were, and most of the pub raised a glass to Mr. O'Driscoll in thanks. With the pints finished, Joan's father paid the tab.

"Well, let's go home, son." Mr. O'Driscoll said. Jack looked around the pub, then raised his hand to Corey, who held his beer up and nodded along with the others at his table.

When they reached the door, Jack could hear Richard telling Joan's mother he couldn't possibly eat another bite, and he really must be getting back to the airport.

"I'll call you tomorrow and give you an update, be safe and relax, for god sake, man, before you have a stroke," Jack told Richard as he walked him to the car. Jack watched as the car carrying Richard drove into the night, its tail lights dwindling to nothing.

"So you met some of the lads, have you?" Joan asked as they watched Richard's car drive away.

"Yeah, I think so, Corey and a couple of them off one of the fishing boats." He answered as he turned to hug her.

"Well, all the lads who were in the pub work for my father. Dad built his first boat, and everyone said he was crazy. Now he and Mom have twelve, and they own the pub." Joan told him.

"Oh, so I've got me a rich chick." Jack joked as they stood at the edge of the road, watching a group of young people walking towards them. The teenagers smiled and said hi as they passed, not knowing just a short time ago, there was a fight for life on the spot.

"We better get in before your mother comes and gets us," Joan said.

"She is excited to have you at the supper table, and so is Lilly." Before he followed Joan into the house, Jack took one more look at the area. He didn't know for sure if this was over; he hoped it was. He just wanted to get past this group. Jack wanted to help others with his friends, and Joan got onto the work of bringing peace to others.

The End

THE GROUP

Don't miss out!

Visit the website below and you can sign up to receive emails whenever Todd LeRoux publishes a new book. There's no charge and no obligation.

https://books2read.com/r/B-A-MMEEB-WSBYC

BOOKS 2 READ

Connecting independent readers to independent writers.

Did you love *The Group*? Then you should read *The Cradle Operation*[1] by Todd LeRoux!

[2]

John had been John his whole life, but when General Chow tortured him, he remembered a lady calling him Jack. How could he have another person's memories? John knew he needed to escape the prison he was in; he didn't know where in China he was being held. He must know he needed to get out. Every day for months, the general would send a guard to get him, and every day he would ask about the damned accounts. Every day, John would say he didn't know about the accounts. John knew what the general was talking about; he wanted to know about the bank accounts John's former chief had around the world.

---

1. https://books2read.com/u/4jYOnl

2. https://books2read.com/u/4jYOnl

Chow-Yang looked out his office windows. A general on his payroll had captured John. The bastard was to kill John as soon as he was found; Chow-yang knew the General was torturing John, trying to get his account numbers. Yang smiled. No one knew the account numbers but him, and once he convinced the CIA that John was killed in the field, he would die as his plane crashed into the South China Sea. Yang was now in complete control of the drugs and weapons trade in half the world. All he and Mike Styles needed was for John Smyth to be dead. Then came the one phone call Yang didn't want to hear: a CIA listening base caught Chinese chatter about an escaped prisoner.

Read more at https://www.toddleroux.com/.

About the Author

Todd lives on the banks of the Miramichi river. After years of working away, he now enjoys his time at home with family and friends.

Read more at https://www.toddleroux.com/.